MW00932284

The Tantalizing Tales of Amanda Sneed

The Diary of Dreams
By J. S. Lorenz
Illustrations by Chris Volion

Imagination Square Publishing
Bluebird House of Children's Books
Ball Ground, GA

For information address
Imagination Square Publishing,
Bluebird House of Children's Books
1031 Laurel Lake Drive,
Ball Ground, Georgia 30107.

ISBN 978-1-516-81201-1
Rev. 150812A

Table of Contents

To my Bluebird, who never stopped dreaming in me.

And to Ian, who made this dream come true.

Chapter 1
One Splendorific Girl

If silence is golden, then this must be the richest moment ever. Rich in fear, wealthy in fright, and abundant in anxiety. Although a moment may be silent, it is during such moments that other things can be heard. It was one such moment of silence where an incredibly brave and gallant prince lay still listening to the effects of panic upon his heart. The drumming of his pulse beat throughout his veins and pounded like a sledgehammer inside his head. The prince was waiting. He was waiting ever so still and ever so silent. He was waiting for a battle to begin. And he was all alone to fight.

Motionless and prone to the ground, the jagged rocks of the earth pierced into gaps of the prince's armored body. On his upper body, he wore chain mail, links of tightly interwoven metal rings that would prevent the intrusion of an enemy's sharp blade. Over the chains on his chest, he wore a leather breastplate, decorated with a crest of a bird with wings of fire. His lower body was dressed in thick leather hide pants and he wore a pair of black leather boots. On his shoulders, forearms, knees, and shins, he had securely fastened metal armor for added protection. Around his hip was a weathered leather utility belt which contained a dagger, a key ring, some rope, a water canteen, and rations to aid in his hunger. Around his neck was attached a blue velvet cape, worn only by royalty. In his left hand he held a shield that resembled the shape of an arrowhead. His right hand was clinched tightly to the handle of his sword, ready to be drawn, as it remained firmly secure within its sheath.

Most individuals have at least once in their life found themselves in an uncomfortable or even frightening situation where they wished they could close their eyes, reopen them, and hope to find themselves free of their current situation - wishing to erase the moment at hand from their lives by merely drifting off into a magical slumber. A wish to drift off to a dream that becomes their reality, and their reality becomes a past dream. But a wish such as this is only a dream reserved for the foolish.

For the prince, this was one such occurrence. But no matter how many times the noble warrior shut his eyes and reopened them, he still found himself in the same location and under the same circumstance.

To make matters worse, a heavy fog settled over the terrain encompassing the noble warrior, keeping his sight limited and his guard in high alert. And although all was silent, the prince could sense danger approaching. He knew that if he were to lose focus, if even for a mere second, he could be handed a terrible fate. It felt as if the silence was wearing a mask of fear and anxiety that stared deep into his valiant blue eyes.

The silence started to break.

The prince could feel the ground begin to vibrate against his chest - a rhythm which soon matched the rhythm of his own breaths. He knew that the aura of a battle was about to settle in on him as he could faintly detect the beating black hearts of an army of goblins, marching their way toward his location.

The panting of heavy breath of these shadow demons made the air around him feel warmer and warmer, as a chill crept up the back of the prince's neck. Overwhelmed by the sweat of his palms, the young warrior's grip started slipping, causing him to attempt to clench tighter and tighter to his sword.

"Be calm, be very calm," the prince whispered to himself. "Trust your sword."

The anticipation of the enemies' approach began taking its toll, as the prince's heart was beating at an unnatural, rapid pace. As his vision blurred and his mouth dried, the prince could detect a disorientated feeling throughout his body.

"Just make your move. Please, just make your move," said the prince with a tone of fear in his voice.

Feeling a nudge against his belt, the prince immediately shouted an alert. "Stop! Who goes there?" To his surprise, brushing up close to him, was a curious light brown rodent. At first it appeared to the prince to be a rat or an opossum or maybe even a weasel. "What are you doing out here little fella?" questioned the prince as his attention immediately focused itself on his unexpected visitor. But before the prince could get a good look at the furry creature, the rodent snagged the key ring from the prince's utility belt and ran away into the thickness of the fog.

"Come back here you thief!" ordered the prince as he stood and ran after the rodent, unsure of which direction he had gone. "I need those keys!" The prince's legs felt stiff having been still for so long. Using all of his energy, the prince sliced his way through the fog like a sharp knife cutting through paper. But then he stopped. He stopped because he had found something. But it wasn't the rodent. It was much worse. The prince found himself face to face, and eye to eye, with a brutally large and grotesquely nasty, monstrosity of a goblin who was resting an enormous wooden club against his right shoulder like a baseball bat.

"Hello, Lucky," the goblin snickered. "I don't have your keys, but I do have a club you can join." The goblin lifted his club to strike the prince. The prince immediately drew his sword and raised it, as he took a defensive stance, countering each blow the goblin swung his way.

"I shall chew off your ears and rip off your nose, noble scum," grumbled the goblin with a wickedly eerie and intimidating voice. His appearance put even more fright into an image that the prince had already found overwhelmingly horrific.

The goblin was taller than the prince, even though he leaned forward due to poor posture. Or maybe that was because he was just crooked. His joints were bent in strange directions and he even had a hunch growing from his back. He had hair, but not much of it. It did not look as if he was going bald, but rather someone or something had torn much of his hair out. Perhaps the same someone or something that had taken a bite out of his pointy left ear. The hunch on his back had more hair growing on it than what was found on his head. His skin was a dark green shade and much of it looked charred and full of scars. His entire body was filled with boils and infections which had a disgusting odor. What teeth he did have were razor sharp, but were brown and yellowed, filling a rotted and decayed mouth of dental horror. The goblin's eyes were only one shade - black - the shade that reflected the darkness of his heart. But a shade that matched the nails on his nine fingers and his eight remaining toes.

"I want to hear you scream as I crush your bones," the goblin taunted, striking his club and nearly landing a perfect blow against the prince's right foot.

More goblin soldiers began to close in on the battle scene. Things were looking very dismal for the royal heir. Within seconds, he found himself completely encircled by tens of hundreds of goblins. "I need a miracle." It was all the prince could say to himself, given the circumstance of his situation.

But ask and you shall receive. For a miracle began to happen. A shrieking sound pierced the air, causing all within in its range to cover their ears. "What is that noise?" the prince asked in confusion. "It's the most appalling sound I have ever heard."

The prince looked up to see a silhouette flickering through the fog, of a small girl carrying a rod-shaped weapon. The shrill of the sound continued to escalate, as the goblins dropped their weapons and began to run away as fast and as far as possible. With the little girl closely approaching, the prince was able to identify what the powerful weapon was that scared off the entire goblin force.

"A clarinet?" The prince was completely puzzled. "You were able to chase off an entire army of goblins with the annoying squeal of a clarinet?"

"Of course silly," the young amateur musician began explaining. "Goblins hate that. It's not just any clarinet either. This one has a broken reed. It makes C major sound just plain nasty and that drives the average goblin nuts."

But there was one goblin who was a bit above average and didn't run away. With a fiendish stare he spoke, "Did you think I'd be prone to your petty stunts so easily little girl?" He then turned his head to the side, smiled an evil grin of delight, and pointed to his deformed ear.

"Shoot - earplugs! I should have known," the clarinet wielding warrior responded with discouragement.

"I shall crush your little horn into tiny splinters," taunted the goblin, "and then pounce on your itty bitty fingers and toes until you beg of me to stop!" With a huge swing forward, the goblin was able to smash the girl's clarinet with his wooden club. Weaponless, she began to move backwards, while still facing her enemy.

The nasty imp reared back his club to hammer down a final blow. But then, the strangest thing happened.

The girl's eyes became bright and shined like two heavenly stars. The goblin and the prince both froze in awe as they had never seen this optical spectacle before. The girl reached into her navy blue jacket with her right hand and pulled out one white rose. Lifting the rose up to her lips, she blew on it and the rose froze into solid ice. The girl covered the frozen petals with her left hand and crushed them into tiny icy pieces, sending them crumbling into her right hand. Then she tossed the crumbled pieces in an underhand motion at the goblin. Upon leaving her hand, the pieces of ice transformed. The ice had turned into hundreds upon thousands of butterflies. Butterflies that immediately swarmed around the goblin. The goblin dropped his club and began to swat at the swarm of butterflies with his hands. But it was no use. The goblin quickly realized that the vast number of butterflies was too great for him to fight back and he took off running into the fog.

"That was the most amazing feat of courage I have ever seen," stated the prince in wonder. "You showed such bravery and determination. I must thank you for everything you've done for me, but I don't even know your name. Please, I must know. Who are you?"

"Amanda. Amanda Sneed." An unknown voice answered for her, causing the young girl to begin losing her concentration on the previous battle she had encountered. The voice continued to speak. "Do you mind not holding a conversation with yourself and rejoin the rest of us here in class? Miss Sneed, do you think you could answer the question I just asked the class?" The voice was none other than Mr. Izzmund, Amanda's fifth grade home room teacher. And now, Mr. Izzmund's entire fifth grade class at Maffet Valley Elementary had their attention focused on Amanda. All of the students laughed and pointed their fingers at their strange classmate who had just been caught drifting off into a daydream during class - the classmate who is labeled "different" by everyone at Maffet Valley Elementary, students and teachers included. The classmate by the name of Amanda Sneed.

"That's enough everyone. Let Miss Sneed answer," said Mr. Izzmund. "Well Amanda, we're waiting." Mr. Izzmund was an average size man, and quite eccentric in his own right. He had bushy dark hair and thick eyebrows to match, both of which where kept in place from using excessive amounts of men's hair cream. His horn-rimmed glasses made his eyes look twice the size that they actually were. He dressed himself in a white collared dress shirt -

heavily starched and absolutely no wrinkles - with one pocket on the left side of his chest. In that pocket could always be found a handkerchief. A handkerchief whose corners were stitched with an array of colors and patterns as if the handkerchief itself might be a family heirloom. Mr. Izzmund was known for having a terrible sinus problem and consistently had a red nose which countered his pale skin. Around the neck of his white collared dress shirt, he wore a black bow-tie, whether it was a school day or not. To top off his wardrobe, he carried a long, black umbrella with him to and from school, rain or shine.

Still being caught somewhere between her daydream and reality, Amanda responded to Mr. Izzmund as if speaking to the prince from her daydream. "Amanda Sneed. My name is Amanda Sneed."

Laughter filled the classroom yet again. "I said that's enough class!" said Mr. Izzmund beginning to sound impatient. "Yes, we know your name is Amanda Sneed. Now, could you kindly explain to me a unique characteristic of an amphibian?" Mr. Izzmund pulled out his handkerchief and blew his nose.

It was then that Amanda heard the laughter of the class and realized that she was not in her dream. She was in her home room. *Oh great*, Amanda thought to herself, *yet another awkward moment. I'll have to add it to a very long list.*

Amanda was different from "normal" kids. Amanda was a dreamer. She fantasized how things could be and not of how things necessarily were. Reality was boring to Amanda. On many occasions Amanda found herself in situations with her peers taunting her. They teased her stringy brown hair - hair held up in pigtails, with each pigtail kept in place by a pair of wire bread ties. They even teased the way she dressed. Amanda's wardrobe displayed the most current fashions that any reputable flea market or garage sale could offer. From her patched jeans to her high tops with the broken shoe laces, Amanda's clothes were anything but new and stylish. But no matter what outfit she wore, Amanda was never seen without wearing her favorite navy blue, hooded jacket. The jacket was at least two sizes too big for her, easily stretching down to the tops of her knees. The arms of the jacket were so long that Amanda had to roll up the sleeves almost half their length just so her hands could be exposed. However, this jacket was special to Amanda. Not only did this jacket have many pockets and secret storage areas within its interior, it had belonged to someone special. This jacket at one time was her father's.

You see, Amanda was an only child who was raised by her grandparents. Her mother died shortly after Amanda was born due to complications with her delivery. She never met her father. She had been told that he was constantly on the road looking for work, but she was never given any details. He never wrote. He never called. Her only memories of either of her parents were merely pictures and stories.

Because of her situation, Amanda had only known her grandparents as a source of parental consistency all of her life. But they were older and didn't have the energy to keep up with the imagination and energy that a spunky ten year old girl had to dish out. An imagination and energy that had caused Amanda to be an extremely creative and gifted child. An imagination and energy that was not accepted as normal by others and gave Amanda the reputation of being "different".

"What a loser," piped Stephanie Graham. "I think the freak girl has gone off to visit another planet. I can answer your question Mr. Izzmund."

Now for Stephanie to give her opinion and volunteer her knowledge of anything, was not surprising. Stephanie was the most popular girl in all of Maffet Valley Elementary's fifth grade class. She was also known to be quite the beauty with her long, golden blond hair and radiating blue eyes. Girls wanted to be like her and boys worshiped the ground she walked on. No, neither popularity nor attention from others were problems for Stephanie, even if tact was.

"No," stated Mr. Izzmund as he began pulling the handkerchief from his pocket. "I want Amanda to answer." Mr. Izzmund was famous for putting students on the spot. His rule was this, if you did not show him respect, than he would not show you any. And by daydreaming in class, Amanda was definitely being disrespectful in his eyes. "Go on Amanda. How would you explain the fact that a frog is born in water as a tadpole with gills and a tail. But as an adult, it grows legs and loses it tail, only to find itself able to live on land, but still able to swim and live in water?"

"Well Mr. Izzmund. I think I would explain it as - well, I think I would... I would say it is splendorific," Amanda replied.

The entire class froze for a brief moment, wondering what possibly Amanda could have meant by that. Then, as before, everyone started laughing. Laughter directed once again at Amanda, the girl who was "different".

"Splendorific?" Stephanie sneered. "What's that supposed to mean anyway?"

"Well, it's really a word I made up," Amanda said in her defense. "But it makes sense if you really think about it." Amanda was doing her best to think exactly what splendorific meant. She had been using this word plenty of times, but never before had she really thought about what it meant. Then it came to her. "It sort of means that something is marvelous or brilliant. When I find something to be splendorific, then it means that nothing could be any more perfect."

"What?" Stephanie questioned sounding doubtful. "Since when do you have the right to make up new words? I bet you're writing your own dictionary too." Stephanie really could not have been more hateful. "It's just like a weirdo like you to come up with your own words. You just have to be different, don't you? I bet you're even going to make something "strange" happen again and try to fool us all. I know better. Those are just stupid stunts of yours. You just like the attention. Why wouldn't a freak like you crave the attention?"

By "strange" happenings, Stephanie was referring to something else about Amanda. The "strange" happenings were incidents that had been witnessed by her classmates. The same classmates that taunted her daydreaming and her appearance. Yes, there were incidents. Incidents that had happened quite recently in Amanda's life. Incidents that were both bizarre and unexplainable. Incidents that had led to embarrassment, ridicule, and question. Incidents that left the other students choosing to cast out Amanda from being any part of them.

The first of these incidents happened in music class. It was during one of Amanda's very first clarinet lessons. Mrs. Oberhosen, or Mrs. O. as Maffet Valley Elementary's music teacher was widely known throughout school, was spending time with each student a few minutes individually. She would get the student started working on a few notes of their respective instrument before moving on to another student. Mrs. O. had finished teaching Amanda her notes to play on her clarinet, and then moved on to the next student, giving Amanda her time to practice. Amanda began to drift off and imagine herself performing a clarinet solo in front of the entire school with everyone applauding and throwing roses at her. Then Amanda realized that all was quiet. When she regained her composure everyone was staring at her - at her and her clarinet. The clarinet that was floating on its own in front of Amanda and playing a lullaby without any interaction from Amanda. Quickly, Amanda grabbed her clarinet and began to play something - anything - hoping that no one would think that she was strange. From that moment in music class, no one sat in the chairs next to Amanda.

"Then go ahead Stephanie," said Mr. Izzmund, "and tell us a little about amphibians. I want to know about frogs and their ability to live in both water and places such as trees. And how ironic that the wood from these trees can float in water as can a frog." Mr. Izzmund sneezed and proceeded to blow his nose.

The second of these incidents was in the cafeteria. Amanda without question was one of the students who brought their lunch every day. Every morning Amanda's grandmother would pack a meal in an old hat box, that she used for a lunch box, filled with an unidentifiable meat sandwich, one large shaved raw carrot, and her speciality - jello surprise. Amanda's grandmother was not known for her cooking. Or maybe she was - her bad cooking. But Amanda had no choice. As her grandmother always explained, "It's just easier on your grandfather and myself to pack your lunch than to pay for those expensive, $1.50 school meals."

Most days, Amanda was not particularly hungry and could satisfy any craving by only eating the shaved raw carrot. But on this particular day, the fifth grade had to eat their lunch later than normal due to a school presentation.

Amanda was hungry. Her stomach had been growling all throughout the entire presentation and she could not wait to eat. Once in the cafeteria, Amanda looked inside her hat box and saw the same unappealing food. She closed the box in disgust and started dreaming of a delicious submarine sandwich filled with ham, turkey, roast beef, cheeses, tomato, lettuce... Her mouth was drooling. She could almost smell the fresh bread. But just like in music class, she once again regained her composure to find the entire cafeteria staring at her. Looking down at the table where she was sitting, Amanda saw that she had pulled out of her hat box, a submarine sandwich that was the length of at least five of the cafeteria tables. From that moment on in the cafeteria, no one sat at the same cafeteria table as Amanda.

"Thank you, Mr. Izzmund, but please call me Stephie," responded Stephanie. "I can make up words too. It's much more glamorous sounding anyway. Hmm, Stephie Graham. Yes, I like the way that sounds. It's so much more pleasing to the ears. I am so clever - and so very cute too." Not only did Stephanie, or is it Stephie, cut others down, but she tended to be quite the professional at self-promotion.

The third of these incidents happened very recently in science class. The fifth graders were tasked with constructing volcanos and demonstrating an eruption of lava from their displays, by using household products to create the lava. Amanda's clay volcano was constructed well, but she ended up being the last presenter in the class - as usual. Her classmates took their time with their respective demonstrations and Amanda began to grow tired. She closed her eyes and dreamed about her project and demonstrating the most beautiful volcano ever. She dreamed of a volcano found on a tropical island, filled with beautiful flowers, butterflies, and rainbows. Then she heard laughter. Opening her eyes, everyone in science class was laughing at her - her and her volcano. Somehow, while she was napping, her volcano had begun erupting.

But it wasn't erupting "homemade lava". Instead, it was spitting out the petals of many different flowers. Flower petals that ended up covering her volcano, her desk, and many of her classmates. From that moment on in science class, no one wished to be Amanda's lab partner.

If only Amanda had one person she could call a friend. Someone to stick up for her. Someone to defend her point of view. But there was no one. It looked like she was on her own. Everyone loved Stephie, including the teachers. No one liked Amanda. Well, almost no one. Maybe there was a friend. Maybe there was a friend who loved Amanda very much and would follow her anywhere. Just maybe...

"AAAAAHHHHHH!!!! A RAT!!!!!" Stephie screamed so loud that many in the class had to cover their ears including Mr. Izzmund as he dropped his handkerchief for the moment. In her fright, Stephie fell backwards into a shelf full of books, sending them tumbling to the ground. "That rat! It's disgusting! It has huge fangs and such large claws! Somebody do something before it bites me!" The chaos had caused most of the students to scream along with Stephie and to jump to their desks to avoid a vicious rat bite.

But this rodent was not a rat. It did not have huge fangs nor did it have large claws. This cute and cuddly creature was quite tame and completely harmless. This bundle of fur was nothing more than a curious little ferret.

The ferret's face was white, almost resembling that of an opossum. The rest of his fur was a tan color, except for a dark stripe of brown down the center of his stomach. On his back he wore a ferret sized, olive green backpack. On that backpack was embroidered a red letter "L".

As tame as he was, in all of the excitement and screaming taking place in the classroom, the ferret became quite frightened and ended up scurrying onto the teacher's cluttered desk. It then took a huge leap forward and landed directly on top of Mr. Izzmund's head, giving him what might become the latest fad, a ferret hat.

"Lawrence, stop!" screamed Amanda. Completely startled by the events that just took place, Amanda could not hold back her concern for the ferret.

"Does this creature belong to you Miss Sneed?" Anger filled Mr. Izzmund's face, making it appear the same red color as his nose.

"Yes Mr. Izzmund, that would be my pet ferret. His name is Lawrence." Lawrence was more than just a pet to Amanda. Lawrence was her best friend and went with her everywhere - well, almost everywhere. Sometimes, such as now, Amanda wished Lawrence would stay put at home.

"Miss Sneed, I believe it would be best for you to get this furry animal off of my head, and take it home and put it in a cage so it cannot cause any more problems than it already has!" Mr. Izzmund sneezed and grabbed his handkerchief. He was at his wit's end. No one in the class had ever seen him this mad before. "I am so very disappointed in you Amanda." Then he blew his nose.

"Take this note to the Principal's office so you may be dismissed early." Again, Mr. Izzmund sneezed and sneezed and sneezed. It seemed as if Mr. Izzmund not only had sinus problems, but was also allergic to ferrets. "I want you to get your things now and go. Don't ever let me see that rodent again."

Knowing it was worthless to argue, Amanda took the note, picked up Lawrence, and grabbed her book bag. She did not look back on her way out of the classroom, nor did she want to. She knew all fifth graders' eyes were staring at her and all the whispers were nothing more than critical, degrading babble in honor of her and her pet ferret, Lawrence. As she left the classroom and headed toward the Principal's office, a tear formed in her eye, rolled down her cheek, and splashed to the floor, leaving a tiny puddle of sadness in her path.

"Oh great! A day's suspension!" exclaimed Amanda as she shut the door, leaving the Principal's office.

"How am I supposed to explain this to grandmother? What's worse, how am I supposed to explain it to grandfather? He won't be happy."

With her book bag secure on her back, Amanda cradled Lawrence tightly with both arms, insuring that the ferret would not make an escape. She continued down the hallway of the school toward the exit near the student bike rack with her head down, pondering in her thoughts and dwelling on her own sorrow.

Passing the school's trophy case, Amanda stopped to look inside at the prestigious collection of awards belonging to Maffet Valley Elementary, all in one place, contained behind glass for all to see. The trophies varied from spelling bee championships to hopscotch competitions. There was even a crab soccer tournament trophy, an event that Amanda had played a small role in. As she continued to stare into the case, she could see a faint reflection of herself in the glass. "Why am I so different? Why can't I be normal like everyone else?" A door shut in the distance and the noise snapped Amanda out of her focus on her reflection. She turned and walked away from the trophy case, unaware that her reflection had remained in the glass and had morphed into a shadowed outline of an unknown figure.

Continuing to the end of the hall, she made a left down a short corridor that led to the exit door that she sought. But upon making the turn around the corner into the corridor, she was startled. Startled to the point that she froze in her tracks. Startled to find that she was not alone.

"Aren't you supposed to be somewhere little Miss?"

Directly in front of Amanda was a very large man. A very large man indeed. Copper colored hair covered so much of his face that only a glimpse of his pale blue eyes could be detected. From his beard to his brow, he was a very shaggy man. He wore brown coveralls which were covered in what looked like sparkling grains of sand. Attached on his hip was a clip of keys. On that clip there was a separate key ring. And on that separate ring dangled a most magnificent looking key. It was larger than his other keys and very authentic looking. It was gold and had a radiating glow about it. Amanda immediately was drawn to fix her eyes upon this key.

"Um, yes, sir," answered Amanda. "I am supposed to be somewhere sir. I'm on my way home and I must be going now before I get into any more trouble."

"Don't call me sir," the man said. "The name's Hemlock. But it would be best if you refer to me as Master Hemlock." His voice was very rough, as if he had a cold in his chest. The mere sound coming from his lips was enough to intimidate Amanda. "Do you find an interest in my key?" Hemlock was a new face, not that there was much face to see, but a new face nonetheless to Amanda. The push broom in his left hand pretty much explained to Amanda that Hemlock was a school custodian, but she had never seen him at school before.

"No, I just seem to um, well, it seems to glow and ..." Amanda replied, stumbling through her words. The fact that he was sweeping the floors and still covered with sand puzzled Amanda. Amanda tried to change the subject. "How do you keep the floors clean if all that sand on your clothes keeps falling off where you swept? Your uniform does appear to be awfully dirty."

"It's quite simple little one. The sand only falls when and where I want it to," Hemlock replied, as he kept his stare directly into Amanda's eyes. A stare that made Amanda feel as if he were trying to hypnotize her.

"I see. That is just..." Amanda did not know how to react. What did he mean the sand only falls when and where he wants it to? "Well, it's just splendorific, I suppose." That was the only fitting response she could think of, with so much confusion weighing in her mind. "I don't really understand, but that's ok. It was nice to meet you Hemlo–, I mean Master Hemlock. I must be going now so that I may get my ferret home."

In her fright, Amanda did not realize that she had lost her tight cradle hold on the ferret and dropped Lawrence upon confronting Master Hemlock. "Did you happen to see where my ferret went?" she asked.

"What ferret?" Hemlock replied.

"His name is Lawrence and he has a backpack and he... Oh, never mind." Amanda didn't wish to discuss anything more with her new acquaintance. She knew Lawrence would find his way home. Amanda stepped to the side as Master Hemlock pushed his broom forward and around the corner from where she came. She watched as the sparkling grains of sand brushed off of Master Hemlock's body with each pounding step he took. But to her surprise, as he walked away, the sand would flow in a motion on the floor behind him, like a stream, as if it were following him. Or at least she thought so. Amanda rubbed her eyes thinking perhaps she was imagining this. But when she reopened them, Master Hemlock was gone, and there was no sand to be found on any floor around her.

In her astonishment, Amanda ran to the exit and outside to the student bike rack. She pulled her purple three-speed with the banana seat and Y-shaped handle bars that curved down on the ends, from the rack, and began peddling home as fast as she could. Amanda's only goal for the moment was to get away from Master Hemlock as quickly as possible. For in her mind, Master Hemlock was a strange man. A very strange man indeed.

Chapter 2
Meet the Grandparents

Maffet Valley was a small community that had at one moment in time thrived on the wealth of the gold mining industry. It was well over 100 years ago that gold had first been discovered in Maffet Valley by a humble storyteller named Logan Parks Sneed. Logan was not a miner, nor was he an adventurer. Logan was known for two things -

fishing and telling tall tales. It was during one of his daily fishing outings at Lumpkin Creek that Logan found his first nugget of gold amidst the creek rocks. A nugget that had friends. Many of them. The hidden portion of Lumpkin Creek where he was fishing was filled with them and it is rumored that Logan lost his favorite fishing pole that day, dropping it in the delight he had taken in the gold. But that rumor is perhaps yet another story started by Logan himself.

However, Logan had been fishing at Lumpkin Creek for almost twenty years. And although this portion of the creek was very secluded and was a secret fishing spot known only by himself, Logan had never seen gold here before. How did this happen? How did all of this gold just appear throughout the creek? He decided not to dwell on his questions. Instead, Logan ran back to Maffet Valley to tell the other townsfolk of the gold that he found in the hills while he was fishing.

But Logan's reputation for storytelling left him with a problem. It made it hard for others to believe him when he spoke of the gold flowing through the veins of Lumpkin Creek. "So much gold," Logan said, "that you can use it to cover the roof of the largest building in town, and still have enough gold left over to buy your family a new pig." One by one Logan told of the golden streams hidden in the hills above Maffet Valley. No one listened. The entire town felt this was nothing more than a made up story courtesy of the dreams of a man named Logan Parks Sneed.

Realizing that no one believed him, Logan decided it would be best to validate his story by presenting evidence of his finding at the next town meeting, held on every other Monday, at precisely 7:00 p.m., at the Maffet Valley town hall. Even though this decision was against his better judgment, Logan felt if he were ever to be taken serious as a storyteller or a resident of Maffet Valley, then he needed to prove his credibility.

At the next scheduled town meeting, Logan arrived 30 minutes early with a gunny sack full of gold. It was so full and so heavy that Logan had to load in onto a wheelbarrow and roll it into the town hall. He decided it was best to keep the gold in the gunny sack until it came time for him to approach the townspeople.

The meeting began with typical discussions and babble. Logan could tell by the smiles and sneers of others, as well as the whispers within the room, that he and his gold were the silent discussion of many. It then became time for new business. Logan immediately lifted his hand in the air and stated, "I'd like to approach the front to discuss the gold in them there hills of Maffet Valley."

Logan came up front to plead his case, pushing his wheelbarrow along the way. Laughter and taunts could be heard throughout the town hall. No one thought there was real gold in that gunny sack. Everyone felt this was just another story of Logan's and that if anything was in the sack, it would be painted rocks.

Logan pulled a large gold nugget from the sack. The laughter stopped. The taunting stopped. The mayor of Maffet Valley walked over to Logan and took the piece of gold, holding it close to his eyepiece for further examination. "Why Logan," said the mayor, "I do believe that you are correct. This is indeed real gold."

Upon hearing the mayor's verdict, all attendees of the meeting jumped from their seats to come up front and take a look. They pushed and shoved each other trying to touch the gold and hold it for themselves. This chaos caused Logan's wheelbarrow to tip over, spilling out the remaining gold in the gunny sack, and making Logan fall to the ground. The townspeople were like scavengers grabbing the gold that had spilled.

Logan shouted, "Wait! That's my gold! I found it!" But it was no use. As quickly as it had spilled it was taken. Others immediately left to gather tools, wagons, and any other necessities needed for gold hunting. Logan's secret was no more. The gold was no longer his claim, but the claim of many. The claim of those who now desired to find it.

This gold fever remained in Maffet Valley for several years. Logan continued to fish and tell his stories to those who would listen, and stayed away from the gold miners and their search. The miners continued to destroy the land around Maffet Valley, creating strip pits in the land and underground mining caverns, until they could find gold no more.

But the days of having gold fever in Maffet Valley were now long gone. The pits that were once filled with shovels, pick axes, and overworked miners were now nothing more than rain filled ponds home to snakes, frogs, mosquitos, and an occasional fish. The entrances to the mining tunnels were well boarded up to prevent any entry due to possible dangers that lie within. However, this does not prevent the curious from trying. There are those who wish to enter the mining tunnels. But their attempts are met with strange results. All who enter say they experience the same occurrence. Upon first entering the mining caves, they begin to grow tired and fall asleep, finding themselves back at their homes when awaking.

The miners were all gone too, as well as their families and descendants. In fact, most of the residents of Maffet Valley from the beginning days of the gold rush had their descendants move away. There was no reason to stay. The gold was gone and work had to be found elsewhere. Bags were packed and families moved. That is, most of them. Although he felt betrayed by the other Maffet Valley residents, Logan ended up staying in Maffet Valley and marrying a woman by the name of Abigail Patrick. Logan and Abigail had five children, fourteen grandchildren, and several more descendants further along the family tree. Most left Maffet Valley except for one great-great grandson named Herbert Sneed.

Herbert was a stocky man, with broad shoulders and a strong jaw. Herbert was known as the "firecracker" in Maffet Valley due to his energetic spunk and quick temper. He had just turned sixty years old and was considered a retiree from working in the construction business for over thirty-five years. But being a spunky "firecracker" also meant not being able to sit still, and Herbert was notorious for not sitting still. Even a simple walk from the front door of his home to the mailbox turned into a quick paced stride with Herbert holding onto his belt buckle with his right hand, mumbling comments and complaints to himself, and gesturing his words by talking with his left hand. Even looking at Herbert one knew that he was a "firecracker". His bushy gray and black eyebrows would shift up and down when he grew excited, and the top of his bald head would turn a deep flush red.

The overabundance of energy that Herbert displayed forced him out of retirement and placed him into a self-employed state as the community's self-proclaimed handyman. Herbert had started his own business to keep busy and drain off the extra energy that he had on a daily basis. But there was a secret about this "firecracker" energy that only Herbert and his wife Martha knew. Herbert had an amazingly precise body clock. At exactly 5:00 a.m. every morning, he arose from bed, he would go for a brisk walk, and then he would be wide awake and ready to attack the day. But at 5:00 p.m., his body shut down and the "firecracker" energy turned into a burned out smoldering fuse. Therefore, Herbert had to set his business hours accordingly and only worked daily until 5:00 p.m. A time which Martha Sneed planned her schedule around every day.

But before 5:00 p.m., Martha could usually be found busy with her favorite past time - gardening. And having a greenhouse and a flower garden as enormous as Martha Sneed had, required constant care and maintenance. That is exactly how Amanda found her grandmother the afternoon she was sent home early from school by Mr. Izzmund, tending to her garden.

Martha Sneed used to own a flower shop in Maffet Valley and was able to use the greenhouse to raise many beautiful flowers and plants from all over the world. Time changes who we are both mentally and physically and for Martha Sneed, time changed her memory. More and more, Martha found herself missing deliveries and forgetting to place orders. This was no way to run a business and soon she found herself losing customers. Martha found it in her best interests to sell her shop and work from home as a "consultant" for the flower shop. She could make suggestions and sell the shop plants and flowers from her own garden, without putting herself at risk of missing a customer order.

Amanda drove up the driveway on her purple three-speed bicycle with the banana seat and Y-shaped handlebars that curved down at the ends, to see her grandmother pulling weeds from a bed of white roses. White roses were a favorite among Grandma Sneed and Amanda knew that her grandmother spent the majority of her time in the garden tending to their care.

"Hello, grandmother," greeted Amanda as she dismounted her bicycle and pushed down the kickstand to keep it from falling.

"Well hello, dear," Grandma Sneed answered startled. "I didn't hear you come up the driveway. You're home earlier than normal. Is today an early release day?"

Amanda froze not knowing how to answer. It wasn't her practice to lie to her grandmother. Nor did she want to admit her guilt either. Perhaps stretching the truth would be the best approach. "Well, no," answered Amanda biting her lower lip. "Today isn't an early release day from school. Mr. Izzmund just felt I needed to get home a little bit earlier today so that I may work on some..., some self improvement techniques."

"Self improvement?" pondered Grandma Sneed. "You should wait until your grandpa gets home and have him join along. He could use all the self improvement he can get."

Just wonderful, Amanda thought. *Now how am I going to explain that I'm suspended tomorrow from school? I can't exactly say I have a whole day at home devoted to self improvement.*

"Could you lend me a hand with these roses?" asked Grandma Sneed. "I wish I could leave them to improve by themselves."

"Sure grandmother," answered Amanda. "I'd love to help you."

"You know," Grandma Sneed stated, "I went to give your ferret a treat today. I couldn't find him anywhere. I looked and looked and looked, but he was nowhere to be found. I thought maybe I forgot where you kept him."

Amanda could sense a different tone in her grandmother's voice. It was as if her grandmother was trying to hint something to her, but wanted Amanda to guess what it was first.

"Animals are quite unpredictable creatures," Grandma Sneed continued. "You can never be too sure what behavior to expect from them sometimes. When I was a little girl, I had a pet myself. It was a dog named Shags. Shags was the most faithful and trusting friend that I ever had. He would have done anything for me and I would have done anything for him. Every day when I came home from school, he was there to greet me at the entrance to my driveway. Then, one day, he wasn't there. I thought perhaps something was wrong. Maybe Shags was hurt or something worse. I ran into the house to find my mother to see if she knew what had happened to Shags. To my surprise when I entered the kitchen, there was trash everywhere. Food wrappers, garbage from the waste can, ripped curtains. But most of all, a freshly baked apple pie that had earlier set on the seal of the kitchen window, existed no more. And standing at the opposite side of the kitchen when I entered was my mother with her arms crossed, tapping her foot, and glaring right at me. I knew from this look that the "renovation" of the kitchen was due to none other than Shags. I never once thought Shags was capable of such a thing. He listened so well and never got into any trouble. I guess he smelled that freshly baked apple pie and couldn't help himself. It turns out since the kitchen window was open, he jumped right up, knocking the pie to the floor inside, and managed to pull himself right on in the house. He didn't stop with the pie though. The point is, animals are definitely unpredictable and we, as the ones responsible for them, are also responsible for their actions. I guess that's why I'm worried about where your ferret might be. I sure hope he hasn't done anything to cause problems for himself and you."

The gig was up. Amanda was busted and she knew it. The whole story about Shags was her grandmother's huge "hint" to confess now or pay the price later.

"Ok," Amanda confessed, "I'm sure the school has already called you. I can tell by the apple pie story that you know Lawrence has gotten me into trouble today."

"Oh?" responded Grandma Sneed laughing. "What makes you think that? But you're right. Your school did call me, and yes, I do know that you were sent home early because of your ferret's disruption. And I also know that you are suspended from school tomorrow. However, your grandfather doesn't know. So it might be best if I break it to the ole' firecracker gently later this evening. He won't be so understanding as I am. He never had a pet growing up. Maybe he should have. That might have kept him from being so cranky in his old age. You can help me on your "day off" tomorrow by working in the garden. A garden this size needs all the helping hands it can get. And be sure to keep that ferret caged up when you leave in the mornings for school from now on."

Where was that crazy ferret anyway? He hadn't been seen since Amanda ran into Master Hemlock on the way out of the school. Oh yes, Master Hemlock. With the apple pie story, Amanda had almost forgotten about the mysterious giant of a janitor. "Grandmother, there is a custodian at school that I met today. I was surprised when I ran into him because, well, he was a bit creepy and I never have seen him before. His name is Hemlock. Have you heard of him?"

"Well, let me see," said Amanda's grandmother. "Hemlock? I tend to remember your grandfather saying that name." Grandma Sneed's memory wasn't always that reliable, and she usually tried her best to hide that fact. If she couldn't remember something, she just pretended and made up an answer. "Why don't you wait until he gets home and you can ask him at dinner. Speaking of dinner, I need to get that meatloaf put in the oven."

Meals were usually very quiet. Grandpa Sneed always brought the daily newspaper to the table, and if he did start a conversation, the subject matter usually had to do with the weather. His energy was drained by this time and the "firecracker" didn't feel much like conversation, nor did he care to be bothered.

Grandma Sneed spent her mealtime up and down from her chair, constantly bringing more items to the dinner table, whether they were needed or not. "Oh wait," Grandma Sneed said jumping up from her chair and heading to the refrigerator, "I forgot the mustard. One of you might want mustard on your meatloaf."

Fearful of bringing up the school episode to her grandfather, Amanda decided to start a discussion of a different subject. "Grandfather, I was curious about something."

"Hmm?" replied Grandpa Sneed with his nose in the newspaper. "You say you're curious. Why are you kids always so curious? Always asking questions. Always wanting to know something irrelevant and useless. Go on, what's got your curiosity?"

Amanda gulped, "Do you know a new janitor at the school named Hemlock?"

"Do I know a Hemlock?" Grandpa Sneed responded lowering his paper. "There's a Hemlock character that moved into the old Wilson cabin right on the other side of our woods. I've never met him, but when I get up in the mornings and go for my walk, I always see a dim light glowing from that place. I figure he's an early riser just like myself. Just why do you want to know about this Hemlock?"

"Um, it's no big deal grandfather," Amanda said as she was shocked to hear that Hemlock lived practically next door to her. "I accidently ran into him at school today. He startled me and he acted a little weird so I was curious if you knew anything about him. That's all." She didn't mention Master Hemlock again and began to finish her meal.

"Whoops," Grandma Sneed hooted jumping up again from her chair, "I forgot to put the asparagus muffins on the table. I sure hope they aren't cold now."

Finishing her meal was a challenge for Amanda. The meatloaf tasted like oven cooked dirt and the asparagus in the muffins tasted like they had been soaked in vinegar - too much vinegar. Of course, any amount of vinegar would be too much for a muffin and the look on Amanda's face reflected just that when she bit down upon them. However, she continued to force the food down, taking a large swig of sweet tea after each bite.

"Do you like the meatloaf, dear?" asked Grandma Sneed. No matter how much disapproval Amanda tried NOT to show her grandmother, she was always asked if she liked the main course. And on this evening, she did not want to upset her grandmother. For by this time, her grandmother had forgotten about Amanda's school problems and having to discuss the matter with Grandpa Sneed.

"Yes, grandmother," responded Amanda trying not to hurt her grandmother's feelings. "It is just incredilicious." Yet another of word courtesy of the Amanda Sneed dictionary. Her grandmother was used to this though and knew that incredilicious meant that Amanda approved.

"Well, I'm glad you enjoyed it," Grandma Sneed said with delight. "Here, have some more." Grandma Sneed then put yet another piece of meatloaf on Amanda's plate as Amanda's eyes grew big. "Oh no, I forgot the cottage cheese and coconut jello." Grandma Sneed jumped up once again from her chair and scurried to the refrigerator. Bringing a large bowl of green jello over to the table, Grandma Sneed scooped a healthy portion onto Amanda's plate and smiled. "There's always room for jello."

"I think I may need another glass of tea," Amanda said cringing in her chair.

Amanda walked out onto the front porch after dinner. It was still early in the evening, but the sun had already set and darkness had made its way to the sky on this early October night. It was a clear night. Many stars could be seen and the moon shown bright in its crescent form. The Sneeds owned a home on several acres of land, just outside of Maffet Valley's town limits. The house was a two story country style home, with at least two windows to every room and two green shutters securely fastened around the outside of every window. There were three porches. One at the front of the house, one along the side of the house, and one to the rear of the house. The sides of the front porch were lined with well-trimmed hedges. The side porch had an old fashioned swing that could hold two average sized individuals. It was fastened to the porch's ceiling by a pair of rusted chains that squeaked when the swing swayed back and forth. The rear porch was screened in so that the Sneeds could enjoy sitting outside without the unwanted bites of mosquitoes that were abundant in the area during the summer months. Near the house was an old red barn with a tin roof. Amanda loved to climb up into the loft of the barn when it rained, and relax to the mesmerizing sound of the drops as they tap-danced against the tin. Since Amanda's grandparents did not raise any livestock, a portion of this barn had been converted to a carport by the "firecracker" of a handyman himself. The remainder of the barn was used for storage. The only other building on the property was Grandma Sneed's greenhouse. It was built close to the house for her convenience. Most of their acreage was wooded, but the portion that wasn't, was filled with Grandma Sneed's flower gardens.

Sitting down on the steps of the front porch, Amanda heard a noise coming from the trimmed hedges to the right side of the porch. There was no guessing who or what caused the noise. "All right you nutty fur ball, come on out." Amanda walked down to the bushes, got down on her knees, and pulled the hedge limbs back with both hands. "There you are." Peering back at her was none other than Lawrence. He sat upright on his hind legs with his front legs hanging straight down. "Where in the world have you been, Lawrence? I've been worried sick about you."

But then, Amanda noticed something swaying from Lawrence's mouth. "Oh no! What have you done now?"

Lawrence, like many ferrets, had an obsession to collect specific items. Lawrence's obsession was collecting keys. From his mouth dangled the same magnificent key that had been attached to Master Hemlock's key ring. "Let me have that!" Amanda exclaimed to Lawrence. Normally, Amanda would place any key that Lawrence brought home into his olive green backpack. But this key was not for keeping. This key must be returned and returned quickly.

Amanda's look said it all. "He saw me eying his key. He'll think I took it. And in a way, I did. Why couldn't you leave this one alone, Lawrence? Master Hemlock gives me the creeps. And now, I have to return it to him and when I do, he'll think I'm a thief. No, I somehow have to keep him from thinking I have his key. But how? How are we going to get this key back to him without him knowing it?"

Amanda pondered and pondered. "There's only one thing we can do, Lawrence. We have to sneak over to his home tonight and leave the key. It's the only way. Let's just hope he isn't home."

This decision made sense to Amanda. At least at the moment it did. Amanda knew what to plan for with regards to her grandparents. The nighttime routine was always consistent in the Sneed household. Very seldom did it vary. Amanda went to bed at 9:00 p.m., being tucked in and read a story by her grandmother. By 10:00 p.m., her grandparents were in bed themselves and quickly asleep. However, if Amanda was tired and went to bed earlier, then her grandparents would also go to bed earlier.

"Listen, Lawrence," Amanda said determined as she explained the plan to Lawrence, "I'll pretend I'm tired and head upstairs to bed early. Grandfather and grandmother won't stay up much longer after that so once they have gone to sleep, we'll sneak out the back door. It's the only one in the house that doesn't squeak when it opens. We'll take my flashlight so we can see. Now this is important. We're going straight there and straight back, stopping only long enough to leave the key somewhere in Master Hemlock's home. No sniffing around his place. No eating his food. And for gosh sake, no more taking his keys. Got it?"

The ferret showed the same expression, or lack thereof, as he always did as he tilted his head and gave Amanda a blank stare. But to this splendorific little girl, that was good enough.

Why do things always happen this way for me? Amanda thought to herself. Maybe it was her nerves, or maybe it was the stress, but Amanda's thoughts began to dwell on the problem at hand. *I wish my real life would be more like my dreams. Things always turn out splendorifically when I dream. I don't have to make decisions, they just happen.* Amanda hated to make decisions and she didn't much care for any kind of confrontation either. She would rather drift off to her dreams and let them take over.

But be careful what you wish for. Because sometimes wishes do come true. And sometimes dreams do become real. And sometimes, magic happens.

Chapter 3
The Well of Wishes

Hearing the television, Amanda knew it was time for her to go back inside and begin her plan. "Ok, Lawrence, grandfather turned on the television," Amanda said to her ferret friend. "That means we can get started. Don't do anything that will give us away either. Just follow my lead."

Just as expected, Grandpa Sneed was comfortably sitting reclined in his chair in the family room, holding the remainder of that day's paper rolled up in his left hand. And in his right hand, he held the remote control to the television, switching from channel to channel, and only allowing no more than two seconds of viewing per channel before changing to another. The television amplified its noise throughout the entire family room which showed another weakness of Grandpa Sneed - his hearing.

Grandma Sneed approached the family room from their bedroom which was on the first floor of the house. She had been getting herself more comfortable for the evening, dressed in a long, lime colored, terrycloth housecoat, which covered most all of her, exposing only the lower portions of her shins. On her feet, she wore matching lime colored slippers.

With too much exaggeration, Amanda stretched her arms above her head, and added a theatrical yawn to grace her performance. "Wow, am I tired," Amanda said. "I think I might just go on to bed if that's ok with both of you."

"So soon?" Grandma Sneed asked. "I don't feel like we visited much this evening. Would you like me to come upstairs to read to you and tuck you in?"

"No, grandmother," replied Amanda, "that's ok. I'm so tired, I'll probably be asleep by the time you get upstairs anyway. I really need to get rested tonight."

"You will need to be rested for your day tomorrow," responded Grandma Sneed winking. "Just be sure to turn your light off before you fall asleep."

Amanda walked over, bent down, and gave her grandfather a hug. "Goodnight, grandfather."

"Hey!" said Grandpa Sneed. "You're blocking my view of the television."

"She's trying to tell you goodnight, Herb," scolded Grandma Sneed. "Quit being so cranky. You sound like you need to get to bed."

"Oh, I guess I wasn't paying attention. Goodnight, sweety," said Grandpa Sneed. "Don't let those bedbugs bite. And for gosh sakes, take those wire bread ties out of your hair before you go to sleep. They'll make your hair rust."

"Goodnight, grandmother," said Amanda walking over to the couch where she was resting.

Grandma Sneed pulled Amanda to her and kissed her forehead. "Goodnight, dear," Grandma Sneed said smiling. "Sweet dreams."

Amanda headed upstairs to her room, got under the covers of her bed, and waited patiently. Within minutes, the sound of the television was gone and the light that Amanda could see from her room coming from downstairs was gone too. She knew this was the first step to her grandparents going to bed.

Soon afterwards, Grandpa Sneed's snoring could be heard bellowing through the halls of the house with a deep bass sound. His snoring was joined in duet with Grandma Sneed's snoring, which made a much daintier sound.

"That's the signal. It's time my little furry friend," Amanda stated anxiously as she flung the covers off of her body and jumped out of bed. "Are you ready?" Lawrence still had on his olive green backpack with the letter "L" embroidered on it, and stood next to Amanda, ready to follow her wherever she might go.

Amanda grabbed a flashlight out of her top dresser drawer. "Better check the batteries," she said as she turned the flashlight on and off again. She put her hand in her pants pocket, checking to see if the Master Hemlock's key was still there. "It's good to be prepared, Lawrence. Let's go." Amanda placed the flashlight in one of the many secret compartments within her navy blue jacket, which she still had not taken off for the day, picked up Lawrence, and tiptoed down the stairs, making her way to the back door.

Sneaking out was not a pastime of Amanda's. In fact, this was a first time experience for her. The darkness of the night did have an affect on Amanda. "Ok, Lawrence," Amanda whispered, "remember, straight there, straight back. Let's be glad I have my flashlight with us." Following the edge of the woods was no easy task with only dim moonlight to lead their way. The cabin was not far. Walking, it would only take about five minutes to make the journey. But to Amanda, five minutes of walking by the woods at night, felt more like five hours. "We should be there any second, Lawrence. I'm pretty sure it's not much farther."

The sounds of the night created an orchestral effect. Crickets and tree frogs sang together in unison, a chorus of epic proportion. The sounds were mesmerizing to both Amanda and Lawrence. It was very chilly for an early October night. The clear skies from earlier were now becoming partially cloudy. A light breeze blew directly into Amanda's face as she marched forward. The air whispered in her ears as she walked, and the faster she walked, the louder these whispers became. The trees sounded as if they were moaning, causing Amanda to feel more nervous than she already was. "It's ok, Lawrence. Nothing to be afraid of out here in these woods," Amanda said bravely, pretending not to be scared.

"See, Lawrence, there it is," Amanda said pointing her finger. Just ahead of her was a tiny cabin. A fire was burning in the fireplace of the cabin. The glow from the fire inside made a pair of windows in the front resemble two orange eyes staring back at Amanda. The limbs from a pair of oak trees which book cased the cabin, hung down like multiple arms with a myriad of crooked fingers, ready to snatch all who tried to enter. This gave Master Hemlock's home the appearance of a living, monstrous beast. "So maybe it is a little creepy. We still have to go inside and put this key somewhere, so no chickening out on me now. You hear me?"

Approaching the front of the cabin, Amanda climbed up the steps to the top of the porch. She stopped when she found herself at the front door and took a deep breath to help calm her nerves. "Let's just slide the key you stole under the door and be on our way." Lawrence pushed his nose against the base of the door which was slightly cracked opened and marched his way in. "Wait! Come back here!" Amanda was perturbed at the ferret for taking the initiative to prance right on in the house.

Amanda hesitantly peered around the side of the door to ensure Master Hemlock was not home. Realizing it was safe to enter, she followed Lawrence inside, then stopped to gaze around at what Master Hemlock called home. "Well, this seems cozy," Amanda said looking around. "He's not much of a decorator."

The cabin was only a two room home - the main room, which included a dining area, and a back room. Amanda tiptoed forward in case Master Hemlock was somewhere in the back of the cabin. Along the left wall, was a fireplace. Judging by the large iron pot hanging over the fire, it appeared as if Master Hemlock used it for his stove. The fire burned brightly and gave the entire main room the same eerie orange glow that Amanda witnessed when she approached the cabin from outside.

To the right side of the main room was a doorway. The doorway led to the back room which Amanda guessed was Master Hemlock's bedroom. But Amanda did not know this for sure from where she stood and she had no intention to walk in back and find out. In front of the wall along the right side of the main room was a large rocking chair made of thick, heavy wood. "You could put an elephant on a chair that size, Lawrence," Amanda said chuckling.

Along the far wall, directly across from the front door, was a shelf. On the shelf were several books, most of which looked to be old and dusty. There were also some dishes, jars of preserved foods, and an hourglass. One item in particular caught Amanda's attention. "Would you look at that chest?" Amanda asked in amazement. "It looks like a pirate chest." The chest on the shelf did indeed resemble an authentic pirate's treasure chest.

In the middle of this room was a dining table with only one chair. "I guess he eats alone most of the time," Amanda concluded. But the weirdest thing about this room was that it had several bags of sand lying around in many different places. Most of these bags were partially opened so the sand inside could be seen. Strangely, the sand glistened just as the sand did that covered Master Hemlock's brown coveralls.

"Lawrence, would you look at all these bags of sand?" Amanda asked with excitement. "The sand, it sparkles like glitter. Just like that sand did at school today. I've never seen sand do that before. I thought I was seeing things earlier today, but now I'm positive what I saw." Amanda found the twinkling of the sand to be very intriguing and almost hypnotic. "Why would he have so much sand in his house anyway? That just seems a little messy to me."

Amanda was so interested in the sand, that she did not notice Master Hemlock approaching from outside.

However, Lawrence did, as the ferret scurried his way behind one of the bags of sand, leaving his tail exposed. "What is going on with you this time?" she asked. "Did you find another key back there or something? I certainly hope not. We're in enough trouble with Master Hemlock." Amanda did not know what Lawrence was doing. It wasn't until she heard the loud stomp of a foot place its mark on the front porch of the cabin, that she realized Lawrence was scared and was not searching for keys behind the bags of sand.

Now Amanda was scared too. "Oh no. Master Hemlock is home. What do I do now?" Without hesitation, Amanda dropped to the ground on all fours and found herself crawling under the dining table. *There's no place to hide*, Amanda thought. *Maybe if I get all the way under here, he won't see me.*

The front door swung open. Master Hemlock stood still for a moment as if he wanted to observe the room completely before entering. He then started sniffing.

"Must be another rat," he mumbled under his breath. "Doesn't matter, I need to find that key." Master Hemlock made a quick dash to the shelves, looking behind each and every item. He picked up the chest and opened it. "Where did it go?" He appeared extremely disappointed in his search. "Maybe I dropped it." Master Hemlock began to look around the floor, thinking maybe the key could have fallen somewhere. "What's this? I think I found my rat problem." Master Hemlock could see Lawrence's tail sticking out from behind the sandbag. "Come here little fella'. Hmm, let me guess."

Amanda didn't move. *Ok, so he found Lawrence*, her thoughts filled her head. *Big deal. I'll just tell him tomorrow that my ferret was still lost and somehow ended up at his house. I have to get out of here*. Amanda curled her body underneath the table, but when she turned with her face looking the other direction, she was eye to eye with Master Hemlock, who was leaning down to look under the table at her.

"I believe I found that ferret you were looking for earlier today at school little miss," said Master Hemlock. "Why don't you come out from under there?"

Amanda was frightened and very upset with herself. "Great, in trouble yet again," she whispered.

"So, Miss Sneed. It is Miss Sneed isn't it?" asked Master Hemlock.

"Yes sir, I mean Master Hemlock," Amanda replied.

"Well then, Miss Sneed, what exactly is the purpose of your visit this evening?" Master Hemlock questioned. "Are you sleepwalking or were you hoping I might be able to read you a bedtime story?"

"No, Master Hemlock," Amanda began to explain. "I was... I was actually returning something of yours. You see, my goofy pet ferret there has this problem. He likes to steal keys and he took this one of yours that he saw today. I just wanted to get it back to you, so you didn't think I took it, that's all." Amanda pulled the gold key out of her pocket and handed it to Master Hemlock.

"You have my key?" Master Hemlock said in disbelief. "I've been looking for it all night. Normally, I would be a bit upset with someone for taking one of my possessions. But getting this key back is so important, that I will make an exception this time. Thank you so much Miss Sneed. I have to have this key somewhere soon. It's an emergency. You have no idea how happy I am right now to have it back. In all honesty, you have done a great service by returning it."

Hemlock took the key and held it up to his eye, giving it a quick inspection. "Yes, this is the one alright." He placed the key in his front left pocket of his brown coveralls and then turned around and walked over to the shelf along the far wall. Once again, he picked up the chest and opened it.

"Most children your age would just keep a key this beautiful," he said. "Not too many have an honest heart like you Miss Sneed. I want to give this to you as a gift for handling things the way you did so thoughtfully."

What Master Hemlock was about to give Amanda was again something she had never seen before. Master Hemlock pulled from the chest a gold coin. Not just any gold coin. This coin had a sensational glow to it. A glow so bright that it hurt Amanda's eyes to look directly at it. "I've never seen a coin glow like this before," she said. "Trying to look at it is like staring into the sun."

"That is because this is no normal coin, Miss Sneed," Master Hemlock stated. "This is a coin that only a child could dream of having. In fact, this is only half of the gift that I have to give you. For behind my house is a well. A well with a magical power. The power to grant wishes. But, you have to use one of these gold coins to make the well's magic work. Only with this coin, will it become a real wishing well."

"You have got to be kidding me," doubted Amanda. She didn't believe Master Hemlock. Who would? It was all too strange to her. The glistening sand, the radiating gold coin, and a school janitor with a wishing well in his backyard. "Ok, Master Hemlock. Let's cut this out right now. Do you really expect me to believe that by tossing this coin into the well behind your home, I will get whatever I wish for?"

"I do not joke around when it comes to magic Miss Sneed." The look on Master Hemlock's face said it all. He did not smile. He did not frown. He did not blink an eye. He stared directly into Amanda's eyes and said to her, "You must listen though. When the moon casts its light on the well, only then can you throw this gold coin into the well. One more thing - be sure to follow the rules the way they are written."

"What rules?" Amanda asked puzzled, as she kept her attention focused on trying to look at the coin without blinking.

"The wishing rules, of course," Master Hemlock chuckled. "You cannot expect to be granted a wish, without having certain guidelines to follow. Just be careful what you wish for." Master Hemlock looked over and glanced at the hourglass on his shelf.

"I'm sorry I cannot help you further," he said. "I must be going now. I am late for work and I still must return this key. Please, forgive me." But before Amanda could raise her head from looking down at the gold coin, Master Hemlock had disappeared into the night.

"Where did he go?" she asked herself. Amanda was confused. "Why did he say he had to get to work? I thought he just got home from working at school. Why does he have to return that key and who does it belong to? Why is that key so important? And why does that sand glisten the way it does? I still don't understand." Master Hemlock was a mysterious man. A mysterious man indeed.

Amanda was not sure what had happened to Master Hemlock or why he left so quickly. But her confusion was quickly overcome by her curiosity. "Wow, Lawrence,"

Amanda chirped with excitement. "Do you think this is really a magical gold coin? Or do you think he told me that just to make me feel better about your stealing his key? It doesn't matter. I'm glad he has his key back. That is what we came over here for. Getting this coin is just a bonus, regardless of whether it is magical or not."

Amanda picked up Lawrence and exited the cabin through the front door, leaving it wide open as she hurried in excitement. The sky had become mostly cloudy as a strong gust of air greeted Amanda immediately upon exiting. The well was just to the rear of the cabin. It looked like a typical well, not that Amanda could tell the difference between a "normal" well and a "different" well that granted wishes. The well had a circular foundation composed of creek rocks. Across the top, there was a crank handle. Wrapped around the crank handle was an old worn rope. The rope hung downward a couple feet and attached to its end was a wooden bucket. The bucket was swinging back and forth in the breeze.

As she headed toward the back of Master Hemlock's home, the clouds blocked the moonlight from time to time, making it hard for Amanda to see. Near the well, was an outhouse whose door was open and swaying back and forth due to the wind. "So we have to wait until the moon shines just right on this thing," she asked. "At least we don't have to throw the coin somewhere in that outhouse. That would be gross."

There's something I don't understand Lawrence. How will we know when it's the right time to make the wish? How much moonlight are we going to need to do it? With these clouds, we might just have a problem." Amanda walked up near the well and could see markings written on a stone placed directly in front of the well. She pulled out her flashlight from her navy blue jacket, and shined the light on the stone. "There's writing on this rock. These must be the rules Master Hemlock was talking about." Amanda glanced over the markings and began reading them to Lawrence.

Know What You Wish For
Make A Wish That You Know
For The Wish That You Wish,
Is The Wish That Will Show

With Two Hands, Drop A Coin
Made of Gold, Made To Glow
But Wait For The Light
Of The Moon To Let Go

"Why that doesn't sound so hard," said Amanda. "Wait, let me think about this. I have to use two hands. But do I let go with one hand or two? Do my hands have to be in the moonlight too? What about the coin?" Without a hint, the wind began to blow fiercely as the clouds above moved swiftly, and the moonlight could be seen creeping its way closer and closer to the well.

Startled, Amanda took a step back, only to fall to the ground, dropping the coin from her hands. "Oh no! I'm not going to make it. This might be my only chance to make the wish with all the clouds moving in. And now I've lost the coin." Amanda scurried around on her hands and knees, desperately searching for the coin she had dropped. The moonlight was touching the base of the well and Amanda began to get much more upset with herself.

"Why am I so clumsy? Why couldn't this simple task be easy for me?" Then, like a revelation, Amanda realized that she was going about it the wrong way. "Wait a minute!" she exclaimed. "The coin glows. Just look for the glow." Sure enough, that was all it took. Looking around her, she could see the glow of the gold coin emitting brightly in a patch of grass nearby. "There it is!" she said in delight as she snatched up the coin and rose to her feet.

Knowing she did not have much time, she made her way up to the well. Amanda grasped the gold coin tightly in her hand, debating in her head, the many wishes she could make. *Should I wish for all the riches in the world?* she thought. *Or for a new bicycle in place of my ugly purple three speed? Or to have a different flavor of ice cream for lunch every day instead of grandmother's jello surprise? Or should I wish to be more popular than Stephanie at school? Now that's a tempting wish.* Tighter she squeezed the coin. She could feel the sweat building on her palms. This decision was driving her insane. "Why is it so hard to make a decision? Why can't my choice of a wish "just happen" like things happen in my dreams? I never have to make decisions in my dreams. Everything just happens."

Then, without any further thought, it came to her. "THAT'S IT!!!" she burst with excitement. "My Dreams! That's what I'll wish for." She held the gold coin up to her lips and kissed it. With it still lightly touching her lips, she looked deep down into the well and whispered to herself, "I wish all of my dreams would come true." The moonlight could not have been more perfect, as it graced its presence upon the well. Amanda let go of the gold coin with both hands and listened for it to reach the bottom. Staring into the well, Amanda watched and waited, hoping for any sort of guarantee that the coin had made a complete journey.

"Kaplunk!" There it was. That was the guarantee she needed.

"Yes!" Amanda looked up and smiled as a huge gust of wind blew toward her, forcing her pigtails backward. She raised both of her arms as if she had been the victor of a huge battle, when the wind caused the bucket hanging from the well's crank handle, to smash against her forehead. Amanda fell backwards to the ground and closed her eyes. No longer did the importance of the gold key concern Amanda. No longer did the glittering sand concern Amanda. No longer did Master Hemlock's quick disappearance concern Amanda. With the sound of the coin hitting the bottom of the well, this splendorific little girl knew that she had made her wish. With that noise, this splendorific little girl knew that her dreams just might come true.

Chapter 4
Awakened in a Dream

Amanda opened her eyes, completely unaware of her surroundings. She had been sleeping on her back, still in her navy blue jacket, with Lawrence asleep on top of her. "Why are we swaying, Lawrence?" questioned Amanda. "My bed doesn't sway." Looking upward, Amanda could see the sky. But given that she wasn't quite awake, she didn't realize that she was actually outdoors.

"Actually, I don't remember going to bed last night. In fact, I don't remember leaving Master Hemlock's cabin. All I remember was Master Hemlock giving me a gold coin and I made a wish in his wishing well and...uh!!! Oh my gosh, Lawrence! Wake up!" Amanda sat up quickly, flinging Lawrence into the air. "The wish, Lawrence! Remember? I made a wish!" The events of the previous evening suddenly filled Amanda's head. That is, most of them. "Wait, I don't remember much after I made the wish. But that makes no sense. I must have blacked out or fell asleep by the well. But if that's the case, why am I not still by the well and instead I'm here? And where exactly is here?"

Amanda looked around and quickly realized that she was indeed no longer at the wishing well, nor was she in her bed, nor was she at Master Hemlock's. She was nowhere familiar. Instead, she found herself in a rowboat located in the middle of a muddy brown pond, without any oars to paddle the boat to shore.

"What is that smell?" Amanda asked grossed out by the scent gracing her nostrils. "Is that you, Lawrence?" But the odor became an afterthought once she heard laughter coming from nearby.

"Looks to me like ya' got yourself in some kind of predicament," chuckled a voice from behind Amanda.

Amanda turned around to see a fish dressed in blue overalls and a straw hat, sitting on the shore. He had a long blade of grass sticking out of his mouth, and was holding a fishing pole that had been cast out into the pond near where Amanda was stuck. "Why, you're a fish. And you're fishing?" Amanda said in complete puzzlement. Amanda did not understand any of this. Not only was this fish out of the water, and not only could he talk, but he was dressed like he was going to go on a hay ride.

"Why, you're a human. And I'm guessin' you're humannin'," the fish said defensively. "What do ya' mean

I'm fishin' anyway? I'm wormin' little lady. And not havin' much luck at it either."

"A talking fish? How is it you talk?" Amanda asked in both fright and confusion. "What type of fish are you? I've never met a fish that could talk."

"Well, first lil' lady, I talk quite a bit," explained the fish. "Don't get two words in 'round my wife though. That woman can really talk, let me tell you. Second, far as what type fish I am, well, can't you tell? I'm a blue gill of course. Just take a look here." The fish turned his head to the side and pointed at his cheek area which showed a large bluish colored spot. "I have ta' say, don't think I've ever heard no human talk myself. 'Course, I ain't never seen no human before, 'cept pictures in my lil' ones storybooks."

The fish's pole began to jerk. "Must be a big'un. Bet it's least a couple ounces." The fish pulled back on his pole and reeled in the worm, landing him on shore. Then after removing the hook, the fish set the worm on the ground. "Look at 'em squirm, would ya'? Just like a worm out of water. This one looks like it'll make some good eatin' too. This one here's a catworm. Makes a mighty fine fillet, specially deep-fried and battered in pond scum."

"Gross," Amanda said with a look of disgust on her face. Amanda didn't care much for the thought of deep-fried worms. Especially deep-fried worms battered in pond scum. "Oh, by the way, my name's Amanda."

"Well, pleasure's all mine Miss Amanda. Ma' name's Monroe. Have to admit. Didn't think no one was in 'dat boat. Let alone, a human."

"It's nice to meet you Monroe...I think." Amanda wasn't too sure what to think. Meeting a talking fish was definitely the weirdest thing that had ever happened to her before. Instead of dwelling on the weirdness of meeting her new acquaintance, she focused her thoughts on efforts of getting out of her current inconvenient situation. "I do have one problem. I was wondering if you might help me out with something. As you can see, my ferret Lawrence and I have ended up out here in the middle of this pond in this boat. The problem is it has no oars. So do you think maybe you could help get the boat over to shore somehow so we're not stuck out here forever?"

"Hmm, let's see. I don't 'zackly have no oars ma'self. 'Course, if I did, don't know how I'd get 'em to ya'." Monroe pondered the problem a bit more, as he put his fin to his chin, and looked upward, with the appearance of complete confusion. "I know somethin'. How 'bout I cast my line over to ya' and you tie it on that boat. Then I'll start reelin'."

"Why that sounds like a splendorific idea Monroe," Amanda said, surprised to hear such a logical idea coming from Monroe. "Let's give it a shot."

"Splendorific?" mumbled Monroe.

"A talking fish?" whispered Amanda.

Monroe cast his worming line out to the water, very near where Amanda was located. Amanda leaned over the side of the boat and reached for the fishing line. She pulled it inside the boat and tied it onto an anchoring hook at the bow.

"Ok, hold on lil' miss." Monroe reeled and reeled until his eyes popped out of his head and the tension in his pole caused the pole to bend so far that it looked like it would break at any moment. "How much you weigh lil' lady? Ain't no worm in 'dis pond ever put that much strain on my line before."

"Trust me," Amanda replied feeling insulted, "I'm very small for a human. I've been told that I'd blow away like a kite if I ever got caught in a brisk wind."

"Why, flap my fins. I been comin' here wormin' every mornin' for da' past 47 years, and I ain't never reeled me in a human before," Monroe said as the boat drew closer to the shore. "Woo wee! Yep, this is a first for me."

"I'm glad I was able to assist you as your first human catch," Amanda responded with a hint of sarcasm. "I'm sure my grandparents would be very proud of me."

"So you have a human family?" Monroe asked. "Tell me a little bit 'bout 'em."

Monroe pulled the boat onto the shore as Amanda proceeded to tell him about her grandparents. "Well, Mr. Fish - I mean Monroe, I live with my grandmother and my grandfather. They don't always understand me and that makes it hard for me to talk to them about things sometimes. Don't get me wrong, they are wonderful and I love them, but it's just not the same as having real parents. At least that's how I feel when I see other kids with their parents. I always feel like something is missing. You see, I never knew my mother. She died shortly after I was born. As far as my father, he was very sad when she died. He was only around briefly after my mother passed away and therefore I don't know him either except what my grandparents tell me. Grandfather says it's complicated and that he works a lot, but in a way, I feel like my father died too. I have no brothers or sisters. Other than that, my only family is Lawrence here." Upon hearing his name,

Lawrence began chasing his tail as if he were showing off. "He likes attention. Can you tell?"

"Wow, you never met your parents," Monroe responded. "I have ta' say, that sounds a bit sad. But at least ya' got your grandparents to live with. Which reminds me, where do ya' live and how'd you get here lil' miss? I am still scratchin' my scales tryin' to figure out how I found a human in my pond dis' mornin'."

"Well, I'm not too sure," Amanda answered with a nervous tone in her voice. "You see, I ran into this janitor at school named Master Hemlock and he had this really cool key. Well, my ferret stole his key and ran off. Lawrence has this problem with keys. He tends to "acquire" all the keys he finds. As far as this key, I couldn't just let Lawrence keep it. So I snuck over to Master Hemlock's house last night, after grandmother and grandfather fell asleep, to give it back. But I didn't want him to know it was my ferret who took the key, so I tried to sneak in his house while he was gone. But that didn't work. He ended coming home while I was still in his home and catching me. So I explained to him what happened and gave him his key back. I thought he'd be mad, but just the opposite happened. He found it very nice that I'd return something of his so he gives me this really cool gold coin and tells me that I could make a wish using the coin in a well in his backyard. So I make a wish and I wake up in your pond, which really smells bad, by the way. And the thing is, I should be in school right now. Mr. Izzmund is going to be so mad at me. He's my teacher. He sneezes a lot and he..."

"Stop, please just stop!" Monroe had to put an end to Amanda's babbling. "You're confusin' me. Walk with me toward my home and we'll try ta' figure this all out."

"Um, Monroe, where am I anyway?" Amanda asked. "What is this place?"

"Well lil' miss, 'dis is the island of Maldderan," Monroe explained, "and 'dis land that we're on is my farm."

"An island? We're on an island?" Amanda asked looking around. "Maldderan. I've never heard of it. How did I ever get here from Maffet Valley? If Maldderan is an island then it must be surrounded by water. Am I right Monroe? Is there an ocean out there? Are there any other islands around Maldderan? Maybe I can travel back to Maffet Valley in a boat. If we can find some oars, I could even use this boat here. I wonder how close are we to my home?"

"Ya' sure ask a lot of questions and I don't know a lot of da' answers to 'em," Monroe responded. "Maldderan is a pretty big island and it is where I was born and have lived my entire life, but I ain't never been off of Maldderan once, so I don't really know if anything else exists around it. As far as I know, Maldderan is an island all on its own. I do know it's surrounded by beautiful blue water known as da' Deliria Sea. I love it here though. Good weather, good friends, good times."

Amanda and Lawrence followed Monroe up a tall hill with much anticipation. "My home is just over the top of 'dis hill here," Monroe told them. "Not too far now."

"I'm so sorry Monroe," apologized Amanda as the trio came to the top of the hill. "I don't mean to be a burden on you. I didn't plan on waking up in your pond. I wanted to wake up in my own bed and get up and brush my teeth and..." Amanda stopped talking and stood in amazement at the sight before her eyes. Because at the top of that hill, Amanda looked down upon the entire land around them and witnessed an image unlike anything she had seen before. "Why, those are...," Amanda said frightened. "Those are..."

"Dragons," said Monroe finishing her sentence for her. "Yep, they are dragons. Welcome, lil' miss to the Dragon Fields of Lysium."

It was breathtaking and yet frightening at the same time. Below were hundreds of dragons of all sizes and colors. There were green dragons with two long prickly horns along the back of their head and scaly wings on their side. Others were brown and had no wings. But the claws on their feet were noticeably larger than the others as Amanda saw one of the brown dragons rip a tree into two with one swipe of its claw. There were red ones and purple ones. There were even blue dragons among the herd. Dragons were grazing in the fields and dragons were flying above, eating from the trees. Several dragons were soaking in a small pond that was located in the center of their grazing fields. Groups of smaller dragons were running together as if they were playing games with each other.

"Lysium's my name," Monroe continued. "Monroe E. Lysium. So 'dis here farm is named after my family. We usually just call it Lysium Fields."

"Why, Lysium Fields is just splendorific, Monroe," Amanda said amazed. "I've never seen anything like this." Amanda's eyes stayed affixed to the field of dragons below her. "I must admit, I am a bit scared though. I can't move my legs."

Amanda wasn't the only scared one. Lawrence did not like the sight of dragons, not a single one of them, as he burrowed his way behind Amanda's feet. He tucked his head low to the ground and let his backpack fall forward to cover the top of his head.

"Don't be nervous. Dragons are really quite timid," Monroe explained. "All it takes is just a lil' trust on their part. They'll do anything for ya' then. There are just certain things ya' always need ta' know 'bout dragons. You see, dragons are very, very smart. They understand everything ya' tell 'em."

"I can't believe this," Amanda said rubbing her eyes. "I must be dreaming. Dragons aren't real, fish don't talk, and I need to wake up right now."

Noticing that many of the fields where the dragons were grazing were not green like grass as she expected, Amanda asked, "Why are those fields yellow?"

"Those fields are dandelion fields," said Monroe. "Dandelions are a favorite among all dragon types. So we grow quite a bit of 'em. We also grow lots of gum balls too. 'Nother favorite among dragons."

"Dandelions and gum balls? Really?" Amanda asked curiously. "My grandfather can't stand dandelions. He says they're a worthless weed. I always loved them. I pick them for my grandmother all the time. She loves all types of flowers. I think they're beautiful. I love it when they turn into a white fluffy puffball so I can blow on them and watch all the seeds float individually through the air. They remind me of tiny ballerinas dancing in sky."

Monroe unintentionally ignored Amanda as he stared at a group of trees near where they were standing.

"Why, look'ee there. You see that group of gum ball trees?" Monroe was a bit upset as he pointed to several dozen gum ball trees to his left. "They been stripped clean. Gosh dern 'dem pirates. Always comin' round here stealin' my gum balls. Don't know why no stinkin' pirate needs gum balls anyway."

"Pirates?" Amanda gulped. "Did, did you just say pirates?" Amanda needed quick verification about this comment. "Monroe, when you said pirates, do you mean like 'walk the plank' pirates?"

"Well, I guess so," Monroe answered. "I ain't never actually seen one of 'der ugly mugs. By the time I get myself out here to catch 'em, they're on 'der way out of here. All I see is 'dat ship that they fly."

"What do you mean, a flying ship?" Amanda asked as her curiosity level increased.

"I mean 'der ship flies," Monroe explained. "Up in da' air."

"Oh great!" Amanda stated nervously. "First I meet a talking fish, then I just happen to bump into hundreds of dragons, and now you're telling me there is a pirate ship flying above me somewhere in the clouds?"

"I would say that's pretty much it lil' miss," Monroe replied nodding his head.

"Hey, these are real gum balls on these trees," Amanda said astonished as she reached out to pick one off of the tree. "I thought these were the same gum ball trees from where I live with the spiky green balls hanging on the tree limbs. But these trees are different. This is bubble gum growing on these trees. How can you possibly grow...? Never mind. I do love bubble gum though. Can I chew one?"

"Of course ya' can lil' miss. That's what 'der for," Monroe replied. "These here are all bubble gum trees. Der's different types too. This one you're about to chew is a cherry gum ball. Some of these over here are blackberry. We actually have 52 flavors we grow on our farm altogether. Plenty of choices for everyone, dependin' on your taste."

"Wow, this is yummy!" Amanda exclaimed with complete satisfaction as she chewed and chewed on the cherry gum ball. "It tastes incredible. It's so delicious. I would say these gum balls are incredilicious. Yes, they're incredilicious. I don't understand what a pirate would want with them? I guess they like to chew bubble gum as much as I do."

Amanda's thoughts of pirates was quickly sidetracked as she began to notice something around each of the dragons' necks. "Are those necklaces the dragons are wearing?" Amanda asked Monroe.

"Well, sort of lil' miss," Monroe answered. "'Dat 'der would be a tag of sorts. It's how we label 'dem dragons. Ya' see, look at that one. It says XA-211. Da' first letter "X" is a label showing that da' dragon belongs to our farm. In other words, da' dragon is part of Lysium Fields. The second letter "A" means it is a girl dragon. If it was a boy, the letter would be "R" instead of "A". The number is just da' sequence that da' dragon was born. So number 211 means that the dragon was da' 211th female dragon born or acquired here at Lysium Fields."

"That's incredible!" exclaimed Amanda. "I see a lot of "XA" tags instead of "XR" tags though. Why is that?"

"Dat's because we tend to raise females only," Monroe responded. "It's our business ya' know? We milk these dragons and sell the milk. Dragon milk is very valuable. It cures lots of ailments and is delicious to drink, especially mixed with chocolate syrup. Only the girls can be milked. So the boy dragons are usually sold or traded. Da' ones we keep we use for working in the fields or for transportation purposes. I'll show you 'zactly what I mean by milkin' the dragons. Let's head on into da' milkin' parlor and I'll show you 'round."

The trio began their walk from the grazing fields and gum ball orchards toward Monroe's home and the dragon milking parlor. Upon approaching the main farm area, Amanda saw many buildings on the property. All of the buildings were composed of hardened packs of dry mud. There were small pebbles or various colors blended into the mud composition giving the buildings a hint of green, red, gray, and black tones. The windows on the buildings were glass and rounded outward like a glass bubble being blown from inside, resembling the side of a round fish bowl cut into half. The doors to the buildings were not rectangular like most doors. These doors were large pieces of coral, shaped in various ways depending on the coral used. No two doors were alike. Most looked like the letter "Y" with minor variations in the shape from one to the other, giving each door its own unique appearance. The coral used on each door was not one complete piece either. The coral had been sliced lengthways into thin sheets like lumber is cut from a tree.

"That's my house 'der," Monroe said as he pointed his fin to an interesting looking three level building constructed of layers of mud. "It's not much. But it's home." Amanda noticed one difference about Monroe's home from the rest of the buildings. At one end of his house was a stack made of mud, like a fireplace, elevating above the top of the roof. But there was no smoke coming from this fireplace. Instead, there were bubbles floating from within the top of the stack into the air above, popping within moments of leaving the stack, and splashing droplets of water with each burst.

Monroe continued to walk up to the largest building on the property. The structure was a huge dome enclosed in mud. It resembled a mud-packed coliseum complete with a roof overhead. "Here it is. This is da' milkin' parlor. Let's go on in."

"Daddy, Daddy!!!" Before Monroe could open the door to the parlor, several young fish came running out to greet Monroe, Amanda and Lawrence. Many tripping over their own tail fins along the way.

"Wow, you have a lot of children," Amanda said in amazement.

"Yep, I have 34 still livin' at home," Monroe responded. "I have 129 altogether. I get 'der names mixed up most of 'da time."

"Daddy, who's that?" said one of toddler fish pointing toward Amanda with her tiny fin.

"Daddy, that looks like one of those humans in our storybooks," said another little one. "Does it bite?"

"No, no, no," replied Monroe. "She's completely harmless. She needs my help though so you kids run along now and play, ya' hear? Between raisin' these kids, milkin' and keepin' up with da' dragon livestock, I hardly have any time ta' be wormin' these days. I was lucky to have had time out 'der 'dis mornin'."

The fish children all ran off, staring at Amanda the entire time. One was even picking his nose with his right pectoral fin as he turned to run away. "Sorry 'bout 'der manners lil' miss," apologized Monroe.

"Oh, don't worry about them," replied Amanda. "They are all really cute. All 34 of them."

Monroe finally got around to opening the door to the milk parlor. "Ok, come on in."

The entrance to the large mud-packed dome was a chunk of coral with a relatively flat bottom and the shape of a half circle rounding its top. On the surface of the door was a picture carved into the coral of a dragon carrying two pails - one in each wing - resembling a measurement scale. The door opened by swiveling on its center as Monroe pushed the right edge of its surface with his fin.

Amanda stepped in behind Monroe with Lawrence. She followed Monroe through a series of mud tunnels, weaving in and out with no logical understanding to the path he was taking. Amanda had to lower her head in many spots within the tunnels. She did however bump her head on a few occasions, causing the dry mud of the overhead to leave a dusty cloud behind them as they passed.

The tunnels of the dragon milking parlor were not lit with conventional lighting. Instead, there were jars attached at various intervals on the walls of the tunnels. Inside of these jars were the strangest looking bugs. They looked like roaches, but their bodies were yellow. The jars had small holes punctured throughout their casing, allowing air to enter, but were small enough to keep the bugs from escaping. What was strange about these bugs was that each one lit up like a light bulb. Each jar had at least a dozen of these bugs inside which was enough to give the tunnels a bright source of light.

Amanda was fascinated by these bugs as she lifted her hand to touch one of the jars.

"Don't touch 'em!" Monroe bursted as he pushed her hand down with his fin. "'Dem is lightnin' bugs. One touch of one of 'dem critters and you'll be knocked out for sure. It's one nasty shock too. Trust me. I get stuck catchin' more of 'em when we need additional light." Amanda listened and instead of touching the lightning bugs or anything else in the mud tunnels, she decided to put her hands in the front pockets of her navy blue jacket.

The trio finally came to the end of the maze of tunnels and entered into a gigantic room - a room known as the dragon milking parlor. The colossal size of the parlor explained why the building appeared to be a coliseum from the outside. The parlor was circular and the mud ceiling formed a concave shape like the inside of a dome. Around the outer edge of the circular room, creating a wide border, was an elevated platform, partitioned off from the center of the parlor. With respect to locations on a clock, this border ran from the 8 o'clock position to the 4 o'clock position, in a clockwise manner.

Amanda, Monroe, and Lawrence were standing at the 6 o'clock position, at the top of small set of stairs that led down into the center of the parlor. Dragons were entering a door at the 8 o'clock position and moving around the platform clockwise, stopping at the 4 o'clock position, fitting eight dragons in the parlor at one time. At the 4 o'clock position was another door which allowed the dragons to exit when they were finished being milked.

Looping around the center of the parlor, down the set of steps, were eight clear, globe-shaped glass tanks, one respective to the location where each one of the eight dragons stood. In the exact center of the parlor, was another clear, globe-shaped glass tank, larger than any of the eight. It was at least ten times the size of all eight small tanks put together. And the eight tanks around the center of the parlor did not look all that small to Amanda.

All eight of the small glass tanks fed into the large tank in the center through a series of glass pipes. A teal blue liquid could be seen through the clear transparent glass of all of the tanks. A liquid commonly known as dragon milk. Amanda watched as the dragon milk flowed from the smaller tanks into the large tank in the center. The entire operation left her amazed and speechless.

Working around the tanks, were several other fish farmers. Most looked like Monroe minus the straw hat. These fish were working hard handling the milk and the dragons that were being milked. Most were so busy that they didn't even notice when a human entered the parlor.

A few did notice as they began to whisper to each other and point fins in Amanda's direction.

"Would you look at that?" Amanda said to Lawrence oblivious to the whispering of the other fish. "So that's dragon milk? It's the most interesting color. Look at it flow from the smaller tanks to the larger one. That's amazing."

"What do ya' think?" Monroe asked. "Milkin' as many dragons as we do is a lot of work. We stay milkin' all day and night. We run shifts though. Almost time for me to start milkin'. My friend Sebastian is milkin' right now. Don't see him in here right now. Must be bringin' up some more dragons or somethin'."

"I guess I'm a little confused. Where I'm from, we get our milk from cows," said Amanda.

"Cows!" exclaimed Monroe. "Why cows are the most disgustin' animal I can think of. The only good use fer a cow 'round here is ta' help fertilize the dandelion crop. I wouldn't drink cow's milk if you gave me all da' worms on this island for my dinner."

Another fish dressed in overalls came into the milk parlor. "What did you drag in here this time?" asked the fish staring at Amanda.

"Sebastian, I'd like you ta' meet my human friend Amanda. I found her while I was wormin' up at ole' muddy pond," said Monroe. "You might say I reeled her in."

"Interesting," replied Sebastian. "How about we put her to work?" Sebastian wasn't quite as friendly as Monroe had been to Amanda.

"Um, how do you do Sebastian?" greeted Amanda. "My name's Amanda Sneed and I must say, this is the most splendorific farm I have ever seen. A bit scary, but splendorific nonetheless."

"Save your breath human," said Sebastian. "I'm not interested."

"Sure," said Amanda as she quickly tried to think of something to talk about with Sebastian. "What type of fish are you Sebastian? Are you a bluegill too like Monroe?"

"Hmmpppffff!!! Do I look like a bluegill?" exclaimed Sebastian with a tone of being insulted as he pointed to his cheek. "No, I'm a sea bass, not that it's your business. What I read about you humans must be true. Always making assumptions."

"Lighten up on our guest buddy," requested Monroe. "She's just tryin' ta' be friendly."

"Whatever. I'll be over here milking if you need me." Sebastian turned his back and walked away from Amanda and Monroe.

"I'm glad it wasn't him that I met first out at the pond," said Amanda, "otherwise, I might still be stuck out in that boat."

"Oh, don't worry too much 'bout him," Monroe responded. "He's always in a bad mood for some reason or 'nother. Don't take it personally."

"Ok, I won't," responded Amanda. "I do want you to know that I'm glad you got me out of that pond though. Now I need to figure out what I'm doing here though and how I can get home. This place is completely amazing to me, but I can't stay. My grandparents must be worried sick about me."

"Well, I don't 'zactly know why you're here or how to get ya' home neither," Monroe said. "But one thing I do know, is that when I have something that needs answerin', I go to da' city. Da' city is full of answers. I suggest you go there yourself and see if you can answer your questions there."

"The city?" Amanda questioned. "What city? Where is it? How do I get there? Who do I need to see? ..."

"Hang on, hang on," Monroe interrupted. "I can only handle one question at a time. You're hurtin' my head. First, the city's name is Meeyor. At least dat's the closest city near here. It's da' one we go to all da' time.

Some call it da' city of reflection. Little bright there. You'll have ta' wear sunglasses. Second, far as where is it, it's only three hours Northwest of here. 'Course, that's walkin' along the main roads by fin."

"Three hours!" Amanda said worried. "I don't have fins, but I'm sure it would take me close to that long to walk it too."

"Well, 'der's 'nother way," Monroe said. "Sebastian, why don't ya' go out and round up 'dat crazy one. We'll be out in a second."

"Sure. Whatever. Anything for the human," Sebastian responded sarcastically.

Sebastian left through the door that the dragons exited the milk parlor, with a disgruntled look on his face. Within moments, loud noises were heard from outside the milk parlor. Noises that included sounds of broken glass, slamming doors, and a deep bellowing roar of a dragon. Noises that were followed by a lot of yelling from a very angry fish named Sebastian.

Monroe, Amanda, and Lawrence ran outside to find a large, extremely active dragon, dragging Sebastian on the ground behind him by a rope. "Dern dragon!" Sebastian said in disgust. "Whoa there! I said whoa there!"

The dragon paced back and forth, smelling everything in his path. The majority of his body was composed of blue scales, with some darker, black scales blending in with the blue ones. This combination of color gave the dragon's body a dark tone, although his blue scales shined when struck by light. Along the sides of his face and neck, were long, thick red strands resembling hair. His ears stood upward, as if he were constantly listening to everything around him. His eyes were like two jewels, bright and piercing, as they gleamed the same intensity and aura of an emerald. His tail extended well beyond his hind legs. Upon the tip of his tail were seven spikes. Three of the spikes were to the right side of his tail's tip, while three others were to the left. The last spike curved upward, like a hook, along the top of the very tip of his tail. The spikes were sharp and Amanda feared any possibility of coming into contact with them.

But perhaps the most breathtaking feature of this creature was his wingspan. When the dragon finally stopped moving and was no longer dragging Sebastian along the ground, Sebastian stood up and positioned himself in front of the dragon, attempting to pull him forward toward Monroe, Amanda, and Lawrence. This attempt was useless as the dragon rose on his hind legs, pulling Sebastian upward and dangling him in the air, and spreading his enormous wings to their fullest extension. This action made the dragon appear almost three times the size that he really was. The trio was left in a dark shadow as his wings blocked all possible light from reaching their presence.

"'Dis here is XR-27," Monroe said introducing the male dragon to Amanda. "'Dis is your ticket ta' wherever ya' want ta' go on this island. Ya' name it, he'll take ya' there. He's a peppy one too. He'll never run out of energy on ya'." XR-27 then pulled his wings back to his body, positioned himself back down on all fours, reached forward with his neck, and licked Amanda on the side of her face.

"He does have a lot of energy," Amanda said. "I think he likes me already. He sort of acts like a puppy. A 9 foot tall, 700 pound puppy that is. He's huge. How old is he? He must be pretty old considering how big he is."

"Why he's just a youngster. He's only 10 months old. His mama however is 312 years old," Monroe explained. "Looks good for her age though. She's a feisty one too, let me tell ya'. Pretty good sign this one here is a spitfire, just like his mama."

"Can he do tricks?" Amanda asked as she knelt down to pick up a stick to throw. "Let's see if he can fetch." Amanda drew her arm back to throw the stick. "Here XR, go fetch the stick."

"No!!! Stop!!!" Monroe yelled. But before she could stop, Amanda's arm thrust forward and released the stick, launching it into the air for the dragon to fetch.

However, instead of fetching, the young dragon reared its head back as if it were getting ready to spit. Then, as quick as a flash of lightning, the dragon blew out a stream of blazing fire, directly centered on the stick. The stick was immediately engulfed in a huge flame, burning it to a crisp, leaving nothing more than a pile of ashes on the ground.

"Oh my, what did I do?" Amanda asked frightened.

"Like I said earlier," Monroe began to answer, "there are certain things you need to know about a dragon. One of those things is never play fetch with a dragon. They have a different idea about what fetchin' is. Dragons tend to use fetchin' as a way ta' do target practice. So be careful and don't go throwin' that ferret around. Might cause him ta' feel a little hot in his seat."

"Gee, thanks Monroe," Amanda stated with a bit of sarcasm. "Nice of you to fill me in on that little dragon tidbit. Anything else I might need to know so I don't burn down a house or something?"

"Nope, not that I can think of at da' moment," Monroe answered. "You might want to keep 'em chewin' some bubble gum though. Dragons love bubble gum. It keeps 'em from breathin' fire. Not ta' mention, sure helps with that breath of theirs. Let me tell ya', when one of 'em gets a hold of some onions in those dandelion fields, their breath will curl ya' fins. It just plain stinks. I'm not sure what's worse, smellin' a dragon's breath or havin' it breath fire on ya'."

Lawrence was scared to death. The dragon and the fire episode had taken their toll on the poor ferret and he jumped into Amanda's arms for safety. "Do you think carrying you will save either of us from a flame like that?" Amanda asked the rodent. "Oh well, you better get used to him. Apparently, we have to fly on that creature."

"Oh right," Monroe perked up. "Ya' need a lesson in flyin' a dragon, don't 'cha? Well let's begin with boardin' a dragon. First ya' gotta let the dragon know you want to ride it. Go up to 'em and rub your hand along side its neck. That'll get its attention ya' want somethin'. Then, pat his wing two times. XR-27 prefers ya' board his left wing, so pat that one."

"We have to board on his wing?" Amanda asked.

"How else ya' 'spect ta' get up on a dragon?" Monroe answered with a question.

"Good point," Amanda said. "I'll be quiet and listen now."

"Ok, once he knows ya' want ta' fly, he'll stick his wing out for ya' ta' climb," Monroe continued. "Don't worry 'bout hurtin' him either. He's one strong dragon."

Then, sit down around his shoulders and get as comfy as ya' can. Them scales don't feel so hot pokin' on the back side, if ya' know what I mean."

"Actually, I don't know," Amanda stated. "But I bet I'm about to find out."

"That's boardin' in a nutshell," said Monroe. "Now comes the tricky part - actually flyin' this creature. Once you're on board and you're ready ta' go, rub the side of his neck again ta' let him know ya' need somethin'. Then, ya' have ta' burp."

"I have to what?" Amanda asked as if she misunderstood Monroe.

"You have ta' burp," Monroe said. "Like this." Monroe let out a huge burp deep from within his fish gut that lasted for at least five seconds. "I'm not sure why that works, but it does. I actually found out by accident. I burp a lot since I got a problem with indigestion and all. Eatin' too many worms will do that to ya'. Haven't found a dragon yet 'dat don't respond to a burp when I'm ready ta' fly."

"But I'm not much of an expert when it comes to burping," Amanda said hesitantly. "I find it a little gross."

"No problem," responded Monroe. "Sebastian, how 'bout you go get a travel canteen with some dragon milk for our friend here."

By this time, Sebastian had brushed himself off of all dirt and grime acquired from being dragged on the ground by XR-27. With his composure and attitude back, Sebastian answered, "Sure Monroe. I'd do anything for a human. Is there anything else you'd like me to fetch for the princess while I'm gone?"

"Nope, that'll do it," answered Monroe. "Just some milk. Might want ta' hurry though."

"Hurry?" mumbled Sebastian walking back into the parlor. "Sure, I'll hurry."

Monroe shook his head in response to Sebastian's rude behavior and continued Amanda's dragon flight training. "XR-27 has been lots of places on this island, so just tell him right after ya' burp where ya' want ta' go and he'll take ya' there. If ya' don't know a name of where ya' want ta' go, just give 'em a direction. He'll get ya' there. When you're ready ta' land, just rub the side of his neck again and then pat the back of his neck twice. Gettin' off of him is similar ta' boardin'. Just rub the side of his neck and pat his left wing twice."

"Ok," Amanda said, "I think I have all of that. Is there anything else I need to know?"

"Oh, yep, matter of fact, 'der is," Monroe said. "Be sure ta' give 'em somethin' as a treat every time he does somethin' for ya'. So, if he lets you board, give 'em a dandelion or some bubble gum. It's proper dragon etiquette. Here, I'll give ya' plenty of raspberry gum balls ta' give 'em as rewards. Raspberry is XR-27's favorite flavor." Monroe handed Amanda a large bag of gum balls which she put in Lawrence's backpack.

"Thank you," said Amanda. "I wouldn't want to insult a dragon, that's for sure."

"Oh, and in case ya' get lost," Monroe continued as he pulled a folded piece of worn brown paper from the back pocket of his overalls, "here's a map of the entire island. Well, almost the entire island. This map's missin' a chunk out of the bottom left corner. Never been ta' 'dat part of the island ma'self, so I'm not too sure what's 'der. If ya' got ta' get ta' that part of the island, don't worry.

Just let XR-27 ya' need ta' fly Southwest. At least it's Southwest from here. Ya' won't get lost on this island though. Not with a dragon like XR-27."

Amanda opened the map and took a look. "So where are we on this map Monroe?" she asked.

"Lysium Fields is right here," Monroe explained just Southeast of the center of Maldderan, "and you are headin' to Meeyor which is right here." Monroe pointed to Meeyor on the map for Amanda to see. Studying the map, Meeyor appeared to Amanda to be exactly in the center of the island and Northwest of Lysium Fields as Monroe had told her earlier.

"Great. Thanks Monroe," Amanda said. "You've been such a great help. I don't think I can thank you enough."

"Well, don't worry 'bout it lil' miss," Monroe replied. "Let's get ya' on board and headin' on your way. Go ahead, give it a try."

Amanda walked up to XR-27 as he turned to sniff the top of her head. She hesitated a bit, feeling as if he might breath more of that fire on her. She took a deep breath and walked forward. "Ok, here goes nothing," Amanda said to herself.

Reaching up toward the side of XR's neck, Amanda rubbed her hand down the side and then patted his left wing twice. XR-27 then let out his left wing, like a plank.

"Go ahead," Monroe encouraged her, "get on board."

Amanda began walking up XR's left wing, carrying Lawrence in her arms, as the frightened ferret tucked his head inside of her navy blue jacket.

"Ok, I'm on his shoulders. Should I give him a gum ball now?" Amanda asked.

"That'd be a pretty good idea," stated Monroe.

Amanda held out a raspberry gum ball toward XR's head and XR reached over and took it from her hand with his mouth. "That wasn't too bad," said Amanda. "Now, passengers please take your seats." Amanda sat down on XR's shoulders, and jerked back and forth, trying to get comfortable. "This really hurts."

"Told ya' so," said Monroe. "Not much I can do ta' help ya' there. Ya' just have to get used to it. The pain goes away after awhile. When ya' land, ya' can just walk it off."

Great, thought Amanda, *just walk it off. What a logical way to handle pain. Haven't they heard of saddles on this crazy island? Or at least attempt to sit on a blanket for a little bit of comfort? I shouldn't complain. Monroe has been a huge help.*

"Looks like it's time ta' get this dragon in da' air," said Monroe. "Remember, after ya' burp, be sure ta' tell XR-27 that ya' want ta' go ta' Meeyor."

Amanda knew she might have a problem with this part. Burping wasn't something Amanda did very often, but it wasn't something out of the question either. She just needed practice. It was at that time, Sebastian returned with the canteen of dragon milk.

"I thought ya' got lost," said Monroe.

"Ha ha," responded Sebastian. "Here's your dragon milk, all packed up and ready for travel."

"Thanks my old friend," Monroe said.

"Not a problem," answered Sebastian. "Now just get that human out of here. She's attracting bugs."

"Ok, just concentrate," Amanda whispered to herself still focusing on her task at hand. "A good burp has to come from deep in the tummy."

"Ya' seem ta' be havin' trouble with burpin' lil' miss," stated Monroe. "Here, ya' need ta' take this canteen with ya' anyway." Monroe handed Amanda a round canvas container with a long leather carrying strap. She could hear liquid swishing around inside when he handed it to her. "'Dat's dragon milk. Like I said, it can be helpful if ya' get sick or somethin'. But it is also known for makin' folks burp. Why don't 'cha take a drink and see if ya' can burp then? Don't drink too much though. It only takes a little bit ta' do the job."

Amanda pulled the stopper from the canteen. *This is just wonderful*, thought Amanda. *I have to drink dragon milk. Talk about a new experience. Oh well, it has to taste better than some of my grandmother's food. It's just the thought of drinking dragon milk. How gross.* "Here goes nothing." Amanda pinched her nose with her left hand and held the canteen's opening to her mouth with her right hand. She closed her eyes tightly and with a grimacing look on her face, took a small swig of the bluish liquid.

"Wow! That didn't taste too bad," she said as the grimace on her face changed to a look of satisfaction. "It tastes like several different fruity flavors."

"Yep," responded Monroe, "I always describe it as a liquid blend of all 52 flavors of our gum balls in one refreshin' drink. It shouldn't be too long before ya' feel like burpin' neither."

Monroe was right. Amanda's stomach began to feel like it was expanding and filling with air. "I think you're right Monroe. I don't think it's going to take long either." Amanda had no control over the effects of the dragon milk as her stomach was about to pop like a balloon. Feeling the burp building inside her, Amanda went ahead and rubbed the side of XR's neck again when... "Burrrrppppp!!!!!" Amanda let out a loud and lengthy burp from deep within her stomach. Her burp caused XR-27 to immediately begin flapping his wings.

"Why, that's a burp I'd be proud of," laughed Monroe.

Amanda reached forward with another gum ball and XR once again took it from her hand. She placed the stopper back on the dragon milk canteen and secured it around her shoulder and back with the carrying strap. XR flapped his wings harder and the dragon began lifting off of the ground. Amanda quickly remembered she needed to tell the young dragon where to go. "Meeyor, I want to fly to Meeyor." XR-27 responded as he started moving forward in the air.

"There ya' go lil' miss! You're doing it!" shouted Monroe. "Hang in there and good luck!"

"Thank you, Monroe! Thank you for everything! Thank you too, Sebastian!" Amanda shouted back even though Sebastian turned his head to ignore her. "You've both been such a great help! Meeyor, here we come!"

And off they flew.

Chapter 5
The City of Reflection

Encountering dragons for the very first time in her life "was" the most breathtaking feeling Amanda had ever experienced, until now. She was flying. And she was flying on none other than a dragon. Not only did this take her breath away, but it had her scared out of her wits. "Oh my gosh! I think I'm gonna be sick. Don't look down. Just don't look down." XR-27 was soaring through the sky with such perfect form and agility, that Amanda really had no reason to worry

However, being a novice at dragon flying did present some problems for Amanda. Sitting on hard, jagged dragon scales was not the most comfortable of positions. "This definitely isn't flying first class," Amanda stated.

The lack of comfort didn't matter one bit to her though. "Actually, this is better than first class. Who can say they've flown a dragon? I would call this splendorific class. Wouldn't you agree, Lawrence?"

Lawrence, however, did not agree with Amanda's verdict. The speed of the flight was getting the best of the ferret. His mouth stretched out wide which looked like an over-exaggerated grin on his face. His lips flapped rapidly as the air forced its way against them. His eyes twirled in a counter-clockwise rotation, hinting signs that Lawrence was experiencing a bit air sickness.

Meeyor was not hard to locate. Meeyor was a city made completely out of glass. The glass gave quite a shine from the air due to its reflection. It was such a bright shine that Amanda strained her eyes attempting to look directly at the city from her perspective above. "Now I know why Monroe called it the city of reflection," said Amanda.

"That's it right over there, Lawrence." Amanda pointed to the bright area in the near distance. Lawrence put his head down and placed his paws over his eyes. "Does the city's bright reflection bother you Lawrence?" Amanda asked. "I know it's hurting my eyes. I can hardly look in its direction."

XR-27 knew exactly where he was going even without the brightness of Meeyor to guide him. Even though he was only ten months old, XR had already visited Meeyor on many occasions with Monroe. The dragon began descending toward the city.

"Down we go, Lawrence," laughed Amanda. "Wowzers, I feel a little dizzy." With XR descending at such a rapid pace, Amanda was feeling the affects on her body. Pressure could be felt against her eardrums and her nose stung due the air blowing upward into it. Her stomach felt like it was being pushed up into her throat and her lightheadedness caused her to become disoriented with her surroundings.

Upon landing, Amanda went through the routine she learned from Monroe of disembarking a dragon, as she rubbed the side of XR-27's neck and then patted his left wing twice. The dragon stretched out his left wing like a ramp. Amanda picked up Lawrence and climbed her way down to the ground.

Amanda looked around to see where she should go. XR-27 had landed outside of Meeyor near a huge gated field which was full of dragons. But the entrance of the city could be seen nearby to the right of this gated field. The city itself could not be seen from Amanda's perspective. Meeyor was surrounded by a wall used as a shield to protect anyone who stood outside of the city from the brightness within its boundaries.

The shielded wall was built like a wall that surrounds a castle or a fortress. The wall was black and angled slightly outward. It was tall and thick. So tall that not one of Meeyor's buildings could be seen from outside of the city where Amanda stood. Amanda could see many individuals on the top of the wall. She thought they looked like guards, but was too far away to make out any detail in their appearance. Even though this wall was meant to shield the brightness and absorb light from within, it became questionable to Amanda that this wall might be used for defensive reasons, protecting the citizens on the inside.

While Amanda was staring toward the city, XR had started making his way toward the gated field. "Hey, where are you going?" she asked. "The entrance is this way." XR-27 pretended not to hear her, and kept heading for the entrance to the gated field.

Amanda began following XR-27 toward the gated field but then stopped as she saw a sign posted in her path. "Well, you are a smart dragon, aren't you?" she questioned. Posted on the sign in front of her was not only the explanation for the purpose of the gated field, but also written on this sign was one of Meeyor's many rules:

DRAGON PARKING
SELF-PARK ONLY

ABSOLUTELY NO DRAGONS
ARE ALLOWED WITHIN
THE CITY LIMITS OF MEEYOR

"So this field is used as a dragon parking lot?" Amanda questioned amazed. "I guess that makes sense considering they obviously don't allow dragons inside of Meeyor. I guess they don't have valet service for dragons either."

The parking field was full of many dragons. Dragons left by both occupants and visitors of Meeyor. A line to an entrance gate of this parking area had formed with many strange creatures. Most of them looked like they were made of glass. The bodies of the glass people were shaped like human bodies except they had defined edges and smooth surfaces, like a perfectly carved jewel. There were different colors of glass people, including blue, red, green, yellow, purple, and orange glass. Even their clothing was the same color as the rest of their bodies. However, as Amanda observed, she noticed that the color of their bodies would gradually change from one color to another, as she witnessed a green glass man change to blue, even their clothing.

Among the other creatures, Amanda saw a few fish, much like Monroe and Sebastian. There was also an individual who appeared human, but had three eyes, pointed ears, and was much taller than any human. There were some creatures covered with thick, brown fur and no eyes on their heads. They did have eyes however. They were on the palms of their hands. Each of the creatures had their own dragon with them and was waiting to park their dragon in the parking field.

"I guess we need to get in line," Amanda concluded. "You seem to know what you're doing XR." Amanda followed XR-27 and positioned herself in the rear of the line waiting to park dragons. The line was moving quickly and Amanda knew it would not take long to reach the entrance to the gated parking area. There did not appear to be anyone assisting the creatures parking their dragons, as the gate would open automatically for each dragon entering.

At least to Amanda, this appeared to be an automatic process until something else got her attention. To the front, left side of the gated entrance, there was an interesting looking machine. The creatures in front of her were placing something into the machine, pulling a lever, and taking something from it in return. After which, the gate opened and their dragon entered the parking field.

What are they doing? she thought. *I hope I don't need any money.*

Then came Amanda's turn. She was confused. She didn't know what to do. Looking at the machine, she saw the slot where the other creatures were placing an item. She pondered what it was that needed to be put in the slot. "Great," she whispered, "it is money. But this slot is so long. It looks too big to fit any coin I've ever seen. Maybe it's Meeyor money that I have to use." Others behind her began to grow impatience with her lack of action.

"Keep the line moving, human!" shouted the green glass man behind her in line.

"What's the holdup?" screamed another. "Come on. Get out of the way."

Amanda decided to just ask for help. "Excuse me," she asked the green glass man behind her in line, "what is it exactly I need to place in this machine?"

"Boy, aren't you a piece of work," the green glass man responded rudely as his body changed to yellow.

"Don't you know that if you're going to use dragon self parking, you need to place a scale from your dragon in the dragon retrieval whistle machine? Everybody knows that. Figures though. You're obviously not from around here. Just place one of your dragon scales in the slot and pull the lever. This machine will grind up the scale and place it inside a dragon retrieval whistle. It'll give you the whistle and open the gate. The whistle's sound is generated from the ground dragon scale. When you need to get your dragon again, just use the whistle and it'll come. Since the inside of the whistle is composed of a scale from your dragon, and the pitch of the whistle is unique to the dragon scale used, your dragon will be the only dragon to respond when you blow it. Now, get it done and get out of the way."

Amanda looked at XR and knew that she didn't want to pull a scale off of him. That might hurt him. Then she remembered. "Wait, those scales were poking me the entire time we were flying to Meeyor." She looked behind her leg and sure enough, there were several of XR's scales stuck to the back of her pants. Amanda pulled one off and placed it in the machine. Then she pulled the lever and listened while the machine ground up XR-27's scale. A trap door at the bottom of the machine opened up and inside of it was a shiny silver whistle.

"Wow, that was pretty nifty," said Amanda. The gate to the dragon parking field opened upward and XR rapidly made his way inside. "Bye XR. We'll be back shortly. I hope." Amanda put the whistle in Lawrence's backpack and walked toward the entrance to Meeyor.

On the path to the entrance was a large box, full of sunglasses. To the right side of the box was another sign with another rule:

ALL THOSE ENTERING
THE CITY OF MEEYOR
MUST WEAR SUNGLASSES

"I definitely understand the need for a pair of sunglasses," said Amanda as she reached into the box to pull herself out a pair. "Meeyor was a bit bright."

Looking down at Lawrence, Amanda said, "Don't worry little fella, I'll get you a pair too. The sunglasses have straps so they won't fall off of you. I wouldn't want the brightness to hurt your eyes and I definitely don't want to break any of Meeyor's rules. We're here for help, remember? We can't afford to get into any trouble." Amanda reached into the box of sunglasses, picked up a "ferret-sized" pair, and fastened them on Lawrence's head.

Amanda watched as many creatures made their way to the entrance of the city. Many of these creatures were the same ones that Amanda had seen at the dragon parking field. Every single creature had a pair of sunglasses fastened on their face, as they walked through a pair of large, wavy doors. Even the creature with three eyes had sunglasses with three lenses. And the furry, brown creature had put two shaded lenses over each eye on the palms of its hands.

Amanda followed the creatures and headed to the entrance of Meeyor with Lawrence close behind. The two huge doors that she had seen others walk through appeared to be the only way to enter the city. The doors were very tall, about half the height of the shielded barrier of the city. However, unlike normal doors, bluish-black waves rippled from the top, all the way to their base, like a waterfall. The rippling motion made the structure of the doors appear to be more liquid than solid.

Two guards dressed in brilliant ceremonial uniforms were stationed in front of the pair of doors. Each wore a puffy, black, cylindrical helmet, that resembled a flattened black q-tip. Their dress jackets were red and full of medals and their trousers were dark blue and starched to a crisp. They carried staffs held tightly next to their bodies in their right hands - hands covered with white mittens. The staffs were lit up like florescent lights and were snapping and popping, indicating to Amanda that these staffs could be used to shock someone. However, these guards were not human. Their heads looked like light bulbs and both were lit and shining.

Amanda reluctantly approached the entrance.

"Excuse me," Amanda said, "but are you two guarding the entrance to the city?"

Both light bulb guards quickly crossed their staffs with each other, forming the letter X, to prevent Amanda from entering the city. The connection of the two staffs caused both to illuminate much brighter than they did individually. The popping and snapping from each staff now became one continuous sound, resembling television static.

"You do not belong here. You cannot pass," exclaimed one of the guards. "And what do you mean, are we guarding the entrance to the city? Is that an insult? Of course we're guarding the entrance to the city, and doing an outstanding job of it. It should be obvious to anyone that we are guarding the city. What you're asking sounds like an insult to me."

"I have to agree with you," said the other guard. "I am certain that was an insult."

"I'm glad you agree," said the first guard. "Now what shall I do with her?"

"What shall YOU do?" questioned the second light bulb guard. "Don't you mean, what shall WE do?"

"Of course...not," responded the first guard. "She did insult me by questioning me, and not you."

"Well," continued the second guard lowering his staff, "maybe you're insulting me."

"Maybe I am," replied the first guard quickly as he lowered his staff also.

"Well maybe you are," said the second.

"Now that's an insult," said the first guard.

"What?" replied the second guard. "Now you think I'm insulting you?"

"This is ridiculous," said Amanda quietly to Lawrence. "Come on, let's go. They're too busy arguing with each other to notice."

"When it comes to you and me there is no question about it, I am the higher wattage bulb," said the first guard. "I am definitely not the dimmer bulb standing here."

"Well, I never in all of my hours of illuminating, have ever been so humiliated," the second guard responded.

"You know Lawrence," Amanda said, "for a pair of light bulbs, they're not very bright." Amanda put on her sunglasses and made her way through the two giant liquid-like doors, with the two light bulb guards continuing to bicker at each other the entire time.

Once inside the doors, Amanda saw a city unlike any other. Meeyor was beautiful. It was a vision that Amanda would never forget. Building upon building decorated the streets, all made of glass material. Many buildings were circular shaped. Some sat on large glass pillars while others looked like stacks of thick dishes laying one on top of the other. The entire city presented a seamless appearance, with its structures all blending together as if they were one fused creation, but each still having its own unique and individual character.

There were people everywhere. Not human people, but mostly glass people, much like Amanda saw entering the city from outside. The different colors of these glass people created a striking rainbow effect. These citizens lined the streets and roads, all moving in a single file, staring straight ahead with no interaction amongst themselves. Each person was in a great hurry as if their agenda was of the highest priority in all of Meeyor.

The citizens could roam the streets and roads, due to their being no vehicles on the ground. Meeyor had a train system intertwined throughout the city. This train system looked like a glass monorail and its tracks were elevated well above the ground below. The people of Meeyor took glass escalators to get to the boarding areas for these monorail systems. There was also a system of lifts, much like ski lifts, that transported people between shorter distances than the monorail system, holding about twenty glass citizens.

Throughout the city, rules were visible everywhere. There were rules illuminating from billboards. Some rules were lit brightly on street signs. Others rules were radiating from neon flyers on the sides of the monorail compartments.

One rule said:

NO INDIVIDUAL WITHIN MEEYOR
MAY STARE AT THEIR FEET
WHILE WALKING

While another rule stated:

NO STEPPING ON CRACKS
WITHIN CITY LIMITS

And another read:

SITTING ON CITY PROPERTY
IS NOT PERMITTED

Meeyor had rules for everything. The more rules Amanda saw, the more uncomfortable she felt about being there.

"Wow, Lawrence," said Amanda, "with so many rules to follow, no matter what I do, it will be wrong. Of course, that's how I feel at school all of the time, so what's the big deal? These strange people are all so busy. How do I get their attention? All I want is to find someone who can help me get home and maybe tell me why I'm here."

Amanda gazed at a neon sign above her that read:

DESTRUCTION OF ANY CITY PROPERTY WILL RESULT IN IMMEDIATE PUNISHMENT!

"You better stay close to me little guy," Amanda said as she picked up Lawrence. "I'd hate to find out what happens if we broke one of the city's rules. Let's just keep moving and see if we can find someone to help us."

Amanda continued walking forward, trying not to stare at her feet or step on a crack. She decided to stop someone and ask for help. "Excuse me, sir," Amanda said to a blue glass man, "I was wondering if you could help me."

"Get away from me," the man replied as he kept walking.

"Excuse me, madam," Amanda said as she tried again with a yellow glass woman, "I'm lost and needed some help and..."

"Don't bother me," the woman replied. "Can't you see I'm in a hurry?"

"This isn't good, Lawrence," stated Amanda. "These people are rude and only concerned with their own lives. I don't think we're going to get anywhere with this crowd."

Amanda continued walking and trying to get the attention of other city residents, but no one acknowledged her. Being creatures made of glass, they were too involved trying not to shatter their own fragile lives. Soon, she began to lose hope and stopped at one of the many mirrors in the city and stared at her reflection.

"Isn't it funny, Lawrence?" Amanda asked. "Even in a world as crazy as this, I still don't fit in. I'm still the one who's different. At least at home, people would talk to me. Even if they did make fun of me, they were at least talking to me. Look at me though. Just look at me. Why is it I get made fun of at home and why is it no one will talk to me here? What is it about me? Why don't I fit in anywhere?"

While staring at herself, the mirror began to darken and black smoke began to appear within the mirror right before Amanda's eyes.

"What's going on?" she asked worried. "What's happening to the mirror Lawrence?"

In the mirror, two hideously eerie amber colored eyes stared back at Amanda. A body formed around these eyes within the mirror, but the image was not completely clear. Not nearly clear enough for Amanda to understand

153

who or what that creature was. Amanda was frozen in fear and could not take her eyes off of the creature's stare. The creature grinned at Amanda and whispered a very eerie sound, "Sllleeeeeeeepppppppp....." The creature opened its mouth wide and Amanda began to feel herself being pulled forward into the mirror as if she was being sucked into the mouth of this frightening monster.

"No, this is definitely not right!" shouted Amanda as she fought hard to pull back. "Help! Somebody help me!"

Amanda's screams startled the creature as it let go of its grasp on her and disappeared, causing Amanda to drop Lawrence and fall backwards into another mirror nearby. The force of Amanda's body was enough to crack the other mirror into several pieces. Amanda's sunglasses fell off of her face as she landed on her back.

Five of Meeyor's finest guards came running after hearing Amanda's screams. These guards looked exactly like the light bulb guards at the front entrance of Meeyor and each had their staff lit up brightly and ready for use. Amanda squinted her eyes tightly in efforts of preventing the glare of the city, as she searched desperately for the fallen sunglasses.

"Ok, who screamed for help here?" asked one of the guards.

"Was it you?" another guard asked pointing to Lawrence.

"No, it wasn't him," answered Amanda patting her hand on the ground on all fours, hoping to feel the sunglasses she had dropped.

"Did she hurt you little rat?" asked another light bulb guard.

"No, I didn't hurt him," Amanda replied, "and he's not a rat. He's a ferret and he doesn't talk. I am the one who screamed for help."

"Why would we believe that?" said the first guard picking up Amanda's sunglasses and handing them to her. "From the looks of things, you are the one who is sitting on city property not wearing their issued sunglasses. And you broke a mirror. Breaking a mirror in itself is a very serious crime. Breaking a mirror requires that we ban you from Meeyor for at least seven years."

"You don't understand," Amanda tried to explain as she stood up and put her sunglasses back on, "it was an accident. I saw this awful monster or something in that mirror over there and it tried to suck me into the mirror so I screamed for help and..."

"Tell it to the Judge," said the guard cutting Amanda off. "Cuff her and send her directly to the courthouse. You know the rule for destruction of city property. It's immediate punishment. The city's leaders will not tolerate it. Not at all."

Amanda and Lawrence were shackled and taken to Meeyor's courthouse.

In the courtroom, Amanda was made to sit behind a table centered directly in front of what appeared to be the

Judge's bench. She had no lawyer. There was no plaintiff. It was only she and Lawrence, constricted by shackles, waiting for their fate to be decided. Many of Meeyor's citizens were there to watch the case. They all glared at Amanda with blank or accusing stares. In the back corner of the wall to the left of the Judge's bench, was a door. Next to the door stood another light bulb guard - the bailiff of the court. The door began to open.

"All rise for the Honorable Judge Roma Shine!" shouted the bailiff throughout the courtroom.

In walked yet another of the strangest looking characters Amanda had ever seen. At first glance, all Amanda could see were a large pair of glasses with a mirror-like coating, keeping anyone from seeing the eyes of the Judge behind them. The two lenses blended together with no appearance of a nosepiece, giving the impression that the glasses were actually part of Judge Shine's body. Her body, covered by a black robe, was very small compared to the glasses. Her legs could not be seen as they were completely covered by the robe. Her arms were so short that her hands barely peaked out from the robe's sleeves. Each of her hands had only three fingers and in her right hand, she carried a large wooden gavel. The top of her head was covered with a white wig that looked more like a used mop.

As Judge Shine approached her bench, the light bulb bailiff, who was three times the Judge's height, quickly hustled to her side and got down on all fours at the back of the bench.

"You better not drop me this time Bailiff Bulb," grumbled the Judge to the bailiff. "I am very deserving of respect and do not wish to be embarrassed in my courtroom."

"No, your Honor, I guarantee that you'll not fall this time," replied Bailiff Bulb. "I've been working out lately, so you have nothing to worry about."

The Judge proceeded to climb up onto the back of the bailiff, with the bailiff moaning the entire time as if he were in pain. Once on top of Bailiff Bulb, Judge Shine made a quick jump toward her bench and mounted herself onto a stool which sat directly behind it. The Judge then made a motion with all three fingers of her left hand, signaling the occupants of the courtroom to take their seats.

How can such a small person carry such large glasses? Amanda thought as she sat down. *This is more like a circus than a courtroom. Not that I've ever been in a courtroom. But if I had been in one, I would think...*

BAM! BAM! BAM!

Amanda's thoughts were quickly interrupted by a very loud and intimidating sound of the Judge's gavel smacking against the top of her bench. Startled, the entire courtroom, including the bailiff, jumped when hearing the gavel. Many had a surprised look on their face to witness such a small individual beat an object with such intensity.

"My court is now in session," stated Judge Shine. "The court will now hear the case of the city of Meeyor versus Amanda Sneed. Will the defendant please rise?"

"Oops, that's me, I think," Amanda whispered to herself as she rose to her feet.

"You are hereby charged with the following crimes. One, improper use of optical shading devices. Two, illegal use of city property for rest and relaxation. And three, severe vandalism of city property. How do you plead?"

"Um, confused, I think," Amanda answered.

"Confused is not an option. Therefore your plea must be guilty, by reason of confusion," ordered Judge Shine.

"But I can't be guilty," Amanda replied. "I mean, I only came to Meeyor for help, not to get into any trouble. I didn't mean to do anything wrong. I would say it's all an accident, not that I'm guilty."

"Did you or did you not get caught within the city limits, NOT wearing your issued set of sunglasses?" asked Judge Shine.

"Well, I guess I did," Amanda answered. "But they fell off and I..."

"GUILTY!!!" shouted the Judge as she slammed her gavel against the bench.

Did you or did you not use the city street to sit down and relax for a moment?" the Judge interrogated.

"Um, I wasn't relaxing. I fell back and lost my balance," Amanda replied.

"GUILTY!!!" shouted the Judge a second time as she slammed her gavel against the bench two times.

Did you or did you not break a mirror within the city limits?" the Judge demanded.

"Yes, I did," Amanda answered once again. "But there was this person or monster or something in the reflection and it wasn't me and it startled me and..."

"GUILTY!!!" shouted the Judge a third time as she slammed her gavel against her bench three times. "There is no need for me to go any further with this case. It is entirely an open and shut case. I hereby sentence you, Miss Amanda Sneed, to the following..."

"Wait!" A shout from the rear of the courtroom stopped the Judge in the middle of her verdict. All heads turned and all eyes were now fixed on the individual who had just interrupted the Judge - an individual who was so amazing in appearance alone, that any one person would stop doing their task at hand to stare at him.

The individual was shaped like a human, two arms and two legs, a body and head. But this man did not appear human. This man was made completely of glass. Not just any glass either. His hair extended past his shoulders and flowed to the slightest bit of air, emitting light like strands of fiber optic material. He wore a beautiful gown arranged in patterns of multi-colored stained glass. But his face and hands were even more amazing. They did not look like glass. They didn't even look like a solid material. His face and hands were composed of light - a brilliant white light. Although brilliant, it was not too bright, allowing others to gaze upon him. His eyes, however, were piercing and sparkled as if they were composed of crystal.

"Did you just say the child's name is Amanda Sneed?" the glass man asked of the Judge.

"Yes, your most honorable one. The child's name is Amanda Sneed," replied Judge Shine. "She is in court today for multiple violations of the Laws of Meeyor."

"I see," said the strange looking glass-like person. "Let the child come with me. I will take full responsibility of all problems she might have caused and ensure adequate justice."

"Yes, your Excellency," said Judge Shine. "It would be my honor to have you deal with this case personally. This case is dismissed. Release the human."

"What about Lawrence?" Amanda said concerned, pointing to her shackled friend.

"I will take the animal too," said the man draped in multi-colored stained glass.

"Consider him yours, your most noble one," responded Judge Shine. "Unlock those cuffs and hand over that smelly rodent Bailiff Bulb."

"Yes, your Honor," Bailiff Bulb said with much respect. "Right away ma'am."

Upon release, Lawrence bee-lined his way to Amanda. "Poor little guy," Amanda said sympathetically, "that was no way to treat such a sweet little ferret like you."

"Come with me, child," the brilliant glass man stated to Amanda as he began to move out of the courtroom in a gliding motion. Amanda followed without hesitation, even though she had no idea who this person, or thing, was. She had no idea how he knew her or what he wanted with her. All Amanda knew was she was free of the shackles and hoped this might be someone who could help her get home.

Chapter 6
The Guardian of the
Dream Diary

***B**oy, that was close,* Amanda thought. *I really hate to imagine what kind of punishment Judge Shine was about to give me. And who is this person? How will he deal with* *me and what kind of justice does he have in store for me? He was so determined to get me out of there. But how does he know me? What could he possibly want?* Amanda was nervous and many questions swirled in her mind. She started to doubt her fate with this mysterious stranger and wonder if this was the better of the two situations to find herself.

However, Amanda did not have a choice in the matter and she knew it, as she reluctantly followed the stranger out of the courthouse, continuing to question in her mind what would happen to her next. Unable to hold back her curiosity any longer, Amanda decided it was time to break the silence.

"Um, sir," Amanda uttered. "Who are you?"

"I apologize, child," the glass stranger said. "How rude of me. Let me properly introduce myself. My name is Gee Lassy."

"It's nice to meet you, Mister Lassy," replied Amanda. "My name's Amanda Sneed. But you obviously know that already. Why did Judge Shine call you your excellency? Are you some kind of ruler?"

"No, I am not a ruler young, child," answered Gee. "Many call me that and other things merely out of respect."

"Respect?" Amanda asked curiously. "Are you a prophet or something like that?"

"A prophet?" Gee said laughing. "No, not a prophet. I wish I could foresee and tell of the future, but that is an impossible task for me. Some have referred to me as a priest. But I am neither a prophet and a priest. I am an elder of both Meeyor and Maldderan."

"What exactly does it mean to be an elder?" Amanda asked.

"Well, to begin with," Gee answered, "I am one of the oldest living creatures on all of Maldderan. There are few older than I. I have seen many things happen in this great land of ours. I have seen many creatures come and make this their home and I have seen others leave, never to return. My knowledge of this island and its history is very thorough. That knowledge allows me to help advise others here and give them guidance. That is why I'm considered an elder. However, I did not always appear in the form I am now. At one time, I looked much like the common glass citizens you see around Meeyor. It was time and knowledge that evolved me into the person you see today."

"Wow," Amanda said amazed, "it's no wonder everyone shows you respect."

"Yes," said Gee, "the others who reside on Maldderan do show me much respect. But I do not expect or demand it. I do however, accept and understand what makes me different from everyone else on Maldderan."

"Different from everyone else?" questioned Amanda. "I tend to have that problem."

"I don't see being different as a problem," said Gee. "You should see it as something that makes you special and accept who you are. Now come with me. We have much to discuss."

Gee led Amanda and Lawrence through a set of doors and into a cylindrical liquid curtain resembling mercury. Once inside, Amanda could tell that this liquid tube's purpose was that of an elevator. Amanda watched as Gee pushed five different buttons onto a control panel. The liquid walls of the elevator hardened and became clear and transparent and morphed into a spherical shape around them.

"Have a seat and make sure you buckle up," Gee requested, as he sat down in a seat in front of the control panel. Amanda sat in a seat next to him, buckled up, and held Lawrence tight in her arms.

The spherical device began moving upward through a tube, like a pod. At first, Amanda was able to gaze out over the city of Meeyor. But the pod soon increased its speed and Amanda could no longer see anything outside of the walls.

"Hang on, Lawrence, we're moving pretty fast." Amanda could feel the movement of the pod but it didn't feel as if it was going upward any longer. Neither did it feel like it was going downward. Amanda became nervous about the pod's movement as she tightened her grip on Lawrence to keep him safe. It felt as if they were inside a marble rolling throughout a maze of tubes. Curious and concerned about what direction the pod was moving, she asked, "Mister Lassy, what direction are we going? Up or down?"

"We're moving in many directions - up, down, sideways, and even diagonally," answered Gee.

How can that be? thought Amanda. "How can an elevator move in different directions? And how come I'm unable to tell which direction we're moving? This makes no sense. Why is it doing that? Where are we going?"

"This is one of many modes of transportation in Meeyor," continued Gee. "This system is part of a network of lumnivators. I guess you could say, we're using light as our medium to travel. The entire network connects every building within the city. So if someone chooses not to travel outdoors, they can take one of the lumnivator pods, like we're doing now, and be transported exactly to where they desire."

The longer they traveled, the safer Amanda felt inside of the lumnivator. Although it made her nervous at first, Amanda found the lumnivator quite interesting. So did Lawrence. The ferret jumped down from Amanda's arms and began sniffing around. "I don't think you'll find any keys in here Lawrence," Amanda giggled.

"Does your ferret have a passion for keys?" Gee asked.

"Well, it's more like an obsession for collecting keys," answered Amanda. "He tends to take any key he can find. I keep most of them in his backpack. I can show you some if you'd like."

"No, I do not need to see any keys," replied Gee. "But his obsession with collecting keys might work to your advantage."

What does he mean? Amanda thought about Gee's comments. *Maybe it's part of my punishment. Maybe he would have me do something with keys to make up for breaking that mirror.*

The lumnivator stopped, as its state began to change again from a sphere to a cylindrical device, with the walls also changing from a solid to liquid. Gee motioned for Amanda to exit, as the entire party walked through the wavy mercury like wall, into a brilliant room of pure light. "Welcome to my home, child," stated Gee.

There was something noticeably strange about this room. The room was completely empty. No furniture. No carpet. No windows. Nothing. Just four walls, a ceiling and a floor, all well lit, as if they themselves were a light source.

"Uh, yeah," Amanda said sarcastically. "I really like the way you've furnished your place."

"Please sit," Gee said pointing directly behind where Amanda was standing.

"Um, where?" asked Amanda. "I don't see a couch or a stool or any sort of furniture."

"Just sit, please," said Gee.

"Ok, I guess I can sit on the floor," responded Amanda.

As Amanda began to squat toward the ground, a cushioned chair appeared under her, catching her fall. "Where did that come from?" she asked baffled.

Gee did not answer. Instead he asked her another question. "Would you like something to drink?"

Amanda looked puzzled. Where could Gee possibly find something to drink in this empty room? But with a chair appearing out of nowhere, why couldn't a drink appear also? Amanda decided to just go ahead and accept the offer for the drink. "Sure, that would be great."

"There's a glass of water next to you on the table," Gee said.

"What table?" asked Amanda. "I didn't see a table in here."

Looking around Amanda did not see a table until she turned to her right. An end table had appeared next to her chair. On the end table sat a glass of water.

"How can this be happening?" Amanda questioned. "How can these things appear when they weren't there before?"

"You must learn to believe," Gee answered. As he sat back facing Amanda, a large, cushioned chair appeared behind him just like the chair had appeared behind Amanda moments earlier.

I wish to discuss your purpose - not your punishment. You child, have a purpose for being here in Maldderan."

"So I'm not in trouble?" asked Amanda.

"Not in the sense you are thinking," answered Gee. "But, unfortunately, trouble may find you."

"What kind of trouble, Mister Lassy?" Amanda gulped.

"Trouble of nightmarish proportions," Gee replied. "Now, where do I begin?"

"I'm getting scared," said Amanda. "What are you trying to tell me?"

"Let me start by saying, I believe I have something of yours." Gee stood up and walked toward one of the walls of the room. Along the wall, a large storage trunk appeared as he approached. Gee knelt over and opened the trunk. Amanda couldn't see inside the trunk from where she was sitting, but she did notice a scarlet silk veil placed over the top of whatever was inside.

"Come here, child. I want you to see firsthand what is under this veil." Gee gazed directly into Amanda's eyes with a crystallized, piercing stare of much seriousness.

Amanda stood up and walked over to Gee's side, awaiting him to show her what was underneath the veil. Gee lifted the veil to uncover a large, old, and noticeably worn book. The book was a dull brown, much like a creek rock. On the side of the book opposite the spine were three locks. Each lock had a symbol engraved on it. Although the symbols were small, the details were vivid, much like the details often found on a large coin. The markings looked like hieroglyphic symbols and had no meaning to Amanda.

"Why, this is just a big old book," Amanda said. "Not the most appealing looking book either. In fact, it looks like a rectangular rock."

"There is a reason it looks like a rock." Gee said. "This book is not always like this. It has turned to stone."

"Why, or how, could some ordinary book turn to stone?" Amanda asked.

"You are about to see why. This is no ordinary book child," responded Gee. "This is a very special book. A very special book to you, because it is yours."

"Mine?" replied Amanda.

"Amanda, this book is a Dream Diary," said Gee. "Your Dream Diary."

"A Dream Diary? My Dream Diary?" Amanda was stunned. "I don't understand."

"Go ahead," said Gee, "pick it up. I'm very curious to see your reaction."

Amanda looked at Gee with concern. Then she glanced down at the Dream Diary, hesitating before reaching for it. "I have to say, I am a bit nervous. I mean, what is it you're expecting to happen?" Amanda asked.

"Don't be scared, child," replied Gee. "No harm will come to you. Go on now. Take the diary."

Amanda reached forward and clinched the sides of the Dream Diary. As soon as she touched the Dream Diary, the book began to brighten, causing it to emit a reddish light all around its cover. Amanda's eyes grew wider as she drew the book closer and closer. A small breeze blew from the diary against Amanda's face, causing Amanda's pigtails to drift back behind her head. The book began to change its form. No longer was it stone. The stone book changed into a beautiful and brilliant, bright ruby red Dream Diary.

"Do you know what just happened?" Gee asked. "Do you understand why this book is no longer stone?"

"No, I don't," answered Amanda very worried by this point. "What just happened Gee?"

"The diary changed back to its real form. You are the owner of this Dream Diary," said Gee. "No other may touch it. If another person touches this diary as it is now, it will turn back to stone and stay that way until you touch it again."

"Turn to stone?" questioned Amanda. "How do you know this?"

"Let me explain," responded Gee. "You may be the owner of this diary, but I am the book's guardian. To be given the task of guarding a Dream Diary is an honor, a privilege, and a huge responsibility. Over the time I have guarded this diary, I have witnessed it change from stone, to the way you see it now, and back to stone again, on many occasions."

"If I am the only one who can touch it, then how have you been able to see it change?" asked Amanda. "I sure don't remember touching this book before."

"There is another way to change it back from stone," hinted Gee. "As you can see, there are three locks on this diary. A Dream Diary is only to be locked if there is a vital reason to lock it. As the guardian, I have to make my best judgement whether the safety of the diary is at risk or not, and will lock it or not based on my decision. If I lock it, the diary turns to stone. If I unlock it, it changes to the way it is now, it's true form. Once unlocked, the diary is vulnerable. Anyone may touch it, not just its owner. What's worse, when unlocked, anyone may read it. By locking it, I prevent this from happening. Once locked, the diary defends itself by turning to stone if touched by anyone besides the owner. It all comes down to the diary's safety. The diary is defenseless when all three locks are unlocked since it cannot turn to stone. What is written inside cannot be seen by others. Especially by others who would use it for their own evil agenda."

"What is written inside that is so important?" asked Amanda. "This seems like a lot of trouble to keep whatever it is safe."

"What is important are your dreams," replied Gee. "The diary is used to record your dreams. Inside of this book, can be read every detail of every dream that you have ever had, since the first day you were born, including your daydreams."

"How could that be?" asked Amanda. "Like I said, I've never seen this book, so how could I write anything inside of it, especially my dreams? I may remember some of them, but I definitely don't remember every dream I've ever had."

"That's because you aren't the one recording your dreams," answered Gee.

"If I'm not doing it," Amanda asked, " then who is recording my dreams in the diary?"

"I am," Gee responded. "I am the one who records your dreams. I am the guardian of your Dream Diary and the watcher of your dreams."

"What do you mean you watch my dreams?" Amanda questioned. "I don't understand at all."

"Dreams of a child are very powerful," Gee explained. "Worlds such as Maldderan rely greatly on these dreams. They are a source of energy to our world and others, providing life-giving power, so that all may exist. Once it was realized that dreams were the source of such phenomenal power, we began to study them. Initially, there was but a small group of wise, scholarly individuals, who did their best to keep track of each and every dream. But the task was too overwhelming. Others were needed to observe the dreams. A recruitment effort was set in place and was met with a tremendous response. Soon, we had thousands upon millions upon billions, watchers of dreams.

181

They came from everywhere. They were of different species and different worlds, but had one common goal - to watch, record, and preserve the power given by the dreams of children. The number of watchers was so great, that we were able to assign each child from your world with their own Dream Watcher. Once a child falls asleep or even daydreams, the Dream Watcher assigned to that child is there to observe. All observations of the dream are recorded in a book. A book which you have already held in your very own hands - a Dream Diary. Each child of your world has an individual Dream Diary, full of every dream or daydream they have ever had."

"This is incredible!" exclaimed Amanda. "I had no idea that dreams could be so powerful. Of course, I didn't even know your world existed until I woke up in that rowboat. And every child has a Dream Watcher and a Dream Diary? I find all of this so amazing, but yet unbelievable. I'll call it unbelazing. It's splendorific too. It's a perfect system."

"Yes, the system appears perfect - too perfect. But it became obvious to all who observed the children that not all dreams were producing positive energy for our worlds. Many children were experiencing nightmares while they slept. Nightmares can also be very powerful but very dangerous, perhaps even more powerful than a dream, as they have their own malicious form of energy exerted. Where a good dream can provide positive energy to a world, nightmares cause an evil presence of darkness capable of consuming all within its reach. It is another responsibility of Dream Watchers to protect their child from these nightmares. We provide a light when there is only darkness. However, Dream Watchers are not perfect. Sometimes the nightmares are too powerful to be driven away by our light and all we can do is watch. I can guarantee that all Dream Watchers do their best, no matter how challenging the task may be. And although some nightmares do manage to slip through our grasps, we never fail to record a dream in a child's diary, should it be needed later in time. And your dreams, child, will be needed."

"My dreams?" Amanda asked bewildered. "What do you want with my dreams? From what you just described, your dream watching system is way too important and organized for someone like me to mess up."

"You must listen to what I still have to say, child," Gee continued. "I have a problem that needs attending. Look closely at the three locks on your Dream Diary. Each one requires a different key. Until recently, the keys were all in my possession. But that is no longer the case. The three keys are hidden away in separate locations around Maldderan."

"Why are the keys hidden?" questioned Amanda.

"You may not want to know," replied Gee. "Let me explain. Please listen and listen very carefully. Like I said, nightmares produce a very powerful, but evil energy. It did not take long for some to see this power, realize it could be used for self empowerment, and give into the power of this dark energy. Most of these culprits were quickly discovered and were thwarted off by the Dream Watchers long before they could learn to use the power or even become organized. But there is one. There is one who did learn to use it. He is a hideous being known as Gamirathen. Gamirathen's desire is to prevent all the children from your world from ever having pleasant dreams, only nightmares. Every nightmare makes his power stronger. And his power is already very strong. That's why the keys for your diary are no longer here. When I realized that the rumors of Gamirathen and his evil were true, I hid the diary and locked it, knowing that he would come searching for it. I then hid the keys. But luckily enough, when he did come, and he did find the diary, it was locked and the keys were well hidden. So when he touched it, the diary turned to stone. Gamirathen tried to pry open the locks, but the harder he tried, the more defensive the diary became. It became so defensive that it began to attack Gamirathen, causing him to burn from within. This however did not stop Gamirathen. It only slowed down his evil agenda. He knew he had been defeated and fled."

"Wait!" bursted Amanda. "Why did he come for my Dream Diary? What is it that makes my diary different? I mean, he could have gone after any of the diaries belonging to one of the other children. Why mine?"

"The same reason I say your dreams will be needed," answered Gee. "You are not like the other children. You are different and have a very special gift. You possess an incredible ability inside of you. Your dreams are not normal dreams. They are very powerful. More powerful than nightmares. What makes you different is you are able to use your dreams. Recreate them at will, so to speak. At least, those you can remember. You are a Dream Caster, child."

"A Dream Caster? No," Amanda responded skeptically, "there's no possible way I have any sort of power. I'm just a kid. I'm not very good at much of anything. I know I don't have any sort of dream power. I don't believe you. Maybe the diary has power, but I don't. Gamirathen only wants the diary because it has power, not me."

"I understand your doubt, but you are the Dream Caster, the one with the power, not the diary. The diary only records your power," Gee said. "Gamirathen realizes that your Dream Diary contains a record of all of your dreams. By reading it, he knows all of your dreams. By knowing all of your dreams, he will understand the potential of your powers and what he should expect from you. "

"Are you saying he knows who I am?" Amanda gulped. "That's just great. How does he know? I don't know who he is. Where is he now? What happened to him after he fled?"

"I do not know for sure," answered Gee. "He was greatly weakened after he was injured due to his confrontation with the diary. It is said he has returned to his castle here on Maldderan, but I have not seen those two horrid amber colored eyes of his since the day he fled from my home."

"Did you say amber colored eyes?" asked Amanda.

"Yes, I did," answered Gee. "Why do you ask?"

"Because I saw two scary eyes in the reflection of the mirror just inside of the city when I first got here. They were amber colored. It's what startled me into screaming for help and bumping into that glass mirror and breaking it. It's part of the reason I was in court when you found me. I broke a rule."

"Then you've seen Gamirathen?" Gee asked.

"Yes," answered Amanda, "from what you just described."

"Then he knows you're here now," said Gee. "His strength must be returning. We haven't much time. Please listen. I must continue to explain why you're here. Gamirathen is wise. He knows I have your diary locked and he'll need all three keys to open it. He'll also assume the keys are hidden, since I would never hold onto the keys myself now that he has tried to open the diary. To ensure the keys were hidden, I recruited the services of three of my oldest and most trusted friends in all of Maldderan. I sent each one of them with a key so that they may take it away and hide it in an area of my choosing. Upon hiding the key, they were each supposed to guard and protect their respective key at its hidden location until Gamirathen could be defeated. Then they were to return the keys back to me. They were each to send word to me once their key was hidden and safe. I have not heard from any of the three as of yet. I fear something terrible has happened."

"It all sounds terrible to me," Amanda responded. "He knows I'm here in Maldderan, he has already tried to capture me, he wants my Dream Diary, and these friends of yours who hid the keys are missing. This isn't good Gee. It sounds like he's gotten a hold of your friends. Which means he might have the keys."

"I disagree," said Gee. "I don't believe he has the keys. I do agree that he may have captured my friends, but I believe the keys are hidden. If Gamirathen had the keys, then he would have returned here by now to attempt to open the diary. But that is not the case. He is searching for the keys as we speak."

"If that's true, then where did you hide them? And who are these friends that hid them?" Amanda questioned.

"Twin siblings, a brother and a sister, hold the first two keys. They are like children to me, and I trust them with my soul. I sent the brother to hide his key, the Emerald Key, deep within a jungle known as Jigsari. This jungle is full of mixed up and puzzling creatures. It is a place that can be quite dangerous. The sister was to take her key, the Sapphire Key, high into the snow-capped mountain region, near a village named Kryogen. This village is full of very friendly folks, but they are what you might consider a bit recreational. It is easy to get distracted there. The third key was sent with my dearest friend and the most responsible man I know. He was to take his key, the Golden Key, to the Beach of the Glittering Sands. This beach is full of magical treasures and sweet surprises. We need these keys back immediately. With the keys, we can open the diary so you may know and remember your dreams, and then learn to use your power to destroy Gamirathen before he grows any stronger."

"Why haven't you gone to get the keys?" asked Amanda. "You did say that you have a general idea where they are located."

"I cannot go," responded Gee Lassy. "My power is better suited here guarding your Dream Diary. Being old and partially made of glass presents a disadvantage. I do not move quickly. Searching for the three keys requires someone young. Someone with lots of energy and can move much faster than I can. Someone with the motivation to find the keys that belong to their diary. Someone who has the power to cast dreams."

"What?" questioned Amanda in shock. "Are you asking me to go find the keys? Are you crazy?"

"No," responded Gee, "I'm not crazy and I'm not asking you either. I'm telling you to go find them."

"But I don't even know this place," Amanda said concerned. "Why don't you get someone else to search for the keys? Someone familiar with Maldderan? Someone you trust? I mean, I'm just a kid. You really expect me to find them?"

"Yes. Yes, I do expect that," stated Gee. "I expect you will find the keys. I expect you will return here with them. I expect you will open your Dream Diary and find the power that is inside you. Yes, Miss Amanda Sneed, from you, I expect there is nothing you cannot dream of doing and therefore there is nothing you cannot do."

"I still don't see how I'm going to be the one to find these keys Mister Lassy," Amanda stated. "What skill could I possibly offer? My only talent seems to be daydreaming."

"That's exactly what is needed," answered Gee quickly. "You are a child. You are a dreamer. There is nothing more powerful than the dreams of a child. And your dreams are very, very powerful. You are able to use your dreams. You must figure that out for yourself."

"I have to be dreaming," Amanda responded. "Wake up Amanda. Wake up. I just want to go home. I don't want to be here anymore. Just wake up."

"I'm afraid that's not possible," said Gee. "You cannot go home right now and this is not a dream. You are here Amanda because Maldderan needs you. If you do not, Gamirathen will find the keys to your Dream Diary, learn of your dreams, and use that knowledge with the power he already possesses to unleash his nightmarish wrath on all of Maldderan. Only you can change that Amanda. You have to discover what is needed to stop Gamirathen. If not, all of Maldderan will surely fall to his power and your dreams will all become nightmares. Please look hard into your heart and soul to discover this. We need you and you need you."

"I don't know about this Mister Lassy," Amanda said worried. "Like I said, I'm different from most people. Very different. I usually end up in a lot of trouble because I'm different. You really need someone who has it all together to do this for you. And that's not me. Trust me. The kids in my class are always telling me how strange and different I am. The truth is, they're right, I'm different."

"Maybe it's not so much that you're different," replied Gee. "Maybe it's that everyone else is the same. And if everyone else is the same, then that would make them ordinary. And if everyone else is ordinary, then that would make you extra-ordinary, young child. You are special and blessed with a gift Miss Amanda Sneed. A gift to dream. You are a Dream Caster. Remember that. Now be gone already. Go and find the keys to your Dream Diary so that you may discover for yourself the power that your gift to dream truly possesses." Upon finishing his thoughts, Gee slowly faded away, as if a light inside of him had dimmed into darkness, disappearing from Amanda's sight.

"Now I'm really feeling creepy," said Amanda. "Where did he go?" Amanda looked around, expecting to see Gee reappear somewhere, but he didn't. "Lawrence, I don't think he's coming back. I guess we're on our own. We should go on and get XR-27."

"I'd hate to think what would happen if I don't do this," pondered Amanda. "But I have to help these people and I have to keep Gamirathen from causing any harm to other kids by making them have nightmares all of the time. That sounds so scary to me. But even if I find the keys, according to Gee, I will eventually have to face Gamirathen. That's something I really prefer not to do. What will I do if I do if I have to face that creature? What will he do with me? And what is this dream casting power Gee is talking about? Maybe it's best not to think about any of this right now and just focus on finding the keys."

Upon her final thought, Amanda picked up Lawrence and smiled at her pet ferret with a hidden look of fear. "Come on Lawrence, we're going key hunting."

Chapter 7
The Jungle of Jigsari

"**K**eys, I have to find keys," Amanda assessed. "In a way this should be easy. I mean, what a coincidence, I just happen to have a pet who is a professional key thief. I guess that's what Gee meant when he said Lawrence's key obsession might be an advantage. He should be able to

197

sniff them out with no problem. But keys are so small compared to the fact that Maldderan is such a large island. At least I do have ideas on their general location. And I do have a map of the island. And best of all, I have a dragon that will fly me to anywhere I want."

Amanda headed over to the lumnivator and entered. "Oh great. How am I supposed to work this thing? Gee didn't mention how to operate the eleva... oops, I guess I should call it the lumnivator." Amanda's doubt was soon dismissed, for once she sat down and buckled, the control panel appeared. "Lawrence, do you feel as weird as I do in this place?" The lumnivator began changing state again, as it hardened and its shape changed to a sphere. "I don't think we're controlling this thing Lawrence." Amanda was right. The lumnivator began to move on its own - jerking and twisting - up and down - side to side – it made Amanda's stomach queasy. It was worse than any amusement ride she had ever experienced. "I don't remember it being this rough when we took it before."

Once stopped, the lumnivator changed again to a liquid cylinder as Amanda and Lawrence exited back into the city of Meeyor. "Good, I'm glad that's over. Come on Lawrence. Let's get some fresh air." Amanda and Lawrence made their way back to the entrance of the city and out the large, wavy, liquid-like doors. They walked past the two light bulb guards, who were still arguing with each other, and made their way to the dragon parking area.

"I sure hope you still have that whistle," said Amanda as she knelt over to get into Lawrence's backpack. "Here it is. It was right at the top of the pack. Good job, Lawrence. I can always count on you. Whoops, I better have some of those raspberry gum balls ready for XR if we plan on having him fly us anywhere. I should take a look at the map too, so I have an idea where we're going."

Amanda pulled out the map to find the three locations Gee had told her the keys were hidden. The Jungle of Jigsari was Northeast of Meeyor, while Kryogen was directly North of Meeyor, on top of a snow-covered mountain range as Gee had said. The Beach of the Glittering Sands was much further away than either Jigsari or Kryogen, as it was far Northwest of Meeyor.

"I say we go to Jigsari first, then head up the mountains to Kryogen, and finish this search for the keys at the Beach of the Glittering Sands," suggested Amanda. "What do you think Lawrence?"

Lawrence didn't care. He was too busy sniffing one of the raspberry gum balls.

"That's ok, I'm sure you'll be happy no matter what we do," said Amanda. "Let's see if this dragon retrieving whistle really works."

Amanda blew into the whistle and before she could even finish blowing, XR-27 came flying out of the dragon parking area and landed right next to Amanda and Lawrence. "Wow!" Amanda said amazed. "Now that's some kind of service. All right XR, it's time to move out."

Amanda went through the dragon ritual of rubbing XR's neck, patting his wing, getting on board, and giving him a raspberry gum ball. Amanda took a small swallow of the dragon's milk and then..."Burrrrppppp!!!!! Whoops, excuse me. XR, I need you to take me to the Jigsari Jungle." Amanda gave XR-27 another gum ball and secured everything safely inside Lawrence's backpack. XR began his ascent and their journey to Jigsari.

XR-27 landed in an open area outside of Jigsari Jungle. Bordering the jungle from this open area was a beautiful blue river. The river's current was strong as Amanda could hear the sound of the rapids beat against the rocks in its path. Beyond the river were many trees extending the length of the river. The trees were green and full of life, giving the feel that one giant green veil was covering the jungle. This dense, green vegetation of the jungle covered the land both up and down the river as far as Amanda could see. A swinging wooden bridge nearby, appeared to be the only way to cross the river into the jungle.

"Where are you going?" asked Amanda as XR-27 started prancing toward a field of dandelions close to where they landed. "Oh, I see, you don't want to go with us. That's ok, go ahead and nibble on the dandelions. If I need you, I'll blow the whistle. You'll probably be happier here eating dandelions than hanging out with us anyway. I'm sure you'll be just fine by yourself."

Setting Lawrence down, Amanda grimaced and said, "It's you and I that I'm worried about Lawrence."

Amanda and Lawrence made their way toward the swinging bridge. Next to the bridge was a sign with a most frightening greeting written on it:

WELCOME TO JIGSARI JUNGLE
LOTS OF DANGER
NOW GO AWAY

"That isn't a very polite sign, Lawrence," said Amanda. "It sounds like we're not welcome here at all. I'm not letting that stop us though. We have to find the Emerald Key."

As Amanda and Lawrence started to step onto the swinging bridge, a creature jumped up from the river and blocked their way. The creature was short, comparing in height approximately to that of Amanda's waist. The creature resembled a frog, but it had legs covered with tree bark. Its arms, body, and head were all covered with a mixture of bark and slimy reptilian skin. Leafy branches grew from various pieces of bark throughout his body, from the top of his head to the surfaces of his webbed feet. The tree bark on his head formed a pattern resembling a widow's peak, coming to a point just above the center of his eyes. From the tip of this peak, extending toward his back, grew a vine in a spiral fashion like a thick, single, green hair.

"Stop right there! Stop right there, now!" ordered the reptilian tree-like beast. "None may pass Timber. None at all."

"Well, why not?" asked Amanda. "Why won't you let me pass?"

"A guardian is Timber. A guardian of this jungle, sworn to protect it. Protect it is what Timber must do," the wooden frog continued to ramble. "And you shall not pass! No, no, no, you shall not."

"Look, I'm not sure who you are or why such a little fellow is guarding such a large jungle," said Amanda, "but I'm really in a hurry. So could you make an exception here and just let me on through to the jungle?"

"Timber cannot do that. Timber cannot do that at all," responded the jungle guardian. "You must turn around now and return from where you came. Timber says turn now. Turn around now and go."

"You don't understand," Amanda explained. "I normally would turn around and go, but I have no choice. I have to enter the jungle. I'm here for a reason. What's your name little frog? Or is it little stump?"

"Well, well, well," said the tree-like frog, "make fun of Timber will you? Go ahead and call Timber a frog.

Go right ahead. Timber's been called worse. Much worse. But Timber is no frog. Timber is a Trog."

"I didn't mean to upset you Timber the Trog," Amanda responded. "I was just curious as to what and who you are. That's all. Now will you let me on by to the jungle?"

"Maybe Timber will. Maybe Timber won't. Let Timber think. Timber will make a deal with you. Yes, a deal Timber will make. Timber challenges you to a test of strength. Timber does love a test of strength. Yes, yes, yes. What do you say? Do you accept Timber's challenge?"

"That depends," Amanda responded. "What exactly is the challenge? How do you wish to test my strength?"

"Oh, very good question. Very, very good question," Timber said hopping around in a circle. "The test of strength is Timber's favorite competition. Yes, Timber's favorite. Timber is so very good too. So very good. Timber will win. Win, win, win. The test of strength is an arm wrestling match. Yes, yes, yes. You must beat Timber at arm wrestling to pass."

"Arm wrestling?" asked Amanda in shock. "Are you sure? No offense, but you have arms that look like sticks. I really don't see you beating me."

"Timber is the best," Timber gloated. "Timber is the best arm wrestler ever. The best, the best, the best. Now put your arm up here and let's get started. Let's get this arm wrestling match started. Timber will be the winner. The winner Timber will be."

"Fine, have it your way." Amanda decided it was better to go along with the test of strength and get it over with so she could get going. Amanda positioned her elbow on a circular post at the corner of the swinging bridge, used to hold the bridge ropes in place. Timber placed his elbow on the post also as Amanda grabbed Timber's webbed hand.

"On the count of three," said Timber. "Timber will count to three and we will begin the test of strength. Not two - not one - but three. Be ready. Be very ready. Here we go. One - two - three."

WHAM! Amanda swiftly flung Timber's arm down winning the match.

"Ok," said Amanda. "There, I won. May I pass now? I'm really in a hurry."

"No, no, no. It's best two out of three. Yes, two out of three," Timber said wanting to continue the competition.

"Why, you little toad," Amanda said with annoyance, "you never said anything about this test of strength being the best of two out of three."

"Yes Timber did," Timber replied. "Two out of three is what Timber said. Timber said two out of three. Yes, yes, yes. You weren't listening."

"Well, I think you're making up rules," stated Amanda. "I never heard anything about it being the best of two out of three in all of your rambling."

"Timber did not make up rules. Did not, did not, did not," Timber rambled some more. "Two out of three. Two out of three. Two out of three."

"Fine!" Amanda was very upset by this time. She needed to move on and find the key and had no patience for this annoying creature and his games, especially one who obviously did not play fair. "Put your arm back up there and let's do this."

"Good, good, good," Timber sang in delight. "Two out of three. Two out of three. Two out of three." Timber placed his arm up, propping his elbow with Amanda's on the platform. They grasped hands tightly again. "On the count of three. Three is the count. One - two - three."

WHAM! Amanda swiftly flung Timber's arm down, winning a second time. Timber stared at Amanda with his mouth wide open.

"What's the matter Timber?" Amanda asked. "Are you speechless?"

"No, no, no," Timber responded. "That was a false start. Yes, a false start."

"Just please move so I can get going," Amanda said. "I really have no more time for this."

"Ok, how about we thumb wrestle?" Timber pleaded. "Beat Timber at thumb wrestling and you shall be allowed to pass. Yes, thumb wrestling. Oh how Timber loves thumb wrestling."

"No way," Amanda replied.

"Hopscotch?" Timber asked.

"Nope," Amanda turned him down a second time.

"Croquet?" Timber tried again.

"No," Amanda said. "Face it frog. I not only beat you fair and square, but you were beat by a girl."

Just then Timber began to cry. "Why, why, why? Why will no one be Timber's friend? A friend Timber does not have."

Amanda quickly realized that Timber's actions were to get attention. The poor creature was lonely and wanted a friend. "You're not really a guardian, are you?" asked Amanda.

"No, no, no," Timber said crying. "Timber is not a guardian of the jungle. Timber only wanted to play. Yes, Timber wanted a friend. That's all. Just a friend."

"I have to admit, I know how you feel," said Amanda. "I don't have many friends, except Lawrence here. Oh, my name's Amanda."

"Amanda," said Timber. "Timber loves that name. Amanda, Amanda, Amanda. Timber could dance and sing your name all day and all night."

"I have an idea Timber," said Amanda. "How would you like to join me in the jungle. You see, I am searching for an Emerald Key that is hidden somewhere in this jungle. It could be anywhere. I don't know where, exactly. I only know it's in the jungle somewhere. And I don't know this jungle at all. I can't say I've ever been here before. Maybe since you live here, you might be able to help me find my way around Jigsari."

"What?" Timber perked up. "You want Timber to help you find the key? You want Timber to be your friend and go with you in the jungle. Why, that's a wonderful idea. Yes, a wonderful idea. Yes, yes, yes. Timber will go with you. Timber will go with you into Jigsari. Timber knows Jigsari very well. Timber knows all of Jigsari. Just follow Timber. Now, hop to it."

Timber hopped frantically across the swinging bridge before Amanda had a chance to respond. "I guess he's going with us Lawrence," said Amanda as she headed across the swinging bridge, trying to keep up with Timber. Once across the bridge, Timber moved even faster. The energetic Trog moved at a rapid pace, hopping back and forth, and never staying on a straight path. It was a huge effort just to follow him.

Jigsari was beautiful and full of life. There were trees everywhere. The leaves of the tops of these trees covered the jungle like a large green tarp. On many of the trees were colorful flowers with the most delightful scents Amanda had ever smelled. Vines covered most of the trees, appearing to move along the trees like slithering snakes.

But the most fascinating spectacle in all of Jigsari, were the many strange creatures that resided within its boundaries. Sounds of these creatures blended and filled the air with orchestral splendor. And, from time to time, Amanda was able to catch sight of some of these creatures.

"Timber, wait!" Amanda said as she stopped to gander at a grouping of some very large beasts. Each beasts had a large trunk like an elephant, using it to pull up bushes from the ground and snack on the roots. Each one had a huge body, much like an elephant. But unlike an elephant, this creature had two massive spiral shaped horns on the sides of it head, pointing out like a pair of ears. On the front of each creature's head, was a large triangular object – metallic in nature – which covered most of its eyes and pointed downward toward its trunk.

"What are those things?" Amanda asked.

"Those are Rammaphants," replied Timber. "Rammaphants are very strong. Yes, yes, very strong. They can knock down a great huge tree in just one blow. Only one blow and the tree would fall down. Very strong - but also very gentle. Not quite as nasty as those Tarachnobats hanging above your head."

Amanda looked up to see several creatures hanging upside down from a branch on the tree next to her. These creatures had wings like a bat. Their wings were all closed as if the creatures were napping. Their feet and legs, however, did not look like those of any bat Amanda had seen before. Their feet and legs – all eight pairs of them – were very hairy and reminded her of a very creepy and crawly spider. The mere sight of the Tarachnobat made Amanda nervous, and as she stared, one of the Tarachnobats stretched out its wings, allowing Amanda to see its hideous face. The Tarachnobat had multiple sets of eyes and ferocious fangs that looked like they could bite into steel.

"I think it might be best to move on and not wake up these critters," Amanda suggested.

"Good idea," Timber agreed. "Very good idea. Tarachnobats are very nasty. Very nasty creatures. Their bite is deadly and they will attack if you bother them. But there are nastier creatures in Jigsari. Much nastier. Much deadlier. Creatures that scare even Timber."

"What would that be, Timber?" asked Amanda.

"The creature Timber speaks of is the Boarilla," answered Timber. "We would be lucky not to run into a Boarilla. Lucky, lucky, lucky. Boarilla's are said to have hearts of stone which causes them to have no compassion for others. They are mean and wicked beasts, from their hairy bodies to their sharp, razor-like tusks. Very wicked. Very, very wicked."

"From what you just said, I agree with you," Amanda stated, "we would be lucky not to meet such a beast like that. Let's keep going and not think about it. We have a key to find. By the way, what is that smell?"

Amanda smelled the most disgusting and the most grotesque aroma her nose had ever had the misfortune to smell. The smell was worse than a blend of dirty socks, dog breath, and manure.

"Smeller's the feller," laughed Timber, dancing and hopping in a circle. "And you're the smeller Amanda. Smeller's the feller. Smeller's the feller. Smeller's the feller."

"I don't think so," Amanda said in her defense. "Come on, what is that smell really?"

"Ok," Timber replied, "Timber will stop teasing. That smell is those Stunkeys playing up in those trees. That would be the smell. That would be the smell right there." Timber pointed to a group of funny looking monkeys with long bushy tails. The monkeys were brownish-black, with a white stripe running down the center of their bushy tails, much like a skunk. "Stunkeys tend to make their odor known when others are around their home," Timber continued. "Stunkeys find it funny. Timber finds it funny too. Funny, funny, funny. Smeller's the feller. Smeller's the feller. Smeller's the feller."

The group continued through the jungle, with Amanda continuing to be in awe over the many fascinating creatures. From the Toucandles – a colorful bird with a light built into its beak – to the Octostrich – an eight headed ostrich like creature that spent most of its time trying to decide which direction it wanted to go. As they continued to search for the Emerald Key, they heard a low pitched buzzing sound in the distance.

"What is that noise?" Amanda asked. "It sounds like a motor."

"That noise?" Timber said shaking his head. "Timber does not know. Timber does not know what that noise is. But that noise is getting much louder. Yes, much louder to Timber's ears."

"It seems to be coming from that direction," Amanda said pointing to her left. "It is definitely getting louder. What should we do?"

"Oh no," Timber said, again shaking his head, "Timber does not like this. This noise Timber does not like. We must leave. Come, we must leave now."

"Wait," said Amanda. "I can see something. Look, it's like a black carpet unrolling its way along the ground in our direction."

Amanda was right. A black carpet is exactly what it looked like. For in the very near distance, a stream of blackness made its way toward Amanda, Lawrence, and Timber.

"It flows like a river," Amanda stated. "A black river? That's weird."

"Oh no," Timber said, still shaking his head. "Not a river. No, no, no. That's not a river at all."

"Then what?" Amanda began asking. "What is it?"

"Bedbugs!!!" Timber shouted. "Run! Run! Run!"

With great haste, Timber began hopping as fast as he could to get away. Amanda quickly grabbed Lawrence and took off running behind Timber with the current of bedbugs closely behind her.

"We must run and run fast," Timber said. "Dangerous are bedbugs. Very dangerous they are. One bite will put you to sleep for hours. For hours. Do you understand?"

"Yes," Amanda said panting heavily as she ran. "I think I do understand."

"This makes no sense," Timber stated. "Bedbugs do not travel in swarms. No swarms. No swarming bedbugs. No. Never. Maybe a few travel together, but not a swarm. And bedbugs are nocturnal. And its daytime. This is puzzling. Very puzzling to Timber. It makes Timber a very confused Trog."

Amanda ran as swiftly as she possibly could run, trying hard to keep up with Timber. Although she did not look behind her, Amanda could hear the sound of the swarm of bedbugs getting louder and louder. The swarm sounded like the propeller of an airplane and that propeller was getting closer. Amanda realized that if she did not hurry, she soon might feel lots of bedbug bites on the back of her neck.

"Where are we running to Timber?" Amanda asked short of breath.

"We must get away," responded Timber. "We must get away fast. Follow Timber. Follow Timber to safety."

Timber was focused on fleeing and did not show any hesitation as if he knew exactly where he was going. As they continued to make their escape from the bedbugs, they found themselves at the edge of a beautiful blue waterfall. The waterfall fed a wide river which divided the jungle and its two shores, like a great castle wall borders two opposing lands.

"Here, this is what we need to do," ordered Timber. "This is what we need to do to keep the bedbugs from biting. Follow Timber into the river. Follow Timber into the river, grab a hold of Timber's legs, and try to keep your head above water."

Timber jumped into the river and Amanda stopped at the river bank, unsure for the moment about taking an unexpected swim. "Are you sure?" asked Amanda. "Are you sure that getting in the water will keep them from biting us?"

"Yes, yes, yes!" answered Timber. "Yes it will. Bedbugs cannot swim. They cannot swim at all. Now get into the river or you will not like the bite. Not like the bite at all. Not at all. The bedbugs are almost here! Almost, almost, almost! Please, just trust Timber and jump into the river! Please, please, please!"

Indeed, the bedbugs were almost there. The darkness of the swarm caused the light of the day to dim quickly, for the bedbugs were not only covering the ground now, but also the trees that happened to be in their path. The noise of the swarm became louder and louder until it was nearly deafening. Amanda froze in fear on the shore, unable to make a decision. Then, Lawrence made the decision for her. SPLASH!!

"Come back here, Lawrence!" Amanda yelled. Lawrence jumped into the river and paddled his way to Timber. "Fine, I guess I'd rather be wet than bit by these nasty things." As soon as Amanda jumped into the river, the bedbugs enclosed the entire area where she had been standing. Had she waited one second longer, she would have been covered and bitten by a multitude of bedbugs.

Amanda swam her way to Timber who was floating on his back, and grabbed a hold of his legs. Lawrence had made his way to the other side of the river.

"Hang on, Timber will show you his backstroke. The backstroke is Timber's best stroke. The best stroke it is. Timber is an awesome swimmer. Yes, yes, yes. A very awesome swimmer."

Timber was indeed an excellent swimmer. Being part frog and part tree made swimming easy. He demonstrated his comfort in the water as he swam on his back like he was laying on a comfortable mattress. Timber pulled Amanda to the other side of the river where Lawrence was waiting. Amanda and Timber got out and looked across to the opposite shore to see the swarm of bedbugs discouraged at the failure of their quest, as the black carpet of bugs rolled back up and returned to the depths of the jungle from which they came.

"Phew, that was close," Amanda said as she sat down on the ground to rest.

Timber's eyes got big as he pointed to Amanda's right shoulder. "Don't move. No, do not move at all. That would be a bad thing. Very bad to move."

"Why?" asked Amanda. "What do you see?"

Moving would be a very bad thing for Amanda. For danger sat on her shoulder. On her shoulder sat one…

"Bedbug!" shouted Timber. "Timber sees a bedbug on your shoulder. On your shoulder – right there. That bedbug must have crawled on you before you got in the water. It crawled on your back and used you to get across the river. It did. It did. It did."

"Where?" Amanda asked as she jerked to see her shoulder. "I don't see it."

CRUNCH!

"Ouch!!!" It was too late. The bedbug bit Amanda's neck. She swiped at it with her hand, making it fall to the ground.

"Oh no," said Timber, "we must get rid of it. Let Timber get rid of the pest." Timber hopped over to the river's edge and sucked in a mouthful of water. He then hopped back to where the bedbug was on the ground and sprayed it with a forceful stream of water, launching the bedbug into the river. As Timber expected, the bedbug sank to the bottom of the river like a rock, proving that his statement was correct - bedbugs cannot swim.

"Timber did it!" Timber shouted with pride. "Timber beat the bedbug! Timber beat the bedbug! Timber beat the bedbug!"

Amanda did not care. Her eyelids looked heavy and tired. Her head nodded forward and her legs weakened like they were made of rubber, as she started searching for a place to rest on the ground around her.

"I'm so sleepy," said Amanda stretching her arms high above her head. "Let me just relax for a minute."

"No, no, no," pleaded Timber. "You cannot sleep. You cannot."

It was too late. The bedbug's venom was flowing throughout Amanda's body. There was no stopping its effects. All Timber and Lawrence could do was watch Amanda place her head on the ground and fall fast asleep.

Amanda opened her eyes and everything was blurry. *What a crazy dream that was,* she thought as she rubbed her eyes. *Dragons and bedbugs and crazy wooden frogs. What a silly dream. Oh well, I better get downstairs for breakfast. I don't want grandfather thinking I slept too late. He doesn't care for late sleepers. He might decide to eat my portion.*

"Hello there sleepy head," said a voice beside Amanda. "Did you have a nice nap? Did you enjoy your shuteye? Did you? Did you? Did you?"

Amanda's vision began to clear as she looked directly into Timber's eyes.

"Oh no!" Amanda said disappointed. "I wasn't dreaming. You are real - and I'm not home. This is all real. Which means I'm still stuck here in Jigsari."

"Yes, yes, yes," said Timber. "Yes, you are still here in Jigsari. Jigsari Jungle. And this is Jigsari Falls. Isn't it beautiful? Isn't it just the most beautiful waterfall you've ever seen?"

"Well, yes it is beautiful," responded Amanda. "But I wish I had dreamt it instead. I really wish I was back home. I miss my grandparents. Being here on

Maldderan is becoming more of a nightmare than it is a dream."

"Did you miss Timber?" Timber asked. "Did you miss Timber while you took your bedbug nap?"

"That's right," said Amanda. "I fell asleep because that bedbug bit me. And yes, I guess I did miss you Timber. If it weren't for you that bedbug situation would have been much worse."

"Yes, Timber saved the day. Timber saved the day. Timber saved the day. Timber saved…"

"Ok, ok," Amanda said cutting off Timber, "you saved the day. But we aren't done, remember? We still have to find the Emerald Key. And that isn't going to be easy."

"The key?" asked Timber. "Find the key? Oh yes, Timber can find the key. Yes, yes, yes. Timber can. Where oh where could the key be?"

"Don't ask me," answered Amanda. "You're the one who knows this jungle, not me."

Looking around, Amanda realized that the group of three, was now two. "Wait a minute Timber, where's Lawrence? I haven't seen him since I woke up."

"Timber does not know. Timber is trying to find the key, not the ferret. You asked Timber to find the key. Now you want Timber to find the ferret. Timber is only one Trog. Only one. Timber must focus on one task."

"Please Timber, you must help me find him," Amanda said. "Lawrence is my best friend. I can't lose him."

"Timber understands. Timber will help. First Timber will help Amanda find her ferret. Then Timber will help find the key. Then Timber will need a rest. Perhaps a vacation somewhere tropical."

"This is somewhere tropical you silly toad," Amanda said shaking her head. "This is no time to joke around. We have to find Lawrence and we... There he is!" Amanda pointed toward the waterfall. Lawrence was at the edge of the fall, sniffing around curiously in sleuth-like fashion.

"Why is he sniffing around?" asked Amanda. "Do you think he found the Emerald Key? We need to go see. Come on Timber."

"Goody, goody, goody," laughed Timber. "That is so goody. The ferret found the key. The ferret found the key. Timber beat the bedbug and the ferret found the key."

"Don't jump to any conclusions," suggested Amanda. "He's only sniffing. Now let's go find out why."

Amanda ran over to Lawrence with Timber hopping behind her singing about ferrets and keys and bedbugs. "Well, he's found something alright," said Amanda, "but it isn't a key."

Behind the waterfall, Lawrence had discovered a hidden cave. It was shrouded from all outside view due to the veil of the waterfall covering its entire entrance. But, there was one way to get into the cave. A small ledge created a path from the edge of the waterfall to the cave's entrance. This is what had gotten Lawrence's attention. Now it had Amanda's attention.

"There's only one reason Lawrence would be sniffing the way he is right here," explained Amanda.

"Why, why, why?" asked Timber. "Why is he sniffing? Timber wants to know why the ferret is sniffing."

"Because the key has to be in that cave," answered Amanda. "Lawrence's sniffing is due to the key being in that cave. There isn't a better key hunter than Lawrence. Which means, we have to cross this ledge and go inside to search for ourselves."

"Yes, yes, yes," Timber responded hopping frantically. "Amanda is right. Timber thinks so. Let's go behind the waterfall. Let's go in the cave. Let's go, let's go, let's go."

"Ok," Amanda agreed, "what can it hurt? I mean, if I'm wrong, I'm wrong and we'll keep searching. But if I'm right, and we do find the key, then I can get going and you can go back to guarding the jungle."

"Yes, yes, yes," said Timber. "Timber is the best guard ever. The best, the best, the best."

It was decided to go behind the waterfall and take a look for the Emerald Key. As they approached the ledge, Amanda realized how narrow it was and grew concerned with crossing it safely. However, Timber showed no concern as he took the lead, hopping right onto the ledge and quickly making his way to the back side of the waterfall. Lawrence followed Timber without any problems either, but Amanda, being the biggest of the three, was a different story. With her back firmly against the wall of the ledge and her hands pressed hard against this wall on both sides of her body, she sidled the ledge, inching her way slowly to keep from falling into the blanket of water in front of her. Her heels were also pressed against the wall of the ledge and even then, only the back halves of her feet were able to make contact with the surface of the ledge while the front halves dangled over the side and the doom that would greet her, should she fall.

The water of the fall sprayed her face as she crept her way across the ledge, making it very difficult for her to move with any speed.

"Hang in there," said Timber. "You're almost there. Not much more. Close, close, close."

"Shhh," Amanda said as she began to lose her footing. Amanda was already disoriented by the splashing water and the noise of the waterfall. "Please, just be quiet so I don't lose my focus and fall off of this ledge."

Timber managed to stay quiet and Amanda was able to make it to the end of the ledge. "Wow, that was scary," she said taking a huge gulp. "What is this place?"

Entering the cave, the trio could see the interior easily due to it being well lit by several burning torches. The cave was large and filled with many large boulders, various sized rocks, and some sticks. The boulders were placed in specific arrangements as they stood on edge, creating a circular pattern around the outer rim of the cave. Strange symbols and drawings were on both the boulders and the walls of the caves. Sounds of dripping water echoed the cave as the liquid flowed down the stalactites covering the cave's ceiling like tears falling from an eye. Skeletons of various creatures were seen throughout the cave in random locations. A sight that gave its new visitors a scare they could do without.

"Timber does not know," replied Timber trembling. "Timber has never been to this place before. Never once. Not one time. Never, never, never. Timber thinks we should not be in here. Timber thinks we should leave and leave now. Now, now, now. Now, and never come back. Never."

Besides the torches, boulders, and skeletons, the cave was otherwise empty – except for one thing.

"Would you take a look at that?" Amanda said with her eyes wide open and fright in her voice. "Timber, what is it?"

"Timber does not know - again. Timber has never seen that before. Remember, Timber has never been to this place. Never. But now, Timber is a very scared Trog."

Amanda and Lawrence were also scared. Centered on the far end of the cave, was a hideously terrifying totem pole, with masked faces of creatures that looked very, very real.

The totem pole consisted of four masks. The first mask on the very top of the pole was a frightening bird face, resembling a falcon, but with a long, narrow beak that looked as deadly as a sword. On the sides of the totem pole, behind the raptorial bird mask, were the wings of this creature, spreading out as if it were flying. The second mask was the face of a lion. The lion's mane was full and dominate in appearance, and his mouth was wide open as if ready to bite down with his vicious teeth. The third mask on the totem pole was that of a snake, much like a cobra. The snake had piercing teeth coming from its mouth and mesmerizing eyes that looked as if they could hypnotize anyone. The last and bottom face was that of a bull. The bull's face was reared back as if it was ready to attack. Its horns extended along the sides of the pole and faced forward, as if ready to pierce anyone in front of the pole.

"Um, that thing sure doesn't look friendly," said Amanda. "And I hope I'm wrong, but I think I see a green glow coming from the lion's mouth. And I can think of only one thing that would give off a green glow."

"The Emerald Key!" exclaimed Timber. "The Emerald Key is in the lion's mouth. Oh no, oh no, oh no."

"Oh no is right," Amanda said. "Which means I have to stick my hand in the mouth of the lion to get the key."

"Stick your hand in there?" questioned Timber. "What if there are bedbugs in there? Or even worse, Tarachnobats? Timber would hate for an Tarachnobat to bite down on his hand. Or maybe something slimy or something that burns your hand? Or maybe…"

"Cut it out," Amanda said stopping Timber in the middle of his atrocious list of possibilities. "I'm already scared enough. I don't need any of your frightful suggestions. Now, let me take a deep breath and just do this."

Amanda took a huge breath and stood directly in front of the totem pole. She rolled up the sleeve on her navy blue jacket and began to stick her hand in the mouth of the lion's face. "You can do this," she whispered to herself. "Just believe in yourself."

Amanda had most of her forearm in the lion's mouth as she turned to Timber and said, "See Timber, nothing to worry about. I'll grab the key and we'll be on our way. I think I'm almost there. I should feel it any moment now."

But before Amanda could grab the Emerald Key, she felt something warm around her feet and something else poking at her knees. She looked down and saw the head of the bull breathing steaming hot air from its snout

235

and the curled tongue of the snake touching her knees. Then she felt something wet on her forearm. A wetness that touched her arm with a rough, damp feeling, starting near her elbow and creeping its way up toward her wrist. It was a feeling that reminded her of a cat's tongue licking her arm - but a much larger tongue. She looked back up and the eyes of the lion were staring directly into her eyes.

"Ahhh!!!" Amanda screamed and pulled her arm out of the lion's mouth quickly, just as it began to bite down with its deadly teeth. The totem pole had come to life to defend the Emerald Key and was now a live beast instead of just a statue. All four heads of this Totem Beast were alive and all four looked extremely angry.

Amanda stumbled backwards to get away, narrowly missing a slice from the bird's beak, that would have spiked her head like a melon. "What do we do?" cried Amanda. "This beast is not happy with us being here."

"Timber does not know," said Timber. "Timber says we should run! This way!"

Timber started hopping for the waterfall cave entrance, but the Totem Beast used the wings of the bird to fly faster than Timber could hop, cutting them off in front of the entrance, before they could escape. Amanda watched as Lawrence ran to hide behind a small boulder. "Smart thinking little guy," said Amanda. "Now somebody get me behind a boulder."

The Totem Beast separated into four individual heads and mutated with the snake's head at the top of the pole. The beast dropped to the ground and slithered toward Amanda and Timber.

"This thing is too fast," said Amanda. "We need to separate. You run that way Timber and I'll run this way."

Timber hopped to the right of the Totem Beast and Amanda scurried her way around its left. Timber found a boulder of his own to hide behind. The Totem Beast again separated into four individual heads and again reformed with the head of the bull on the top of the pole. The Totem Beast took a stance with the horns of the bull pointed out

237

front. It charged at the boulder Timber was hiding behind, smashing it into tiny pebbles and launching Timber backwards toward the wall of the cave and to the ground.

"Ok, maybe no one should find me a boulder," Amanda said.

Timber stood up and brushed himself off. Again, the Totem Beast heads separated and reformed so that the head of the lion was on top of the pole. Amanda saw that the lion was about to pounce Timber so she ran quickly to his aid. Just as the lion was in mid-air, Amanda grabbed Timber and ran with him to the far side of the cave, while the Totem Beast tripped on its landing and fell against the wall.

This fall only staggered the Totem Beast for a moment as it stood up and mutated again with the bird's head on top of the pole. The bird used its wings to fly toward Amanda and Timber.

"Oh my gosh!" Amanda screamed in fear. "How are we ever going to stop this creature?

"Timber has no clue. No clues at all," responded Timber. "But, there are four creatures, not just one. Yes, four very ugly creatures. Eek, four very ugly, very nasty creatures."

"Ok, then how are we going to stop these FOUR creatures?" asked Amanda.

"Timber still has no clues," said Timber. "Still no clues at all."

Amanda debated desperately and as quickly as she could. "Wait, I have an idea. Try to distract them while I get something out of Lawrence's backpack."

"Oh boy," said Timber, "Timber gets to be a distraction. The Trog is a distraction. Timber is a very good distraction. Very, very, good."

While Timber drew the attention of the Totem Beast, Amanda opened Lawrence's backpack and filtered through its contents. "Just where did that thing go? I don't have time to spare. Ah, there it is!!" Amanda pulled out the dragon retrieving whistle and immediately blew it with all the power her lungs could produce.

Within mere seconds, XR-27 came flying through the backside of the waterfall with his wings spread wide, ready to be of assistance. Amanda reached down and picked up a stick lying on the ground. She stretched her arm back and threw the stick at the Totem Beast. "Here XR! Fetch the stick!"

The stick went hurling directly at the Totem Beast whose attention had now turned to the dragon that had just entered its domain. XR-27 reared his head back and blew out a scorching stream of fire, meant for the stick. But, because of Amanda's perfect throw, the stream of fire targeted the Totem Beast. The flame impacted the Totem Beast with a devastating blow, causing its wooden structure to burn to ashes, and crumble to nothing more than a pile of smoldering soot on the ground.

"XR, you did it!" exclaimed Amanda. "You stopped that creature. That was so splendorific!"

"Oh wow, oh wow, oh wow," said Timber. "Timber did not know Amanda had a dragon. Timber's so happy the dragon didn't mistake Timber for a stick. That would have been bad. Yes, very bad. A very, very, bad thing for Timber."

"Don't worry Timber," said Amanda. "You might look a little bit like a tree, but I wouldn't have made that mistake."

"Good, good, good," Timber rambled. "Roasted Timber would not be a good thing at all. No, not at all."

The Totem Beast had been destroyed, but Amanda still needed to complete her mission in Jigsari. "I'm so happy and thankful you saved us XR," she said, "but now that the totem pole is gone, we might have another problem. You see, the Emerald Key was inside of it and now it's nothing but ashes."

"Yes, yes, yes," said Timber. "Just a pile of ashes. Just a big ole' pile of green glowing ashes."

"What?" said Amanda. "Did you say green glowing ashes?"

Amanda walked over closer to the pile of simmering ashes. "Wait a minute. Those ashes are still burning and glowing, but they aren't red, like ashes normally would be. They're green just like you said, which means – the Emerald Key is still in there. It's in that pile of hot ashes. But how do we get it out? It's much too hot to touch."

"Wait right there," said Timber. "Timber has an idea. Yes, yes, yes, a very good idea. A very good idea from Timber."

Timber hopped over to the back side of the waterfall and sucked in a mouthful of water. Then he turned around and just like XR, he reared his head back and let out a forceful stream of water, hitting the pile of ashes with a direct shot, leaving a harmless, wet, soggy mess.

"See, Timber can shoot things from his mouth too," Timber said with a grin on his face. "Timber saves the day again. Timber saves the day. Ha, ha, ha. Timber saves the day."

"Yes you did," Amanda said. "You have saved the day many times. Thank you Timber. Now let me see if I can find the key in this mess."

Amanda stuck her hand in the soggy pile of ashes and reached around. "Ick, this is gross," she said, "but well worth it." She pulled her hand out and held up the Emerald Key which was covered with black soot. "I got it!"

"Amanda found the key!" exclaimed Timber. "Amanda found the key! Goody, goody, goody!"

"Well, Timber," said Amanda, "I hate to leave so quickly, but now that I found this key, I have to find two others before I can get home. I hope you understand. I really thank you for all your help."

"Timber understands," responded Timber. "Timber is happy to have found his friend Amanda, even for such a short time."

"Amanda is happy to have found Timber," Amanda said. "But it's not just for a short time. Timber will be Amanda's friend forever."

Amanda gave Timber a hug and turned to XR-27. Amanda and Lawrence boarded the dragon and waved goodbye to Timber. "Goodbye Timber," Amanda said with tears in her eyes, "I hope I can come visit you again sometime."

"Goodbye, Amanda," Timber said with many tears falling from the Trog's eyes. "Timber hopes you visit Jigsari again, too. Goodbye."

Amanda took a quick swig of the dragon milk and... "Burrrrppppp!!!!!"

XR swooped through the backside of the waterfall, just the opposite direction as he had entered, with Amanda putting her head down to keep from getting wet and to shelter Lawrence. They exited the waterfall cave and flew high into the air above the Jigsari Jungle. Their next destination – Kryogen.

Chapter 8
The Village of Kryogen

The further the group distanced themselves in flight from Jigsari, the colder the air clamped down around them. Amanda stuffed Lawrence into her jacket like a mother kangaroo would its young. Even with all of his fur, the poor little rodent did not like the cold one bit. His eyes squinted, his nose was runny, and his teeth were chattering like an engine in desperate need of oil.

Amanda, unsettled and shivering against the rapidly decreasing temperatures, pressed herself against XR-27, making use of the warmth radiating from the dragon's body. Attempting to keep Lawrence warm, Amanda pressed forward against XR-27 even closer, hoping to give added comfort to her pet ferret. However, Lawrence felt more like he was caught in a vise as he let out a yelp due to being squeezed too tightly. Amanda eased up, realizing Lawrence's dissatisfaction at being in the middle of an Amanda and XR sandwich.

"Settle down little guy," said Amanda, "I'm just trying to make this easier on both of us and keep us both warm."

A tiny snowflake landed on the tip of Amanda's nose. It was followed by another, and then another, until many snowflakes swirled around her, dancing a wintry waltz of delight. Amanda stuck out her tongue to catch a flake. As she looked down, she could see the color of the ground change to white and she knew that they must be getting close to Kryogen.

Amanda was right, for XR-27 started descending and landed in a snow covered area, near the top of a mountain, and next to the village of Kryogen. Here the cold temperatures even caused XR to shiver. Amanda looked around for a comfortable place for XR to stay while she and Lawrence went into the village, but there did not seem to be proper shelter for a dragon anywhere in the area. But when she turned back around, she found that XR had already taken the initiative to find his own shelter.

"Hey!" shouted Amanda, "Where are you going?"

The dragon turned his head around and gave Amanda a quick nod to let her know it was ok. He then took flight, heading down the mountain, gliding only mere feet above the tops of the snow-covered trees.

"All right then," said Amanda, "I'll just blow my whistle if I need you. You go on now and find somewhere warm to hang out until we find the Sapphire Key. I'm sure you have better things to do with your time anyway."

Amanda continued to watch XR fly down the mountain until she could see him no longer. She gulped and whispered, "I'm sure we'll be safe without you."

Preoccupied with XR, Amanda had not paid any attention to the village next to where XR had landed. Turning around, she stood to take a look at the village of Kryogen, as the snowflakes continued to fall around her.

Kryogen was a small and beautiful village. There were several cottages inside of the village. These cottages were unique structures as they appeared to be part of the mountain itself. They were rounded on top and all were covered with snow. This made them appear like giant white mushrooms growing on the mountain. Each cottage had a chimney protruding from the top, but only a few of these chimneys had smoke filtering from them. Amanda walked through the village, hoping to find a helpful person in one of the cottages.

She came to a cottage where she could see smoke coming from the chimney. In front of the cottage stood hedges made of ice, not of green vegetation. Several of these ice hedges were sculpted in shapes of hearts, stars, and four-leaf clovers. The front door was very strange looking. It was not a normal shaped door, but rather a very wide, rectangular wooden door.

Amanda knocked on the front door. But no one answered.

"I'm really cold," she said. "I sure hope someone is home, Lawrence."

Amanda knocked again. Still, no one answered.

"Maybe they can't hear us," Amanda suggested. "Maybe they're sleeping or something. I hate to bother them, but I really need to warm up."

Amanda knocked one more time. Still no one answered.

"It's no use, Lawrence," she said, "we need to move on and try a different house."

As Amanda turned around to walk away, she slipped on the ice under her feet, causing her to fall backwards into the front door of the cottage. The impact of her fall caused the front door to open, leaving Amanda on her back with her legs outside of the cottage and the rest of her inside. Lawrence, still safe inside her jacket, stared down into her face.

"Owwww," Amanda said painfully. "I'm guessing that didn't hurt you that much, huh, Lawrence?"

Amanda stood up, shook herself off, and looked around the room of the cottage with curiosity.

"I guess since we're here, we might as well stay a bit," she said as she closed the front door.

Amanda stood inside a small, but heavily decorated living room. The room was painted in warm, earth colors and felt very cozy. Along the far wall was a fireplace with a huge fire burning. In front of the fireplace, a polar bear rug covered the floor. Centered in front of the rug was a flat couch with no back. An ottoman sat on both sides of the couch. The wall to the left held a built-in shelf resembling a shrine, for it was covered with trophies, ribbons, plaques, certificates, and rewards a plenty. There were so many that the shelf looked as if it might collapse under the weight of all of its contents. On the other wall were two doors leading to other rooms and between these doors sat a long rectangular chest.

"Wow," said Amanda, "whoever lives here must be quite a competitor. I wonder what type of competition they're involved in?"

The fire crackled noisily, drawing Amanda's attention away from the trophy case.

"Well, I think I know where the warmest spot in this cottage is, Lawrence," she said. "What do you say we go have a seat over there on that rug?"

Amanda pulled Lawrence out of her jacket and the two of them headed over toward the fireplace. She sat down on the polar bear rug and Lawrence snuggled up next to her. She stared into the fire and watched it burn as the flames danced a mesmerizing sequence of heated steps. Amanda began to feel relaxed and even began to tire, and she stretched out her arms and yawned.

"This rug is so soft," she said. "I sure could use a nap."

Amanda laid down and stretched her body over the polar bear rug.

"It's still a little chilly down here on the floor, even with that fire," Amanda said as she started to pull the polar bear rug around her body like a blanket.

"Just what in tarnation do you think you are doing tugging on me like that miss?" a voice asked from very nearby.

"Aaahhhhh!!!!!" Amanda jumped to her feet still wrapped in the rug, looking around for who it was that just spoke to her. "Who's there? Who did I tug? Who are you?"

"I'm right here," said the voice. "You tugged me. And my name's Bertrand."

"Right where?" asked Amanda. "I don't see anyone. How can I tug you if I can't even see you?"

"Because you're wearing me," said the voice.

Amanda hesitantly took the polar bear rug off of her body. She closed her eyes and turned around to face it. As she lifted up her head and opened her eyes, the polar bear rug was looking directly into Amanda's face with a huge friendly smile of razor sharp, pearly white, polar bear teeth.

"Hello," the polar bear rug grinned.

"Aaahhhhh!!!!!" Amanda screamed again. "You're a rug! And you're a bear! And you're alive!"

"Don't be scared now," said Bertrand. "Yes, I am a rug. I sort of like being a rug. But it's me who should be scared of you. I mean, you broke into my home. You were sitting on me. And you were trying to use me as a fur coat. Now that's scary."

"Oh," said Amanda. "I didn't mean to break in. It was an accident. I was cold. When I got in, I saw how comfy it looked in here and the fire was so warm and then I saw the rug - I mean I saw you, I guess - and I thought I could warm up that way."

"It figures," Bertrand said. "Just a rug? You three-dimensional types are all alike. You treat us two-dimensional types with such disrespect. We are either your rug or your blanket or your curtain. Never treating us with any respect. Just something to be used. Something for you 3-D's to wipe your feet on. I got news for you girly. I'm three-dimensional too, just like you. I have feelings, just like you."

"Hey, Mister Bertrand, I'm sorry," Amanda apologized. "I didn't mean any disrespect to you. You see, where I come from, I would never come across a rug that talked or walked - or had feelings for that matter. This is new to me. There are so many things about Maldderan that are new to me and I don't understand them."

"So you're not from Maldderan?" asked Bertrand.

"No," answered Amanda. "I'm not. I'm sort of here, well, because I wished to be here."

"Interesting wish," Bertrand said. "I think I would have wished for money. Or maybe something potent enough to get these shoe scuffs off of my backside. So many folks think they can just wipe their feet on me. Anyway, how did you wish for something like that? I mean how did you ever know about Maldderan if you weren't from here? Have you been here before?"

"Well, it wasn't exactly like that," replied Amanda. "You see, I wished for all of my dreams to come true and I ended up here in Maldderan."

"Whoa, this is an interesting wish," Bertrand said fascinated. "So, are you telling me Maldderan is your dream?"

"I don't know," said Amanda. "It only makes sense. If the wish came true and this is real, then Maldderan is my dream. If not, I may only be dreaming and this may not be real at all."

"So you made a wish in a different place other than Maldderan. And you feel that world may be real and this one is a dream?" asked Bertrand.

"Yes, I think it is," Amanda answered. "Why do you ask that?"

"Well, I'll tell you why," Bertrand explained. "I am as real as they come. What you see is what you get. I am definitely not part of someone's dream. I feel the same about Maldderan. It is my home and not some dream. So maybe you should look at what you know from a different perspective. Maybe you have been a part of Maldderan all of your life. Maybe what you feel is your world is merely a dream and that this so-called dream that has come true for you, is really your world. Maybe that waking life of yours that you feel is real, is nothing more than a dream."

"What are you trying to say?" Amanda asked. "That everything I know as real is not. That it is merely a dream? That my grandparents aren't real? That my school isn't real?"

"Not necessarily," answered Bertrand. "It's only a theory. I like to theorize things. Some of my friends would rather say I just like to argue a lot. Don't worry too much about it, though. What's your name anyway?"

"Oh, my name's Amanda. Amanda Sneed. I really do like your home Bertrand. It's very cozy."

"It's a pleasure to meet you Miss Amanda Sneed," said Bertrand, "and thank you. I must admit, I do enjoy relaxing in the comforts of my own home."

GRRUUUMMMBBBLLEEEE!!!!!

Amanda started laughing upon hearing the peculiar noise coming from Bertrand.

"Oh, pardon me," apologized Bertrand. "That would be my stomach. You know us bears. We can sleep for a long time and nothing ever disturbs us, but when we wake up, look out. We're usually pretty grumpy, very hungry, and ready to roll. And I am starving. Not to mention, I have a big game today so I need to get my energy up. How about you? I bet you must be hungry. Come over here and pick out something to eat."

Bertrand headed over to the chest that stood between the two doors along the side wall. Amanda followed him, curious to see what he had for her to eat.

"Actually, I am a little hungry," Amanda replied. "What do you have?"

"Come on and take a look," said Bertrand. "There's quite a variety in here."

Bertrand opened the lid to the chest and a gust of cold wind blew out frantically.

"Just wait a moment and it will pass," said Bertrand. "I keep my ice chest pretty chilly."

The wind did subside and Amanda was able to look inside, but all she saw were large blocks of ice. Nothing more. Nothing less.

"This is just ice," said Amanda.

"Well, it is an ice chest," replied Bertrand.

"I guess I was hoping for something a bit more tasty," said Amanda.

"I'm just messing with you," said Bertrand. "These ice cubes are actually frozen foods."

"Frozen foods?" asked Amanda with a look of disgust on her face. "Those are nasty."

"What?" Bertrand asked. "You mean you don't like frozen foods?"

"Well," replied Amanda, "my Grandmother used to feed me those frozen food meals and they tasted gross. I just don't know if I can eat anymore of those. And besides, this just seems a bit too frozen. It's like everything in here is a popsicle."

"I bet you'd like it if you tried some of what's in here," Bertrand suggested to her.

"Well, what kind of frozen food is this one?" Amanda asked pointing to one of the large ice cubes.

"That one is frozen popcorn," answered Bertrand.

"Frozen popcorn?" Amanda asked. "I've never heard of freezing popcorn."

"Preservation," Bertrand replied. "It's all about preservation. I freeze all of my food. I can sleep for pretty long periods of time and I'd hate for any of my food to spoil, even popcorn. So I just freeze it. Hey, this brand has extra butter too. Yummmmmy."

"I guess I'll try the popcorn," said Amanda. "I love popcorn."

"Good choice," said Bertrand. "I think I'll have the same thing."

Bertrand grabbed two metal sticks with spiked tips that were sitting next to the ice chest. He thrust one of the sticks forward into the chest as if he were spear fishing and he pulled the stick out with a large ice cube on the end. After handing it to Amanda, he did the same with the other metal stick, then they went back to the fireplace with their frozen popcorn.

"Just hold the ice cube out over the fire like this," explained Bertrand as he held his metal stick forward with the large ice cube hovering over the roaring flame.

"Ok, I don't get it," said Amanda. "Won't the ice just melt?"

"That's what I'm hoping for," replied Bertrand. "Just be patient."

The ice did begin to melt, and along with melting something very interesting began to happen.

POP!

POP!

POP! POP!

POP! POP! POP! POP! POP!

"Oh my gosh, this is splendorific!" exclaimed Amanda. "These ice cubes are really melting into popcorn. They really are."

"I told you to be patient," said Bertrand. "Wait until you taste it."

The ice cubes did melt and popcorn was the result. What was left was a ball of popcorn stuck to the end of the metal stick which looked like a popcorn lollipop. Amanda and Bertrand sat down in front of the fire to eat their popcorn and talk further about Amanda's reason for being in Maldderan.

"So, I understand that you made a wish and you ended up here in Maldderan," Bertrand began, "but what brings you to Kryogen?"

"I'm here to find a key," answered Amanda.

"A key?" asked Bertrand. "I don't understand. What kind of key?"

"Well it's not a normal key," explained Amanda. "It's a Sapphire Key. You see, when I arrived in Maldderan, I realized that there was this evil person after me named Gamirathen. I also met a very wise and friendly ally named Gee Lassy who has a Dream Diary that belongs to me. Well, this diary requires three keys to unlock it and only I am able to do that. The three keys are hidden throughout Maldderan. I have found one. One is somewhere here in Kryogen, and the other I still have to locate. With the keys, I can open my Dream Diary and use its power to stop Gamirathen from destroying this world and mine, with his evil nightmares."

"Wow, this is quite an undertaking for you," said Bertrand. "Good thing you did stop by to warm up and to get a bite to eat. This Gamirathen character must be pretty nasty. Where did you run into him?"

"I actually saw him in a mirror within the city of Meeyor," replied Amanda. "I haven't seen him since but I know he's out there."

"Meeyor you say?" asked Bertrand, "I've been to Meeyor several times. Not the friendliest place, but I sure do love the shades."

CHIP, CHIP, CHIP - CHIP, CHIP, CHIP!!!

Amanda looked around to see where the noise was coming from.

"I promise that's not my stomach this time," chuckled Bertrand. "I believe it's coming from outside."

Bertrand walked over to the windows at the front of his cottage and looked outside. "Hey, it's my buddy Russell. He's come over to work on my ice hedges."

"Work on your ice hedges?" asked Amanda.

"Yes, he's an ice sculptor, among many other talents," replied Bertrand. "Come on outside and meet him. Oh, by the way, he's really shy and doesn't talk much."

Amanda, Lawrence, and Bertrand went out the front of the cottage and found a small penguin chipping away at one of the ice hedges with a small hammer and an ice pick. The penguin wore a blue and yellow stocking cap and matching scarf. He also wore black boots and a jacket that looked like a tuxedo jacket. He had just finished one of the hedges and it resembled a flamingo. The hedge he was currently chipping away at looked like it was to become a dolphin.

"Well hello, Russell," said Bertrand. "I didn't expect you to come work on the hedges today. Especially right before the big game."

Russell waved at Bertrand with his flipper and looked strangely at Amanda.

"Oh," said Bertrand, "this is my new friend, Amanda Sneed. Amanda, this is Russell."

"It's nice to meet you, Russell," Amanda said holding out her hand to shake Russell's flipper.

Russell reached inside his tuxedo jacket and pulled out a balloon. He quickly stretched and pulled and stretched and pulled on it. Then he blew it up, twisted it into the shape of a heart, and handed it to Amanda.

"I think the penguin likes you," said Bertrand. "I've never known him to give out a heart before. Most people just get a balloon square when they first meet him. You must be special."

"Thank you, Russell," said Amanda. "I do feel special. Wow, you make ice sculptures and balloon figures, too?"

"I did say he had other talents," said Bertrand.

BONG! BONG! BONG!

"I can assure you that noise wasn't my stomach. That was the village clock and wow, I almost lost track of time," said Bertrand. "It's almost time for the game. And what do you know? Here comes part of my team now."

Three shadowy-dressed female characters approached from the near distance. However, the three were not walking, but rather, gliding above the snow covered ground below them.

"Wow, they are an interesting trio," said Amanda. "Who are they?"

"They are sisters," answered Bertrand. "We call them the Ice Sisters Three. You know, I don't really know their real names. Anyway, they're a little bit strange, but awesome crab soccer players. Whatever you do, try not to stare."

The Ice Sisters Three were an interesting looking trio and appeared identical to any observer. Each sister wore a black hooded cloak, covering their face, including their eyes. However, their faces were not entirely covered by the cloak. Each had a white nose that was way too large to be hidden. The mere size of these enormous, deformed, carrot shaped snouts, could not be covered by the cloak, but were instead, covered by many hanging icicles. The cloaks settled just below their waists and their legs were plainly visible. Nylons in alternating, horizontal striped patterns of light and dark blue were worn on each leg. Each sister wore a pair of black leather boots which fit high above the ankle. The tip of each boot gradually spiraled to a pointed toe, looking very much to Amanda like the boots of an elf. But the strangest feature of the Ice Sisters Three were their arms. Their arms were so disproportionately long that their hands dragged the ground. And their fingers were not like normal fingers. Their fingers were piercing and pointed and looked extremely brittle. It was as if they were not fingers at all. But rather, icicles.

"We bring a message to you, a message quite sad."
"For today one you know suffers a sickness quite bad."
"Our friend Barnaby is very ill and quite sore."
"Now our team which was five is now down to four."

"The Ice Sisters Three are famous for saying everything in rhyme," Bertrand explained to Amanda. "The first sister says the first verse, followed by the second sister saying the second verse, and the third sister saying the third verse. To end the chant, all three sisters recite the fourth verse in unison. A bit strange, but you'll get used to them."

"What do you mean Barnaby isn't able to play today?" Bertrand asked in disgust. "This is the most important game ever for us. This is the for the Crab Soccer Cup. It's the village of Kryogen versus the village of Marsays. And if we don't have a fifth team member, we will have to forfeit, which means we will automatically lose the cup."

"Why doesn't Russell play?" asked Amanda.

"Russell is usually a bit busy during the games," Bertrand answered. "You see, he's the referee. And the scorekeeper. And the timekeeper. And the water boy. And the ..."

"I get it," said Amanda. "Russell has many talents."

The Ice Sisters Three surrounded Amanda, making her feel both uncomfortable and nervous.

"Do our eyes play tricks? Is this the child? Yes, it seems."
"This is the one with the nightmares. The one with the dreams."
"Has she come here to save us? Or will our world she disrupt?"
"For our souls feel in this child is an evil that's corrupt."

"This little girl is not evil," Bertrand exclaimed. "Now quit suggesting such nonsense and start getting your heads focused on the game."

"This child has great power, a power to dream."
"But this power if used by evil can cause many to scream."
"To use this great power, she must have faith, this she must."
"But the faith that she must have is in herself she must trust."

"Bertrand, these sisters scare me a little bit," said Amanda.

"Don't be scared of them," Bertrand replied. "I sure am not scared of them. What I am scared of is forfeiting this game and losing the Crab Soccer Cup to the village of Marsays."

"Look, I can see that this game is really important to you, Bertrand," said Amanda. "I know I'm in a bit of a hurry and all, but you've been a big help to me so I was thinking maybe I could help you by being your fifth player. I played crab soccer a few times at my school. I'm not the best player, but I do know how to play."

"Given the fact that the game is about to start, I would say that's a perfect idea," said Bertrand. "Barnaby normally plays goalie, but I'll switch to that position. You play the field and try to work with the Ice Sisters Three the best you can and don't be scared."

The Ice Sisters did not like the idea of Amanda becoming the fifth team member as they voiced their disgust.

"The dreamer will fail, she will fail and cause harm."
"Her presence today is cause for alarm."
"She must go now, she must or we are all in great doom."
"The mere mention of her name will cause evil to loom."

"Ladies, could you be any more depressing?" Bertrand asked. "Besides, I'm the captain of this team and I'm responsible for filling vacant spots. So I say she's staying and playing today's game. We'll discuss the matter after we win the Crab Soccer Cup. Now come on. We have to get to the field and warm up. The game is about to start."

The Ice Sisters Three said no more and all three glided their way to the Kryogen Crab Soccer Field, looking disappointed, worried, and very troubled. Bertrand and

Amanda followed closely behind with Russell and Lawrence bringing up the rear.

The Kryogen Crab Soccer Field was an outdoor field and had plenty of spectator seating. The seating ran along the length of near side of the field and the two ends of the field. Four large lights were posted at each corner of the field and the heat of the lights could be felt from a respectable distance. The heat from the lights kept the field warm, preventing the snow from forming on it and allowing grass to grow. On the far side of the field there was no seating, but rather, several rows of hedges. On the far side of these bushes, there was a steep hill that dropped sharply away from Kryogen.

The seats were already filled with fans as Amanda made her way to the field to stretch out her muscles. She knew that in the game of crab soccer, she would have to walk on her arms quite a bit, so she spent some time loosening up her arm muscles. As she was sitting down and leaning forward to stretch out her calf muscles, she felt something tap her shoulder.

"Bon jour," said a voice from behind Amanda. Amanda turned around to see a crab three times her size, smiling with a large toothy grin, at Amanda. "Bon jour, Mademoiselle. I am Peppee. I am the goalee'."

The large crab put out his right claw, as if he wanted to shake hands with Amanda. Amanda was not sure what to say. "Um, bon sure," she attempted in reply, "I'm Amanda and I don't know what position I'm playing. But it's nice to meet such a large crab like yourself, Peppee. You must be the goalie for Marsays."

Peppee may have been the largest crab on the team for the village of Marsays, but he was not alone. He had four other snow crab teammates who appeared to be very strong competitors as well.

"Who are your friends Peppee?" Amanda asked as she stretched to prepare for the game.

"Oh pardon me Mademoiselle for being so rude," answered Peppee. "Cac'est Jacques et cac'est Remy. Et cac'est Camille et cac'est Mimi."

"It's nice to meet you all," said Amanda. "I'm Amanda."

Meanwhile, Russell entered the field with the crab soccer ball, blew hard into a whistle, and motioned with his wing to have everyone get down and get ready to play.

"Well, good luck to all of you today," Amanda said as she hurried back to Kryogen's side.

"Oui," said Peppee, "good luck to you, Mademoiselle."

Ice Sister One matched up against Camille for the opening face-off. The sisters' advantage at crab soccer became apparent, because their hands dragged the ground as they glided quickly over the field. This allowed them to move with less effort and more speed than other players, while still complying with the game's rules. The crabs were all naturally built to play a sport created for crabs. As for Bertrand, his physical structure as a rug made it easy to position himself with his back to the ground, while both his arms and legs were used to maneuver quickly.

Russell let go of the ball and Ice Sister One immediately took control. Swiftly she dribbled the ball toward the center of the field and then passed left to Ice Sister Two.

Jacques, defending Ice Sister Two, stole the ball and moved down field toward Kryogen's goal. Bertrand braced himself as Jacques passed to his right, toward Mimi. Mimi drilled forward to make a power kick, but Bertrand blocked it at the goal. Bertrand passed the ball out to Amanda who began dribbling the ball up, toward midfield. Ice Sister Three came up behind Amanda and pushed her, causing Amanda to lose control of the soccer ball and allowing Ice Sister Three to take over. The three sisters then set up an offensive triangular formation, targeting the goal. Ice Sister One was up front to the left and Ice Sister Two was up front to the right. Ice Sister Three had control of the ball and stayed back at the point of the triangle. All three moved forward together at a medium pace. Jacques, Remy, and Camille defended the sisters. Ice Sister Three passed the ball off to her right to Ice Sister Two. Ice Sister Three then glided quickly down the center of the field, directly toward the goal. Ice Sister Two passed the ball immediately back to her. Ice Sister Three kicked it with all the power she had, but Peppee blocked it and took control of the ball. Peppee threw the ball out to Camille who kicked the ball down field to Mimi. Mimi and Amanda were alone at the other end of the field, near Kryogen's goal, which was defended by Bertrand.

Mimi dribbled the ball using many fancy steps trying to intimidate Amanda and show her up. Amanda didn't let it bother her, though. In the meantime, the sisters made their way to the Kryogen end of the field to help defend the goal, too. Mimi got around Amanda and headed toward the goal guarded by the three sisters and Bertrand.

Amanda went back to the other end of the field awaiting a possible offensive flurry.

Mimi's fancy footwork made it past Ice Sister One, then Two, then Three, and then Mimi set herself up for a goal. Mimi reared back one of her right crab legs to kick the ball, but Bertrand came out from the goal to steal the ball. His timing was perfect. Before Mimi could kick the ball, Bertrand managed to kick it, and kick it hard. Bertrand kicked it so hard that it ended up on the other side of the field right in front of Amanda with absolutely no one defending her. Only Peppee stood in front of the Marsay's goal to prevent her from scoring.

Amanda dribbled the ball quickly toward the goal. Peppee came out to guard it with all that he hard. He was very large and it would be very difficult to get such a small ball past such a large crab like Peppee. Amanda got right in front of the goal and Peppee, pulled her leg back to kick, and let go. Peppee held down his right claw to block and kept his left claw up in the air, hoping to cover as much of the goal as possible. The ball left Amanda's foot and rolled up Peppee's right claw, up his back, over his left claw, and directly into the goal, using Peppee's body as a ramp the whole way.

"GOAL!!!!!!!!!!" screamed Bertrand.

The crowd went crazy. The fans were jumping up and down. Russell blew his whistle to stop play and then ran over to the scoreboard to place a "1" under the Kryogen side. Then he ran over and grabbed water for everyone.

"Way to go!" shouted Bertrand. "You are quite a little firecracker."

"Thanks!" said Amanda.

Russell got the ball and let Mimi corner kick it in. Amanda was now pumped and ready for more excitement. Her adrenaline was in overdrive. She hadn't had this much fun in a very long time. Mimi passed the ball to Jacques, who immediately had it stolen by Ice Sister Two. Ice Sister Two kicked it to Amanda just to see if she could repeat her performance.

Amanda was charged with nervous excitement. She kicked the crab soccer ball so hard that it left the field and rolled past the row of hedges on the far side of the field. Russell blew his whistle to stop the play. "I'll get it," said Amanda as she hurried over to the bushes to retrieve the ball. But before Amanda could get there, the soccer ball came flying out of the bushes like a missile and landed near the center of the field. However, the crab soccer ball wasn't the same as it had been before Amanda kicked it. It was completely flattened.

"How do you think that happened?" Bertrand asked. "Who's the wise guy in the bushes messing with our game and our ball?"

"I have no idea," Amanda said discouraged, "but I'm going to find out."

Amanda went back to the hedges where the ball came from. "Ok, can you please come out of there and tell us why you were kind enough to flatten our ball?"

No one came. Amanda became annoyed. "I know you're in there. Come out here now and explain why you did this."

A darkness settled over the field and the air became very still. The bush immediately in front of Amanda began to burn and was soon completely engulfed in flames. Another bush did the same, then another, and another. Smoke rose from the flames and through the smoke, creatures marched their way onto the field, dressed in dark, shadowy armor - knight armor. There appeared to be several individual creatures approaching, but as they marched, they shadowed together, appearing as one seamless unit. Their armor covered them from head to toe and each carried a spear in one hand, and a hatchet at its side. The creatures' armored helmets were ferocious. They brought fear into the hearts of all who were unfortunate enough to view them. They had horns that extended outward and then upward, with piercing tips. They had fiery red eyes that could be seen through a small slot in their helmets. What Amanda and the others did not realize at this moment is that these were no ordinary soldiers. These horrid combatants were Gamirathen's Shadow Knightmares.

"Maybe we should have used a different ball," Bertrand said.

"For some reason, I think they would have flattened that one too," said Amanda.

"Amanda, I don't know who or what these things are," said Bertrand, "but I don't think it was just the crab soccer ball they were after. From all you told me earlier about your Dream Diary and those keys and that Gamirathen character, my guess is that this welcome wagon is here in your honor. And if we don't want to be part of a shish-ka-bob on one of their spears, I suggest we hightail it out of here as far and as fast as possible."

"Monstres! Monstres!" shouted Peppee.

"Folie! Folie!" screamed Remy.

The snow crabs of Marsays ran desperately about, scurrying back and forth chaotically, doing their best to avoid any and all contact with the fierce Shadow Knightmare force. The stadium crowd stampeded for the exits, stepping over each other and screaming for their lives.

"Those poor snow crabs," said Bertrand. "I wish I could help them, but I have to get you out of here."

But Bertrand didn't need to play hero to everyone. The Ice Sisters Three stepped in and began launching sheets of ice at the Shadow Knightmares, stunning them briefly and allowing the snow crabs to flee to safety.

"This is our chance," said Bertrand. "We can't get out of the stadium because there's too many of them surrounding the field, but we have another option."

"What's that?" asked Amanda.

"While the sisters have them distracted," Bertrand began to answer, "we can make our way to what is left of those hedges over there and hide for now. I think I can get us down the hill on the other side of them safely. Just follow me."

The Ice Sisters Three continued their attack against the Shadow Knightmares while Bertrand and Amanda took Lawrence and Russell and found a safe spot to hide in the hedges along the far edge of the crab soccer field.

"Now, listen up," said Bertrand. "The sisters won't be able to hold them up forever. We're going to have to go down this hill."

"Oh no!" exclaimed Amanda. "Would you look at that hill? It's too steep. We'll never make it down safely and these creatures have the soccer field surrounded."

"Too steep?" Bertrand asked. "There's not a hill nor mountain too steep for the number one belly bob-sledder in all of Maldderan. Just get on my back, hang on as tight as you can, and close your eyes if you wish."

Bertrand braced the ground firmly while the crew boarded him. Amanda immediately got on top of Bertrand

and held onto Lawrence. Russell waddled over and positioned himself in front of Amanda.

"Hurry and get yourselves secure," ordered Bertrand. "We've no more time to spare. I believe we've been spotted."

Bertrand was correct. One of the Shadow Knightmares had seen Amanda in the hedges and was now gathering a posse to swarm in and surround them. Bertrand turned his head around to see the enemy quickly approaching them.

"Duck!" shouted Bertrand.

Amanda ducked her head instinctively, narrowly avoiding the likely fatal blow from a Shadow Knightmare's hatchet.

"Now hang on!" Bertrand pressed forward with all of his strength in all four of his short, stubby, polar bear legs. He glided down the steep hill with speed and agility, weaving back and forth, avoiding tree after stump, rock after boulder. Amanda closed her eyes for fear of the many quickly approaching objects Bertrand could possibly hit. However, Bertrand was not just a good bob-sledder. Bertrand was the best and Amanda had nothing to worry about as long as they kept moving.

Behind them, the Shadow Knightmares were no match for Bertrand on this snow covered hill. Many tried to follow Bertrand's lead and slide down the hill after them. Most smashed into trees, rocks, or each other. Others tripped, rolling themselves into giant snowballs and getting trapped inside.

Feeling he had reached a safe distance from the Shadow Knightmares, Bertrand stopped near a level area of the hill to check on everyone. "I believe we left those fellas way behind," he said. "How's everyone holding up? Want to ride it again?"

"I think I'm gonna be sick," said Amanda. "That was worse than XR."

Russell just teetered back and forth, his eyes spinning, and showing signs of dizziness. Lawrence knelt to one side and looked as if he were gagging on a hairball.

"So I guess that's a 'No' on another ride," Bertrand chuckled. "Well, then, we do need to find somewhere to hide out for a bit in case those hideous things do make it down the hill this far. Follow me this way."

Bertrand headed through the snow-covered forest looking for a place to hide from the Shadow Knightmares.

"Well, would you look at this?" Bertrand grinned.

Bertrand spotted a secluded cave behind several trees. The cave was not obvious to the average observer, but to a bear like Bertrand, it was instinctively easy to spot.

"This looks perfect, Bertrand," said Amanda. "How did you ever find it?"

"Just call it my instincts," Bertrand responded.

The group entered the cave and Amanda immediately stopped and pointed at something she found truly magnificent. "I can't believe it," said Amanda.

"With the crab soccer game and those ice sisters and those creatures chasing us, I had almost completely forgotten about it."

What Amanda had almost completely forgotten about was the object she came to Kryogen to get in the first place - the Sapphire Key. Now, without looking for it, it came to her and was in the same cave that Bertrand had selected to hide inside. But there was one problem. It was frozen deep inside a huge chunk of ice.

"How do you suppose I am going to get that key out of that chunk of ice?" asked Amanda.

"I'm not sure," answered Bertrand. "Wait for warmer weather?"

The ice chunk formed a portion of the far wall of the cave. The key emitted a bluish sapphire glow, making it easy to see inside the ice.

"I know," said Amanda. "I can call my dragon and he can get the key for me."

"You have a dragon?" Bertrand asked surprised.

"Yes, I do," answered Amanda. "Well, I'm sort of borrowing him. Anyway, I can call him and he can blow fire on this chunk of ice and melt it in no time at all. I can get the key and be on my way."

"No way," said Bertrand. "It's out of the question. Dragon fire can be dangerous for all of us right now. It wouldn't take much to melt enough snow to start an avalanche. We'd be trapped in here forever. No, we must find a different way for you to get your key."

Russell waddled up to the chunk of ice and took a look at it like an engineer surveying a problem in search of a solution. Then he pulled out his small hammer and ice pick from his tuxedo jacket and started picking away at the ice chunk.

"Of course!" exclaimed Bertrand. "Mister talented himself. Why didn't I think of that? All it takes is an ice sculptor to whittle down a chunk of ice."

Russell whittled and picked and chipped away. Chunk after chunk broke away freely until finally, the Sapphire Key was partially exposed.

"You're almost there," encouraged Amanda. "This is great. No, this is more than great. This is splendorific."

Russell continued to chisel until the Sapphire Key was completely exposed and could be pulled out of the ice chunk. Amanda reached in and pulled. As she pulled, the ice from the back side of the large chunk also broke free, leaving a small passageway to the rear of the cave.

"Awesome, I have it," Amanda said overjoyed. "Now I wonder where that goes?"

"Let me see," said Bertrand sticking his head into the hole that Russell had chiseled out of the ice chunk. "From the looks of things, I'd say it goes down."

Bertrand was right. The passageway on the other side of the ice chunk did go down. But the passageway was covered in ice, creating a slippery slide.

"I guess it's a good thing we don't have to leave that way," said Bertrand as he turned to walk out toward the entrance of the cave. "Um, maybe I better think twice about that."

Bertrand had to think twice because when he looked at the entrance, he could see shadows moving from the outside. The Shadow Knightmares were approaching from outside and the group knew that it was only a matter of time before they were discovered hiding in the cave.

"Those things just don't give up," Bertrand said. "Russell, chisel away some more so we can all fit through that opening."

Russell quickly chipped away at what remained of the ice chunk, enlarging the opening to the slippery passageway behind it. There was not much time and he had to work fast.

"That will have to do Russell," said Bertrand. "They're coming."

The Shadow Knightmares were beginning to come into the cave. Amanda put Lawrence through the opening and watched as he slid down the icy slide. She did the same with Russell and then climbed into the hole and held on, waiting for Bertrand.

"Let go Amanda," ordered Bertrand. "Let go and slide down to safety. You have your key."

"I have to make sure you make it through the hole," Amanda said. "How are you ever going to fit?"

"Don't you worry about that," said Bertrand. "I can't get through until you move though."

Amanda understood and let go. The slope was slick and made her slide faster than any playground slide she had ever tried. It was like a frozen water slide. The experience would have been fun if she hadn't been so concerned about Bertrand's safety. Amanda landed safely at the bottom, which emptied to an open area far down the mountain from Kryogen. Lawrence and Russell were waiting patiently at the bottom for her.

"I sure hope he makes it ok," Amanda whispered to herself. "He's such a fighter."

A bellowing noise could be heard coming from up the slide. The noise grew louder and louder as it slid closer to Amanda. Amanda's eyes grew big hoping it was Bertrand, but also concerned it might be one of the Shadow Knightmares. The noise was definitely getting closer and Amanda looked up the icy slide to see Bertrand tail first, sliding toward her at high speed.

"AAAAHHHHH!!!!" screamed Bertrand as he hit the ground upon his exit.

"Are you ok?" asked Amanda. "I was so worried you wouldn't make it. How did you ever fit through that hole?"

"Well, you should know me better by now," answered Bertrand. "I may be big and wide, but I am a rug. And rugs can be rolled up. I can roll myself up tighter than any newspaper. The problem is once I got through the hole all rolled up, I became disoriented and ended up sliding down backwards, so it was a bit scary."

"I'm just happy you made it out of there safely," said Amanda. "I'm sure those creatures will try to follow us too. I think we better get going."

"I agree. Maybe it would be a good idea for you to signal for your dragon now," suggested Bertrand. "I mean, those monsters are after you and they aren't going to stop until they find you. You have the key you were looking for so it might be best for you to get as far away from them as you can while you still have a chance."

"You're right," agreed Amanda. "I need to go ahead and call XR and move on so Kryogen can return to being a peaceful place to live. I really made a mess of things coming around here."

"Quit being so hard on yourself," said Bertrand. "We all have a purpose. Your purpose is of such great importance and comes with such a huge responsibility that you're bound to disrupt a village or two from time to time. I do have a favor I'd like to ask, though."

"Sure, anything," replied Amanda. "I'd help you with anything considering all you've done for me. What's the favor?"

"Could Russell and I hitch a ride on that dragon of yours to my cottage before you leave for good?" Bertrand asked batting his eyes.

"Of course you can," answered Amanda.

Amanda pulled the dragon retrieving whistle from Lawrence's backpack and blew into it long and hard. XR-27 appeared within moments as if he had been right next to the group the entire time. Amanda went through the dragon boarding routine and everyone got on XR.

"Burrrrppppp!!!!!"

"What was that?" Bertrand asked.

Amanda just smiled. The dragon then made his way with all four members of the party back to the village of Kryogen to drop Bertrand and Russell back at Bertrand's home.

"Thank you for the lift," said Bertrand. "I have to admit, that was my first experience ever flying on a dragon. I'd like to do that again sometime."

"Maybe we can do it together again," suggested Amanda. "I hope we will be able to see each other again one day."

"I hope so, too," Bertrand said. "I really am impressed by you little girl. You have a lot of spunk. Feel free to bust into my cottage and plop on top of me while I'm asleep anytime."

"You're a nut," replied Amanda as she leaned over to give Bertrand a great big bear hug. "Thank you for being such a wonderful friend and looking after us. Things wouldn't have turned out so great if you hadn't been here to help me."

"Ah, I didn't do anything that any other average polar bear rug wouldn't have done," Bertrand said blushing. "Now you better get yourself moving along and go get that third key so you can complete your mission here in Maldderan. I'd hate to think what will happen to all of us if you fail."

"You're right," replied Amanda. "Come on, Lawrence. Let's get going. Goodbye, Bertrand. Goodbye, Russell. It was 'cool' meeting you."

"Goodbye, Amanda," said Bertrand while Russell waved his flipper rapidly. "I wish you the best."

Amanda and Lawrence boarded XR, heading West, toward the Beach of the Glittering Sand and two of the keys in their possession. "Burrrrppppp!!!!!"

Chapter 9
The Pirates in da' Skies

"That's two keys down and only one to go, Lawrence."

Amanda was thrilled at the thought of only having one key left to locate. However, she shuttered to think what obstacles lie in her way to get the third, Golden Key, knowing quite well how difficult the first two were to obtain.

"I certainly hope finding this key goes a bit smoother than it did in Jigsari and Kryogen, Lawrence," said Amanda. "Hey, aren't you supposed to be the key thief here? I guess you did sniff out the location of the Emerald Key."

Amanda could see an ocean of water in the distance and looked down, knowing that the beach had to be approaching soon. XR-27 flew briskly and the ground beneath them began to change from forest green trees to brown sandy shores. Within seconds, the dullness of the brown sand disappeared and was gradually replaced with sparkling, copper grains. The glistening of the shore told Amanda that she had reached her desired location.

"Lawrence, would you look at this beach?" Amanda asked. "It's just beautiful. It's just plain beautiful. I'm sure XR will be landing soon."

XR-27 began his descent toward the beach like he had many times before in the other locations around

Maldderan, but this time, landing would not be quite so simple.

BOOOOOMMMMMM!!!!!!

A deep muffled cannon blast came shooting from behind XR and was quickly followed by another and then another.

BOOOOOMMMMMM!!!!!!

BOOOOOMMMMMM!!!!!!

"XR those noises did not sound good!" shouted Amanda. "We have to get out of here now!"

XR-27 made a valiant attempt to escape, but was directly hit on his left wing by what appeared to be a very large, chewed-up piece of bubble gum. When XR flapped his wing down, the bubble gum stuck against the side of the dragon's body and held it firmly in place. Now XR couldn't use his left wing at all, as his body spun around and he began flying in the opposite direction. Amanda held on tight to Lawrence and to XR, hoping that the young dragon could land them safely with just one wing.

But then another blast of bubble gum mush splattered all over XR's face, completely covering his eyes, and most of his nose and mouth. Now the dragon was flying blind and could barely breath. He definitely couldn't use any dragon fire to help him, not that it would help him in this predicament. They had no idea who was attacking them. XR was out of breath. He could take no more and began to fall to the ground.

"No!" screamed Amanda. "You have to keep fighting XR! You must keep fighting!"

It was no use. The bubble gum was stuck on the dragon, making it impossible to fly. He had no fight left in him. But as they fell to the ground, a different object flew toward them at a much faster speed than the gum wads. It was a net - a red net - directly above them moving toward them at a lightning pace. The net passed below the falling dragon and opened up beneath him, catching all of them, stopping their fall, and cradling them like babies in a crib. Lucky for Amanda and Lawrence they had not fallen off of the dragon. Or were they? For now the net was pulling them up, back into the sky and into the clouds above.

"XR, are you ok?" asked Amanda, concerned for the dragon. "Hang in there. I don't know what's waiting for us on the other side of these clouds."

The net continued pulling the group up when Amanda noticed a familiar smell.

"Why does it smell so good in here?" she asked. "Why would it smell good in this net? It smells like, hmm, let me see. I know this smell. Yes, it smells like licorice."

Amanda reached out and tore off a splintered piece of the netting and held it to the tip of her tongue.

"What do you know?" Amanda asked herself. "I was right. I did smell licorice. This netting is made out of cherry licorice. But how?"

As she pondered the strange events, the netting made its way through the clouds. The identity of the bubble gum launching culprit was revealed. Facing the netted trio was a gigantic, floating pirate ship. An amazing ship, indeed. The ship was made completely out of candy and sweets. Its hull was constructed of sugar cookies and the masts were long, thick, peppermint sticks. The sails were thin slices of taffy and even the shell of the Captain's bell was a hollowed out gumdrop. Absolutely everything was made of candy, which explained the cherry licorice netting and the bubble gum cannonballs.

The netting landed gently in the center of the quarterdeck, but Amanda, Lawrence, and XR remained inside as prisoners to the ship and its crew. And what a strange crew this was, for on this pirate ship, there did not appear to be a pirate in sight. Amanda looked all around the ship's deck. She saw many men. She saw a baker and a carpenter and a plumber and even a cowboy. There was a doctor and a painter, a chimney sweep and a mechanic. There seemed to be every occupation represented from her world - but no pirates.

The crew stared and mumbled, agitated, but none would talk to Amanda. This made her very uncomfortable.

She felt like a caged animal at the zoo. She could hold back no longer.

"Will one of you geniuses please tell me why we're here?" Amanda requested.

A fireman walked over to Amanda and said, "We are awaiting the Captain's orders. Now you just hush yourself up and be patient."

"The Captain?" Amanda whispered. "I wonder what the Captain of a bunch of bozo pirates like these is dressed like. A circus clown maybe?"

"Attention on deck!" shouted a voice from the rear of the ship.

All of the crew immediately stopped what they were doing and stood at military attention, with right hands saluting as the Captain of the ship made his way toward Amanda and the others. Amanda listened closely to the sound of his steps across the ship. She could sense his confidence and authority in the rhythm and pace of his steps. Perhaps he was a truly respectable Captain. She looked down as he approached, afraid to look at the Captain directly in the face.

"Aren't you supposed to be somewhere, little miss?" asked the Captain.

"Um, yes sir," answered Amanda staring at the Captain's boots, "I am supposed to be somewhere sir, and I was on my way when my dragon and I were captured by your crew."

"Don't call me sir," ordered the Captain. "The name's Hemlock. But it would be best if you refer to me as Master Hemlock."

"Oh my gosh!" shouted Amanda as she raised her head up to see for herself that it was, truly indeed, Master Hemlock, who was the Captain of the pirate ship. "I cannot believe this! It's you Master Hemlock! It's really you!"

"And greetings to you, Miss Sneed," said Master Hemlock. "As the Captain of this vessel, I'd like to welcome you to my ship. Welcome aboard the *SS Sweet Dreams*, Miss Sneed."

"Why thank you, Master Hemlock," Amanda said somewhat distracted. XR began to squirm and struggle. "Listen, I don't mean to sound rude, but it doesn't exactly feel welcome being caught in a net and my dragon, XR, all bound-up in gum like this."

"Oh, right you are," agreed Master Hemlock. "Undo these licorice nets!" he ordered. "Square away this dragon! And prepare the ship for feast and celebration! We have guests!"

The crew immediately snapped to the orders and unfastened the netting holding Amanda, Lawrence, and XR. Several crew members brought scrub brushes and buckets with soapy water to give XR a much-needed bath.

"Don't give them any problems, XR," said Amanda. "They're only helping you. Make sure they get behind your ears."

"Why don't you come with me, Miss Sneed?" suggested Master Hemlock. "And bring your rat with you. He might end up on the wrong end of a mop handle with this crew."

Amanda followed Master Hemlock to his Captain's quarters. She had many questions for her strange school janitor who apparently had his own floating pirate ship. Master Hemlock opened the door to his quarters. The door was made of pure milk chocolate and was outlined in brilliantly colored pieces of rock candy. Inside his quarters were many treasures. Much like his home, there were bags of sand everywhere - sand that glistened - just like the sand she had seen on the beach below the ship. In the center of the room was a large, business-like desk. An open chest sat on top of the desk. It was a pirate chest filled completely with golden coins. The coins looked exactly like the coin Master Hemlock gave Amanda to make her wish and begin her journey in Maldderan.

Ruby-colored couches trimmed in white etching lined both side walls. At first these couches appeared to look like normal couches, but as Amanda looked closer, she realized that they were actually very large cakes shaped into couches, and that the white etching was frosting.

"Why don't you have a seat on one of those couches, Miss Sneed?" Master Hemlock said as he took a seat behind his desk. "And if you're hungry, go ahead and have a bite of the furniture. It's edible and quite delicious."

Lawrence had followed the delicious sugary scent that greeted his nose as soon as he entered the Captain's quarters. He was already licking away at the icing on the couch, thoroughly enjoying himself. Amanda had some troubling questions to ask, though. "Master Hemlock, why did you attack us out there when we were flying over the beach?"

"Well, Miss Sneed," Master Hemlock started answering, biting into a caramel apple, "I actually didn't attack you. Rather, I saved you from what could have been a huge disaster."

Amanda's eyes grew big and she knit her brow in confusion. "What do you mean, a huge disaster?"

"You see, Miss Sneed," continued Master Hemlock, "if you had fallen on the sand - the glittering sand - you would have fallen asleep. And no one knows how long you would have stayed asleep. You see, that sand is magic. That sand is sleeping sand."

"Sleeping sand?" Amanda questioned, even more confused. "How do you know this? And if you were trying to save us, why did you attack my dragon XR-27?"

"I had to stop the dragon, Miss Sneed," answered Master Hemlock. "I had no other choice. Dragons are very loyal to those they love. If he had seen my ship he would have attacked us in defense of you. I could not allow that. If he had not attacked, he would had taken you far into the beach to hide, only causing you to bury yourself further in the sleeping sand. I had to secure him somehow and do it quickly. You all were safe. I was seeing to that. Am I wrong? I mean, you are here safe and sound now, aren't you Miss Sneed?"

"Yes, I guess you're right," answered Amanda. "I understand that this all has to do with sleeping sand. But my question is, what do you have to do with sleeping sand? From the looks of things, these bags here are full of it, the bags that were in your house were full of it, and you had sand all over you at school that day. It's the same glittering sand found on the beach below. Why is that? Who are you?"

"I guess it's only fair to let you know who I really am, Miss Sneed," Master Hemlock said openly. "I am what the people of your world call the Sandman. Well, I am one of them anyway. I am the lead Sandman. Everyone on this ship is a Sandman. I am just the leader, the Captain, as they call me."

"You're the Sandman?" Amanda asked in shock. "You put people to sleep at night. Oh my gosh."

"Well, not really all people, Miss Sneed," explained Master Hemlock, "just children. Once a child from your world grows up, there's not much need for us anymore. You see, it's worlds such as Maldderan that rely on the dreams of children such as yourself. Your dreams are magical. They give this world energy. So it is our duty to put children like you to sleep at night so you can dream. That way these worlds, these magical worlds like Maldderan, will always exist. As for adults, well, they still dream. But they aren't the dreams that we prefer. Their dreams are missing the magic that is found in a child's dream. So we don't put them to sleep. As adults get older, they tend to have less energy and usually fall asleep in the evening with no extra help needed. It's all of you children that are so hard to get to sleep at night, always full of energy and fighting to stay up late and play. Plus all of that sugar most of you eat. Of course, who am I to talk? I have a ship made completely of candy."

"Then how is it you are my school janitor?" asked Amanda.

"You see, Miss Sneed," Master Hemlock began to answer, "being a Sandman isn't easy. We have to blend into your world during the day. You might think of it as going undercover. I call it wearing a disguise. The Sandmen are just a bunch of pirates in disguises. That's why you see so many of my crew out there dressed in different outfits from different jobs of your world."

"This is amazing," said Amanda. "So there may be other sandmen that work around my home that I have seen and I just don't know it, because they're actually wearing disguises."

"That's right, Miss Sneed," agreed Master Hemlock. "Now you know what to look for. See, you know to look for those with sand on their clothes or someone possibly wearing an eyepatch. And the biggest giveaway would be someone who has a huge sweet tooth. Chances are, that person is one of my crew. When you

311

work on a ship made of candy, it tends to cause you to be addicted to sweets. Thank goodness we have a dentist on board."

"So why do you call yourselves pirates?" asked Amanda. "You don't exactly steal anything."

"On the contrary," responded Master Hemlock. "Why, we do steal something. We steal the waking time of children. That causes them to sleep. Maybe you can think of us as sleep pirates."

"This is all too amazing," Amanda said. "I still cannot believe I found you and you are the Sandman and my school janitor. How splendorific is that?"

"Well, Miss Sneed," answered Master Hemlock, "I don't know how splendorific that is, but I do know I'm getting hungry and I think we should head back and see if my crew has the festivities ready yet."

Master Hemlock swung open the door to his quarters and headed back to the quarterdeck. Amanda picked up Lawrence who was still nibbling on the couch's icing, and followed immediately behind.

"Attention on deck!" shouted one of the crew as Master Hemlock made his way out.

"At ease!" shouted Master Hemlock. "My brothers! My friends! My crew! May we feast today! May we dance and sing and enjoy the company of our guests! For tomorrow we must continue the never-ending task of putting children to sleep so that we may enjoy moments like this yet another day!"

Along the quarterdeck, the crew had set up two long sets of tables full of food and drinks. There were meats and vegetables, fruits and cakes. Everything from corn on the cob to grapes to cookies to stacks of assorted chocolates. Amanda's eyes lit up and she smiled bigger than she had smiled in a very long time. This was a festive occasion. She was going to eat and eat a lot.

Some of the crew played dinner music for the occasion. A construction worker played the piano and a garbage collector strummed a guitar. The band also included harmonicas, tubas, trumpets, and bells. There was even a baker juggling cupcakes. All the pirates appreciated the music as they danced around and sang songs about putting little boys and girls to sleep.

"Us pirates is a sandy bunch.
We're a sandy bunch indeed.
But helpful too, that's what we are,
if sleep is what you need."

"At night children try to stay awake,
and never shut their eyes.
But our magic sand, it does the trick.
We're the pirates in disguise."

"A butcher, a baker, a candlestick maker,
We're exactly what you see.
'A jolly ole' rancher is what I am,
and I mean that literally.'"

Even XR danced. The dragon was clean and free of all gum. The crew had managed to completely square away XR while Amanda was inside Master Hemlock's quarters. And now the dragon was in great spirits.

Amanda saw several bowls full of different colored gum balls and began sampling the assortment in front of her. One by one, she tasted the gum balls. Each gum ball was a different and unusual flavor. The tan ones tasted like cookie dough while the pink ones tasted like cotton candy. The brick red gum ball was fiery hot but had a hint of cherry flavor to it. Amanda named that one the fire blast cherry gum.

"Here," said Master Hemlock, "try this one. It's my favorite flavor." Master Hemlock picked up one of the brown gum balls and handed it to Amanda and she placed it into her mouth.

"Wow!" exclaimed Amanda. "This is by far the most incredilicious flavor I have tried yet. I can really see why this one is your favorite, Master Hemlock. Good choice. Very good choice. But, what is it?"

"It's called Double Dunkin' Chocolate," answered Master Hemlock.

"All of this food is so incredilicious, Master Hemlock," said Amanda. " I don't know how to thank you for feeding me and my friends like this. I really was hungry. I had just traveled from a village named Kryogen and I had some popcorn there. But after getting chased by those shadowy, armored monsters with the red eyes, and then finding the Sapphire Key and running some more, I really worked up a big appetite."

"What did you just say?" Master Hemlock asked as he stopped chewing on a drumstick in the middle of a bite. "Did you say shadowy armored monsters with red eyes were chasing you and you found a Sapphire Key?"

"Yes, I did," said Amanda. "I found an Emerald Key, too. I actually came here to the beach to find a Golden Key. That's when I ran into you."

"Why is it you're looking for these keys?" asked Master Hemlock.

"Because they belong to my Dream Diary," answered Amanda. "I met this glass man who said he was my Dream Watcher. His name is Gee Lassy and he sent me to find the keys. He said he sent three of his best and most trusted friends out to hide the keys. I am trying to find them. Once I find all three, I am supposed to return to Gee who is guarding my Dream Diary."

"Then it is true," Master Hemlock said as he knelt down before Amanda and bowed his head. "I ask you to forgive me if I have shown you rudeness of any kind Madam."

"What are you doing?" asked Amanda. "What happened to calling me Miss Sneed?"

"Beg your pardon Madam, but Gee Lassy is a very good friend of mine," answered Master Hemlock. "I am one of the three he sent out to hide your keys. I was sent to hide the Golden Key. Funny thing, you actually had it at one time. Do you remember?."

"You mean when Lawrence took it off of your key ring at school?" asked Amanda.

"Exactly, Madam," answered Master Hemlock. "I have known Gee for a very, very long time. He trusted me to keep the Golden Key safe. He said that it belonged to the diary of the chosen child - a child with the power to use their dreams and make them real. He referred to the child as a Dream Caster. I had no idea that the chosen child was you. It all makes sense now. Those monsters. Those monsters that you saw are very evil. Those are Gamirathen's soldiers. They are called Shadow Knightmares. They will not rest until they find you. You must get the third key and return to Gee and open your diary. You are the chosen one. You are the Dream Caster. Gamirathen will strike so you must be ready. You must leave immediately. I will follow and help in your aid with my crew."

"Wait," said Amanda, "you're forgetting one thing. I don't have the third key. You hid it somewhere, remember? Any chance you might want to let me know where it is?"

"I did hide it, Madam," answered Master Hemlock. "I hid the Golden Key in the safest and most secure location throughout all of the Beach of the Glittering Sand. There could be no safer place than where I hid it."

"Where?" asked Amanda. "Where did you hide it?"

"Right here." Master Hemlock reached into the chest pocket of his brown coveralls and pulled out the Golden Key, the third and final key to Amanda's Dream Diary, and handed it to Amanda. "Take it, Madam. It belongs to you."

"Thank you, Master Hemlock," said Amanda. "I never would have guessed it was in your pocket this whole time."

Amanda quickly placed the Golden Key inside Lawrence's backpack along with the Emerald and the

319

Sapphire Keys. All three keys needed for the Dream Diary were now accounted for and in her possession.

"General quarters! General quarters!" shouted Master Hemlock. "All hands to your battle stations! Set the ship's course for Meeyor and all ahead full!"

The sandman crew quickly snapped to Master Hemlock's orders. Each crew member knew what to do and what their responsibility was in a time of crisis.

"Now go, Madam!" ordered Master Hemlock. "Go and take those keys back to Gee. I am on my way right behind you. I will be there as quickly as I can. You will move much faster on your dragon than I will with my ship. Now move and move quickly Madam!"

Amanda boarded XR-27 and gave Master Hemlock a look of great concern. "Burrrrppppp!!!!!" With all of the food she had just eaten, Amanda didn't need any dragon's milk to burp.

Amanda and Lawrence held on tight as XR took off like a lightning bolt from the ship. He flew faster than he had ever flown before as Amanda held on tight. She had her three keys but she wasn't happy. She knew that having the keys meant opening the diary. And opening the diary meant that she must sooner or later face Gamirathen. But, despite these fears, she was determined to complete her mission. She is the chosen child. She is the Dream Caster.

Chapter 10
Return to Meeyor

"This is it, Lawrence," said Amanda with a serious look on her face. "We have our keys. Now all we have to do is get back to Gee and open the diary. I just hope the diary tells me what I need to know to defeat Gamirathen. Maybe then we can go home. Right?"

Amanda did her best to sound confident. But her nervousness grew as they approached Meeyor. Amanda could see the city reflect from the air as she did the first time. But this time, she felt no excitement. XR needed no direction as he descended to the city below and landed directly outside the entrance right next to the dragon parking area just as he had done before on Amanda's very first flight with the dragon.

Without hesitating, Amanda led XR up to the entrance gate of the dragon parking area and pulled off one of XR's many dragon scales clinging to her clothing. Like she had before, she put the scale into the machine next to the gate and pulled the lever. After much grinding, the familiar dragon retrieving whistle appeared in the trap door of the machine, giving Amanda a second dragon retrieving whistle. The gate to the dragon parking area opened and XR walked on inside. XR turned around to see Amanda off but Amanda was walking away with her head down in worry.

After picking up a pair of sunglasses for herself and Lawrence - ensuring that she would at least not break this Meeyor rule again - Amanda made her way to the bluish-black rippling wave doors. The same two light bulb guards were still guarding the entrance and were now standing at full military attention and no longer arguing with each other.

"Well, look who it is," said the first light bulb guard to the second.

"If it isn't our little insulting friend," said the second light bulb guard.

"Look guys, I'm here to see Gee Lassy," sighed Amanda. "Please let me through."

"Oh, Gee Lassy," replied the first guard. "That sounds very serious. But, I don't believe he's here today. I heard he was on a vacation or visiting relatives or something like that. So why don't you turn around and go back where you came from?"

"I'm not turning around and I'm not going back anywhere," demanded Amanda. "And he is too here. I know it. He's expecting me."

"I think she's lying," said the second guard. "Just look those beady eyes of hers. No one sees the most Royal Gee Lassy without our knowing."

"Honestly fellas, I'm not lying," pleaded Amanda. "I am only here to see Gee Lassy. Nothing else. I'm not here to cause any problems or insult anyone and I'm definitely not here to break any rules."

"Did we say you were here to break rules?" asked the first light bulb guard.

"I don't believe we did," agreed the second light bulb guard. "I think she is trying to insult us again."

"I do believe you're right," said the first. "She is trying to insult us again. I do not think she shall be granted permission to enter Meeyor."

"You cannot enter," said the second. "I do not allow you to enter Meeyor. Now go."

"No, it was I who said she could not enter," said the first light bulb guard. "I do not allow you to enter Meeyor."

"No you did not say it," argued the second guard. "You merely suggested it. I am the one who said it."

"Are you insulting me again?" asked the first light bulb guard to the second. "I do believe you are insulting me again."

"I do not think so," responded the second light bulb guard. "It is you insulting me once again."

As the two guards bickered with each other, Amanda, once again, slipped through the wavy mirror doors completely unnoticed.

Amanda didn't hesitate to find the lumnivator. She made her way through the crowd of citizens pacing their way through the streets of Meeyor. Amanda actually looked as if she fit in this crowd for she walked forward, in a direct manner, never speaking to anyone and looking as if her agenda was of top priority.

Once inside the lumnivator, Amanda looked at the keypad, trying once again to remember what five buttons Gee had pressed on the very first ride she had in it. But before she had the opportunity to push even one button, the lumnivator's state changed and it began to move on its own, just as it had when she left Gee's home on her way to Jigsari.

The lumnivator moved side to side, and up and down, in many diagonal directions. But, it didn't phase Amanda at all this time. Her mind was focused on one thing - opening her Dream Diary. The lumnivator stopped and changed back to a cylindrical liquid device, allowing her to enter Gee Lassy's home.

The home was not completely empty this time. At the far end of the room was a table and Gee stood in front of it with his back to Amanda.

"You do realize, child," began Gee, "that no ordinary person could have found those keys." Gee turned around to face Amanda. "Only someone truly extra-ordinary could perform such a feat of this magnitude. Only someone who is different from all of the others."

"But I have no powers, Mister Lassy," Amanda tried explaining. "Yes, I found the keys, but I didn't use any dream casting powers like you said I had."

"Your dream casting power will awaken in time," smiled Gee.

"Wait, how did you know I had the keys?" asked Amanda. "Were you controlling the lumnivator?"

Gee didn't answer. Instead he walked toward Amanda. As he walked, Amanda could see her Diary of Dreams on the table behind him.

"It is time," said Gee. "Your diary awaits you my young Dream Caster."

Amanda did not ask any more questions. She knew it was time to open the diary. She walked slowly over to the table, with a determined look that focused solely on the book. While Amanda searched for the keys, she noticed that the diary had again turned to stone.

"Pick it up, child," Gee said convincingly. "Pick it up so it may return to its true form. But this time, once it does, I want you to unlock it, open it, and read about all of your wonderful and amazing dreams."

Amanda picked up the diary with both of her hands and held the book tightly in her grasp. As before, as soon as she touched the diary, it glowed red and a magical force blew Amanda's hair. The ruby red book was now in its true form as she set it down on the table in front of her.

Amanda reached inside of Lawrence's backpack and pulled out all three keys - the Emerald Key, the Sapphire Key, and the Golden Key. She inspected the three locks on the opposite side of the book's spine. Each lock was the color of one of the keys, indicating which key went to which lock. The top lock was emerald green, the middle lock was sapphire blue, and the bottom lock was golden yellow.

Amanda started with the Emerald Key and inserted it into the top lock. Slowly she turned the key counter-clockwise.

'Click.'

The first lock unlocked.

Second, she inserted the Sapphire Key into the middle lock and once again turned the key counter-clockwise.

'Click.'

The second lock unlocked.

Last, she took the Golden Key, held it up to her lips, and kissed it, just as she had kissed the gold coin she used to make her wish. She inserted the key and turned it counter-clockwise.

'Click.'

The third lock unlocked and now the diary could be opened.

Amanda looked up at Gee confused, uncertain of what to do next.

"Go ahead, child," Gee grinned, "open it. Open your Dream Diary and start reading. Read about the dreams that you have had so that you may remember them and use their power when needed."

Amanda put the three keys back into Lawrence's backpack, placed her hand on the front cover of the diary, and attempted to open the book to its first page. With the cover partially open, Amanda could see words written on the page inside. She lifted her head and smiled at Gee. But this smile quickly became a look of fear.

Suddenly, the room darkened and the wall behind Gee began to crack like a mirror. Then another crack formed - followed by another - and another. Soon the entire room was filled with cracks. Cracks that oozed out a black fog that took the form of many Shadow Knightmares.

One of the Shadow Knightmares immediately threw a black cloak over Gee Lassy which tightened snugly around his body. Gee fell to the ground, trapped. The darkness and fog that filtered in with the Shadow

Knightmares, now filled the entire room. It appeared as if the darkness was consuming the light.

Amanda shut the diary as soon as she saw this and tucked it away inside of her navy blue jacket before any of the Shadow Knightmares noticed. Lawrence jumped into her arms and she also tucked him securely into her jacket, masking the bulge of the diary.

One of the Shadow Knightmares picked up Gee and slung him over its shoulder like a sack of potatoes. Two others got on each side of Amanda and began pushing her with their speared staffs, herding her out of Gee's home. Another Shadow Knightmare smashed a hole with his spear against the cracked wall, large enough for Gee and Amanda to fit through. The rest of the Shadow Knightmares began to search around Gee's home, desperately looking for the Dream Diary. Gee and Amanda were taken out through the hole in the wall and then escorted through the city.

The light of the city had faded to black as the thick, evil fog settled over it. The Shadow Knightmares had taken full control of Meeyor. Not a sound could be heard throughout the city and many of the citizens were seen laying among the streets as if they were unconscious. Many cracks had formed in most of the glass structures and buildings. It appeared as if the impact of an earthquake had taken place.

As they passed the wavy mirrored entrance to Meeyor, there was no sign of brightness from the light bulb guards. They both lay on the ground in front of the entrance, completely unconscious and burned out, as if turned off by a switch. Amanda and Gee were forced out near the dragon parking area where a dozen or more Rammaphants stood waiting, guarded by a small squad of Shadow Knightmares. A metal cage was mounted on top of one of the Rammaphants.

With his staff against Amanda's back, one of the Shadow Knightmares pushed her toward a rope ladder hanging from the Rammaphant with the metal cage. Amanda climbed the ladder with Lawrence tucked away inside of her jacket. At the top of the Rammaphant, another Shadow Knightmare was holding the door to the metal cage open, waiting for the her to walk inside. The Shadow Knightmare carrying Gee followed Amanda up the ladder and set him inside of the metal cage after Amanda had entered. Once Amanda and Gee were confined in the cage, the Shadow Knightmare holding the cage door slammed it shut and secured it with a thick chain and large padlock.

The herd of Rammaphants began moving away from Meeyor. Each step of the mighty beasts left the ground trembling. The Rammaphants moved slowly but deliberately. The pounding of the their steps sounded like the slow beat of a bass drum. Amanda looked around for signs of life - any signs of help. She saw nothing as she looked back at Meeyor. The life of the town was gone except for three shadowy figures gliding away from the mirrored entrance. The darkness that had embraced the city of Meeyor followed the caravan, covering the land with darkness, like the approaching darkness before a great storm.

Amanda was crushed. She had been through so much. She had her keys. She completed the quest for their discovery. She even had opened the diary. But now, she felt as if all her efforts were for nothing. She was captured and she had no idea how to escape. Except maybe one.

Remembering that XR had been left behind at the dragon parking area, Amanda pulled out the dragon retrieving whistle from Lawrence's backpack. She hoped her desperate call for help would work as she blew into the whistle. Within moments, Amanda saw the young dragon approaching from the parking area and toward the rear of the herd of Rammaphants.

"Yes!" Amanda cheered silently. "You are such a faithful dragon, XR. I can always count on you."

Unfortunately, several of the Shadow Knightmares also noticed XR approaching and lifted their speared staffs to strike the dragon. Seeing this, XR stopped his motion in mid-flight, turned around, and flew away fast to avoid being speared. Amanda watched in both horror and shock.

"He left me," she whispered to herself. "He just left me."

XR stopped for one brief moment to give Amanda a quick and reassuring nod - much like he had done when he had left her in Kryogen, but Amanda had already turned away, disappointed.

The Shadow Knightmare mounted on the prisoner's Rammaphant reached inside the cage to confiscate the dragon retrieving whistle from Amanda. She placed it into his palm, knowing it was no use to try to keep it from him. The Shadow Knightmare clinched his fist around the whistle with a quick and mighty squeeze, crushing the dragon retrieving whistle into a small pile of dust and crushing Amanda's morale with it. She sat down inside of the cage and put her head on top of her knees.

"Try not to be discouraged, child," Gee said to her in a very weak voice. "I need you to be strong. We all need you to be strong. You mustn't give up hope."

"I'm trying my best," responded Amanda. "I really am. This is not what I wanted. I only wanted my dreams to come true, not my nightmares. I just want to go home now. I only want to go home."

"I'm afraid that is not an option at the moment, child," said Gee. "It won't be easy but you must face Gamirathen. You have to face this nightmare. Don't let him take your dreams from you. Don't you dare let him do it. He will try. I can guarantee you that. But be strong. Believe in yourself. You are a Dream Caster and you must believe in your dreams."

"What about you?" asked Amanda. "What does he want with you? What is that black veil those monsters have used to cover you?"

"I do not know what Gamirathen has in store for me," answered Gee. "I try not to think about it, because anything is possible. I only know that he is a very evil creature with great power. He has trapped me in a Veil of Darkness. My power comes from the light. Without it, I grow weak. I grow powerless. Being draped in a Veil of Darkness prevents my body from absorbing light. Gamirathen knew what he was doing by covering me with this veil. He is very familiar with the powers of a Dream Watcher and knows what it takes to defeat one."

"Why don't I just take it off of you?" asked Amanda.

"You cannot, child," answered Gee. "The Veil of Darkness is not as much a real veil as it is a curse. This curse was created by Gamirathen and only he knows how to break his own spell. Trying to remove it would only cause me further harm. Besides, damage is already done. The longer I wear it, the weaker I become. I have become very weak already. Even if it is removed, I don't know how much help I can be."

Amanda began to feel light gusts of warm, dry air and saw sand covering the ground. It appeared to her that they were now crossing a desert region. As the caravan of Rammaphants made their way across the sand, Amanda was able to peer out the side of her cage and see glimpses of the residents of this barren, arid region. The sight of them made her shudder with chills. Their thick, fleshy green bodies were shaped like cacti and covered with prickly thorns. In the center of their bodies, near the location of a person's heart, was a large hollowed out area that contained a dull shaded bell. Many wore turbans, and different types of veils covered much of their faces, giving them the appearance of a group of bandits.

"Mister Lassy, you have to see these things," shuddered Amanda. "We're in some sort of desert and there are these creepy cactus looking things staring at us with the most devious eyes."

"Be thankful you are in the cage," responded Gee. "Those things you see are called Cactolls and this desert is their home. This is the Desert of Nod. Those Cactolls are very evil. They are thugs, marauders, and thieves. They travel in gangs across this desert searching for prey lost in their travels. They steal their money, their food, their clothes - and you don't want to know what finally happens to the pour souls that they torment. Once they become bored with the lost travelers, they issue a final conviction. You will know when that time comes if you hear the bells tolling - the bells that are found on their bodies, where most have a heart. When you hear their bells toll, you know that some poor desert traveler met their final fate at the hands of these Cactolls. They, my child, are wicked for sure. Yes, be happy you are in this cage and not alone in the desert."

From a distance within the reaches of the desert, a bell tolled a dozen clangs. The sound put a shiver up Amanda's spine. It was not a joyous sound, but more a sound that was meant to mark a moment of grief, like the sound of a funeral bell. Amanda gulped and continued to stare at the Cactolls as they stared back at her with malicious smiles of mischief and delight.

"Another lost soul," whispered Gee upon hearing the bell. "Don't worry too much. They won't bother this crowd. Those Cactolls know better than to try to attack Gamirathen's army. They may be cunning and evil, but they are not stupid."

I wonder where we are going, Amanda questioned. *I haven't traveled in this direction before.* Amanda decided to pull out the map that Monroe had given her to see exactly where they were located. Looking at the map, she could see the Desert of Nod to the Southwest of Meeyor. But the bottom left of the map was missing, preventing her from not only knowing how large the Desert of Nod was, but also what awaited her on the far side of the desert.

"I remember," Amanda pondered, "Monroe said that part of the map was missing. That must be where we are heading. Maybe it was missing on purpose. Maybe

Monroe was trying to protect me so I wouldn't try to travel this way."

The herd of Rammaphants continued making their way across the Desert of Nod. A bitter stench started to fill the air. Amanda looked up to see the outline of a gray and gloomy castle in front of the caravan. It became apparent to Amanda what the missing portion of the map conveyed.

Gamirathen's castle had a life of its own. Or was it death? The castle was surrounded by a moat filled with boiling black liquid. Each pop of a heated bubble from the burning, flowing fluid made a horrifying shrieking sound. Round towers filled with rooms stood at each of the castle's four corners. The roof of each tower was alive with devious eyes and gnashing teeth, acting as lookout guards for the castle. The castle was bordered by mountains with razor sharp rocks and craters that erupted the same boiling black liquid found in the moat. Flames were shooting from these craters like a blast from a cannon and the black liquid crawled its way down the sides of the mountain, creeping into the moat. In the center of the castle was a larger circular tower with a outer spiral staircase leading to the top. The staircase branched off into several passageways and doors leading to other areas within the castle. The top of this circular tower was bordered with at least a dozen enormous spiked structures. The only way inside the castle walls was through one main gate. When opened, the gate would create a bridge across the boiling liquid moat, allowing entrance into an area that most would regret entering.

But there was no choice for Amanda. The gate began to open while two mammoth chains holding the sides of the gate unwound slowly, until the gate made solid contact with the ground below, creating a bridge for the Rammaphants to cross into the castle grounds. The herd moved its way inside, assembling together in one row, side by side. Once all of the Rammaphants had made it inside, the gate entrance shut quickly with a deafening blow as it struck against the castle's walls. The sound was so loud that Amanda covered her ears to lessen the pain on her eardrums.

The inner castle grounds were huge, much larger than Amanda had expected when approaching from outside. Hundreds of Shadow Knightmares were inside, all formed in military alignments. Two battalions of these Shadow Knightmares stood at attention, each battalion facing the other with a open row between them. The open row made a passageway which led to a door at the base of the large circular tower in the center of the castle grounds.

The Shadow Knightmare guarding the metal cage holding Amanda and Gee, unlocked the padlock and unfastened the chain securing it. He motioned for Amanda to exit, then went inside, picked up Gee, and placed him over his shoulder again. Amanda climbed down the rope ladder from the Rammaphant and was ordered to follow the Shadow Knightmare carrying Gee, up to the door of the circular tower. As they walked toward the door of the circular tower, the two battalions of Shadow Knightmares beat the base of their staffs against the ground in perfect unison, creating an eerie and morbid, marching rhythm. The Shadow Knightmare with Gee opened the door and Amanda followed him inside with another Shadow Knightmare right behind her.

They entered into a foyer of sorts, but not a very welcoming one. The room was dark and cold and Amanda could still smell the awful stench that she noticed when approaching the castle. A set of double doors led from this foyer. These double doors opened on their own and the Shadow Knightmare with Gee walked through them. Once he was inside, the doors slammed shut in Amanda's face, preventing her from entering. The Shadow Knightmare that was following Amanda, then made her stand against the wall of the foyer, holding his spear against her, keeping her from moving.

The room inside of the double doors was a long hallway. On the floor of the hall was a blood red carpet leading to a large chair - a throne - the back of which faced them. Along the sides of hallway were pillars made of bone with flames shooting from the tops, giving the room its only source of light. Skulls of various creatures hung along the walls, and Tarachnobats hid in the corners of the room, spinning webs of fright and waiting for their prey to be trapped in their webs.

The Shadow Knightmare walked to the end of this hallway and set Gee down on the floor, facing the back of the throne. Then the Shadow Knightmare saluted in the direction of the throne and marched over to the side wall where he stood at attention.

The throne turned in a counter-clockwise direction to face Gee.

In the throne slouched a creature with a devious grin on his face. He was dressed in a torn black suit and wore a black rose on its left breast pocket. His hands were covered with hair, like a man-wolf. His fingernails were dirty and grotesquely long, so long that they curled at the ends. He held a black cane in his right hand. His face was not human. He had lava red skin that appeared to boil like a simmering volcano. He wore a triangular beard. Both his beard and his hair were black and grey and noticeably unkept and swayed back and forth as if filled with liquid. And his eyes. These were the eyes known by many. These were the amber eyes with the frightening glow, which gave the appearance of a shadowy, flickering flame, like is seen from a candle burning within a jack-o-lantern. It is a vision of evil that leaves a piercing blow of pain in one's heart, when gazed upon.

"Hello, my old friend," smiled the creature. "What's the matter? Feeling a little weak? Maybe we're not getting enough to eat these days."

"Gamirathen, I don't understand your madness," answered Gee. "And you know quite well that I am powerless while covered by your Veil of Darkness. Once again though, you choose to fight unfairly."

"Oh, a fair fight is what you want?" questioned Gamirathen. "Fine, I'll remove the cloak. Darkness be lifted!"

As Gamirathen chanted the three words needed to break the curse of the darkness veil, the veil removed itself from Gee's body. It then folded itself in half - then half again - then half again - and again and again until the veil folded itself into nothingness and disappeared.

"You know it's a bit too late," voiced Gee. "Your veil did its damage. I am in no condition to fight you now. I'm sure that is what you wanted, for me to face you practically defenseless. That way you may destroy me as you wish, and break my body into many pieces just for your own pleasure."

"Now don't you worry, Mister Lassy," sneered Gamirathen, "I wouldn't dream of breaking that delicate body of yours. Oh no. I need you to stay in perfect condition."

"You monster!" Gee screamed in anger. "I know you better than that. Why would it benefit you not to harm me?"

"Who said I wasn't going to harm you?" Gamirathen responded with an evil grin. "You are a trophy to me. One of my most prized possessions. No, I won't break you. I won't break any of that beautifully colored glass that makes up your body. Oh, I would be such the fool. For you I have a special purpose. I plan to make you into a window and place you, in all of your splendor, right here, in my throne room. That way when I sit at my throne, I can stare out onto the world once known as Maldderan. A world which will be my very own. And I will stare at it through you."

"You're a beast!" shouted Gee. "A beast! Did you hear me? There's no possible way you'll get away with this. None!"

"Hmm, pity," responded Gamirathen as he turned his back to Gee and walked away. "Get this fool out of my throne room! Send him to the dungeon!" As Gamirathen shouted, his lava red skin boiled even more, as if it were ready to erupt.

The Shadow Knightmare that was at attention against the wall responded instantly to Gamirathen's orders and escorted Gee, who could barely walk in his weakened condition, to the dungeon.

"Good," smiled Gamirathen calmly. "Now that the trash is out, I have a Dream Caster to speak to."

Immediately after Gee was sent to the dungeon, the Shadow Knightmare guarding Amanda escorted her into Gamirathen's throne room and to the foot of Gamirathen's throne. Suddenly, she could hear screams, the screams of many children. It was simply terrifying and caused Amanda to shiver in fear.

"What's wrong my little angel?" Gamirathen asked. "Do you not care for the way I treat my guests?"

"What are you doing to those children?" Amanda cried out. "They sound as if they are in pain."

"Maybe they are. Maybe they aren't," teased Gamirathen. "But I will say this. Those aren't actually children that you hear."

"They're not?" Amanda questioned puzzled. "It sounds like children to me, you monster. What game are you playing?"

"This is no game," explained Gamirathen, "and those are not children. What you hear is what is left of the children's dreams. But now, they are - well, you might say they are a little bit uncomfortable at the moment."

"You mean you're torturing them!" screamed Amanda. "You fiend! Why would you do such a thing? Why?"

"Torture?" Gamirathen asked sarcastically. "Is that what you call it? I guess we all perceive things differently, now don't we angel. Well, you see, I have stolen the dreams of many children and imprisoned those dreams here in my dungeon, my Dungeon of Darkened Slumber. After my persuasive efforts, there is little left of the dreams, so

352

they are easily replaced with nightmares. Nightmares of my choosing."

"Why?" asked Amanda. "Why would you do something so horrible?"

"Because," answered Gamirathen, "if I can steal the dreams of the children of your world and prevent them from ever finding them, I can fill their souls with fear and evil. Fear and evil in the form of nightmares that I choose and control. It's the ultimate power. Their dreams won't come true. Their nightmares will. These children will grow and run your world one day. Or will they? No, they won't. It will really be me running it. I will be controlling it with my nightmares. I will fill your world with hate and violence and crime and war. Through nightmares, I will burn buildings and corrupt lives and destroy families. Isn't it great? Isn't this the most wonderful idea you've ever heard?"

"You're mad," accused Amanda. "You're completely mad."

"Perhaps," agreed Gamirathen. "Perhaps I am. But there isn't much you can do about that now, now is there?"

"Wait," Amanda said. "So it was you that I saw in the reflection of that mirror?"

"Well, of course," answered Gamirathen. "You might say that I've had my eyes on you for a very long time."

"And you were trying to put me to sleep so you could steal my dreams too, weren't you?" asked Amanda.

"Why, aren't you the smart one?" Gamirathen asked sarcastically.

"I'm smart enough to know that you're not going to get away with this, Gamirathen," warned Amanda.

"Oh no?" asked Gamirathen. "I'm not? Well little miss smarty pants, how do you plan to stop me? With that book of yours? Yes, don't think I haven't forgotten about your little Dream Diary. I mean, that is the main reason I drug you all the way back here - alive. Now, angel, tell me, where is the Dream Diary?"

"I don't know what book you're talking about," answered Amanda.

"I'm sure you don't," sighed Gamirathen. "I'm sure you don't. Well, how do I make this easier? I tell you what. Why don't I send you downstairs and let my dungeon guards try to see if they can get you to remember anything about that diary? Huh? Sound like a plan?"

"Well, I don't..." Amanda began to answer.

"Shut Up!!!" Gamirathen roared with his lava red skin erupting. "Guards! Take the child to the Dungeon of Darkened Slumber and get her to talk! I want to know where that Dream Diary is and I want to know immediately! I am tired of talking! Get her out of my sight!"

Amanda was shocked at Gamirathen's sudden personality change. She had felt for a moment she could actually handle him and his monstrous ways with her own wit. She realized now that she figured wrong. To deal with Gamirathen, she would need something much stronger and much more powerful than a mere wit of a child. But what? She still had no idea how to cast her dreams. For now though, Amanda focused on her present situation, wondering what was in store for her as two Shadow Knightmares came to escort her and Lawrence away from Gamirathen, to the Dungeon of Darkened Slumber.

Chapter 11
The Dungeon of
Darkened Slumber

Amanda was forced down a set of stone stairs into a creepy, damp cellar deep beneath the throne room of Gamirathen. The passageways were narrow and the only light within the dungeon confines were illuminated by caged Toucandles, found at random intervals along the dungeon walls, whose candle beaks were lit with dim, dancing flames.

The odor that Amanda had smelled grew worse as she was forced into the Dungeon of Darkened Slumber. The source of that awful smell must linger somewhere here, deep within the dungeon. The two Shadow Knightmares pushed Amanda forward into the dimly lit corridor. The Shadow Knightmare that escorted Gee to the dungeon was waiting for the others to arrive.

"Mister Lassy, is that you?" Amanda asked, barely able to see anything in front of her.

"Yes, child, I am here," answered Gee.

Amanda continued to hear much screaming, the screaming of the tortured children's dreams. She also heard grunting and snorting coming from the shadows around here, but could not see who or what, was making these sounds.

The corridor was lined with cells on both sides. Each cell held a ghostly outline of a different child. Some of the ghostly outlines were bright as if they were filled with life, while others had grown dark and dreary and stared out into nothingness. These ghostly outlines were the dreams of the children that Gamirathen had stolen, and were now being held captive in his Dungeon of Darkened Slumber.

Amanda attempted to get a better look at one of the dreams in the dimness of the dungeon. As she turned her head, she felt a very warm, disgustingly smelly breath, gracing the side of her neck. Something was next to her and this something was not a Shadow Knightmare.

Amanda cautiously turned her head back, to confront what was breathing on her.

"ROOOOAAAARRRR!!!!" screamed a beast whose drooling fangs were only a couple of inches in front of Amanda's face. Its scream was so terrifying and so intimidating that Amanda was too frightened to even scream herself. Two other beasts soon joined the one in front of her, as they surrounded Amanda and Gee. These were the beasts that Timber had warned Amanda about when she was in Jigsari. These beasts were Boarillas. And Gamirathen was using these Boarillas to guard the Dungeon of Darkened Slumber.

Each Boarilla wore a helmet with five large spikes protruding in random directions. These spikes looked as dangerously piercing as the tusks extending from their mouths. They had collars with spikes also, at least a half dozen spikes on each. Each wore armor around their elbows and knees. This armor also mounted single spikes which extended outward from the Boarillas' joints.

And the smell of the Boarillas was atrocious. It was the worst smell Amanda had ever smelled. Even worse than the Stunkeys in Jigsari. In fact, the smell reminder her of the smell of a Stunkey mixed with the worst smell of body odor one could imagine, as if the Boarillas were never concerned with bathing. Their breath was even worse. It smelled as if they had been chewing on a mixture of rotten potatoes, tainted meat, and spoiled milk. Their fangs were decayed and their gums reeked of rotted flesh. Amanda now knew that the stench she had encountered approaching Gamirathen's castle was due to the presence of the Boarillas. The Shadow Knightmares turned and left, knowing they had left the prisoners in perfect hands.

"Look at this," grunted the first Boarilla. "Why, if it isn't a little girl. Let me have her hair. Please, can I have her hair?"

"Pipe down, Wim," growled the second Boarilla. "You know the master wants us to get the book from her. Then she is his - nothing more. So no, you may not have her hair. That is, unless I get upset."

"No problem, Guido," responded the Boarilla named Wim. "I changed my mind anyway. Everyone knows I don't need anymore hair. I'm quite perfect the way I am."

Amanda could tell there were other Boarillas within the dungeon, but due to the dim light, she could barely see the three that had surrounded her and Gee. The Shadow Knightmares had all but vanished from the dungeon and she was now in the care of a trio of Boarillas.

"Get a move on sweets," grumbled the third Boarilla with a hag-like voice, as she pushed Amanda and Gee forward toward what would be their cell home in the Dungeon of Darkened Slumber.

"Careful, Margie," warned Guido. "We don't want to break the old man either. The master wants him in perfect condition."

"Don't worry, Guido," responded Margie. "Me's wouldn't think of harming either one of these two lovelys."

Amanda and Gee were forced into a cell and Wim took a set of keys tied on his hip and locked the cell door. All three guards stood outside of the cell guarding them from any possible escape. Amanda could hear them talking to each other, but much of it was in a language Amanda

362

could not understand. However, from what she did understand, Amanda could tell each Boarilla had its owned personality.

First there was Wim. Wim spent most of his time babbling about himself and how wonderful he was at everything. He felt he was the most perfect individual in existence. He also boasted on how great of a homeland he had, unlike the cesspool known as Maldderan.

Guido was the cynical one. He was very shrewd, stubborn, set in his ways, and did everything by the book. He was missing most of his teeth and spent much of his time picking the lice off of his body hair. Guido was known to be the meanest of the three guards. Never did you see Guido smile. Never! Unless of course, he was watching a the torture of a prisoner. Or worse, doing the torture himself. Then one might see Guido laughing out loud with a deep, hideous belly laugh.

Then there was Margie. Margie was known to be the direct link between Gamirathen and the Boarillas.

Maybe that was due to her evil charm. She looked out for her Boarilla types and their well being, but she looked out for herself first. Margie was one who pretended to be friendly. But this hag was the type that would be friendly to your face, then destroy your credibility by saying things behind your back, and undermine you when you were not looking.

"Better keep an eye on your pet there sweets," whispered Margie licking her lips and pointing to Lawrence. "If Wim gets a hold of that rat, it's as good as gone." Yes, Margie would appear to be doing one favors, but Amanda quickly learned that it may be Margie who had her eye on eating Lawrence, and not Wim.

The three did have one thing in common. All three were self absorbed. So self absorbed that they failed to realize that others, including prisoners, could be clever and witty too. Even prisoners that you would least expect. Even prisoners they considered only a pesky rodent.

Amanda went and sat near the rear corner of her cell with her arms crossed over her knees and her head resting on her arms. Gee sat in the other rear corner, still very weakened by the effects of the Darkness Veil.

"This place makes me want to throw up. It smells so disgusting," Amanda grimaced. "Why do those Boarillas smell so bad Mister Lassy? I didn't know anything could smell that bad."

"Well, child," answered Gee, "a Boarilla's body just naturally has a bad odor to it. They don't do much to make it better either. They never bath. And they hunt Stunkeys for pleasure. Since Stunkeys can only defend themselves with their spray, the Boarillas get sprayed a lot during the hunt. The Boarillas think it's funny."

"That's not the only thing they seem to find funny," said Amanda. "They all get a kick out of the torture that goes on. That screaming is terrifying to me. But those guards love it."

"Just be glad it is not you they are torturing child," replied Gee, whispering the word "yet" to himself, as he finished his sentence.

Amanda stayed quiet and listened to the rambling of the three Boarilla guards from outside her cell.

"What do you mean I have to work double shifts?" piped Wim. "I thought you were going to do something about that Margie."

"Hold on," Margie responded, "I'm doin' what I can. I got us plenty from the master so far. Am I right?"

"I don't think you're doing enough," answered Wim. "I think we should all approach him for better working conditions, shorter hours, and better benefits. That's what I think. If we went to the master as a group, we'd get better results. Maybe that's what we should do. Form a union. We could call ourselves the Darkness Organization or DarkO for short. Who's with me?"

"Me's think that is a bloody good idea Wim," responded Margie. "DarkO, the union of Boarillas. I kinda like it."

"Fine," Guido added, "start a union. I'll be interested in seeing how far you get with it before the master roasts you into a pile of ashes - or all of us for even mentioning it. Since you're so fond of teamwork at the moment, why don't you come with me and get the torture chamber ready for our little guest here. If we don't have answers on that diary of hers when the master asks us, we will be in for a fate far worse than burning to a pile of ashes."

Wim and Guido walked away from Amanda and Gee's cell into the darkness of the dungeon. Amanda stood up and began pacing within the dungeon cell with the look of despair on her face. She could tell she was being watched.

"What's wrong sweets?" asked Margie. "Don't look so gloom. Im's in charge of assigning work for the prisoners here and I haves a special job fer ya'."

Amanda looked up into the Boarilla's eyes and was quite surprised by her friendly tone. "Why are you being so nice to me?" Amanda asked as she walked up to Margie by the dungeon cell door.

"'Cause you're a pretty girl just like meself," answered Margie winking, "and us pretty girls have ta' stick together, ya' know. Now as far as your special job," she continued with much slobber running out of the sides of her mouth, "fer you, I gots the best job in the dungeon, I do. You gets ta' scrub all the feet of the dungeon guards - three times daily - and I know me's feet's in need of a real good scrubbin'."

"Ewww!" exclaimed Amanda with a look of disgust. "That's just plain gross. And you're gross - and not very nice either."

"Well, talk about bein' stingy," boasted Margie. "Me's thought it was mighty kind to give my sweets such a noble job as scrubbin' us Boarilla feet. Me's guessed wrong. So much fer me bloody favors. Maybe Guido should just handle ya' by the book. What do ya' think sweets?"

"I think you're crazy," answered Amanda, "and I think someone needs to handle you by the book."

"Well sweets, I don't think you're going ta' be the one to do that," laughed Margie, "given that you're stuck on the wrong bloody side of these bars. What do ya' think glass man?" asked Margie of Gee who had kept his silence through all of her babbling. "How would ya' like ta' scrub me's feet?"

"You should not mock this child, beast," answered Gee quite directly with a strong sense of firmness. "You are not even worthy to be speaking to her."

"Bah! Listen ta' the old fool!" piped Margie. "He thinks Im's not worthy ta' speak to the child. Why, me's wishes that the master would let me's melt you down to a blob and lets me's turns your melted self into my bloody new teacup. That's what me's should do with you old fool. But the master seems ta' have a different 'genda. He wants ta' make a window or somethin' out of ya'. Bloody well figures."

BOOOOOMMMMMM!!!!!!

A deafening noise came from outside of the castle and startled all of the Boarilla guards, leaving them scurrying in a tizzy. Margie took off running as Amanda looked up in amazement and curiosity. She had heard that noise before. Was it? Could it be? Wait, where was Lawrence?

"Lawrence. Where's Lawrence?" Amanda asked looking frantically around the dungeon cell for her ferret friend. "Mister Lassy, is he near you?"

"No, child," answered Gee, "I have not seen him since him for quite some time. I became distracted by that babbling idiot of a guard."

"Oh no, I sure hope he didn't get trampled in that chaos out there," said Amanda worried. "Those Boarillas will crush him if they step on him."

Amanda was right. One stomp from a Boarilla foot would crush Lawrence into a flat pancake. But the ferret was not in the cell, so Amanda had every reason to be concerned. Then she noticed something.

"Mister Lassy, I don't hear the guards anymore. It's like they all left or something."

"Perhaps you're right, child," agreed Gee. "I believe that sound caused their curiosity to get the better of them. I too, hear no more grunting or snorting. Nor do I hear any screams. Perhaps the torturing has stopped also."

"I wish we could get out of this cell now," hoped Amanda. "This would be as good a time as any with none of those guards around."

BOOOOOMMMMMM!!!!!!

A second blast was heard and this one made the walls of the dungeon cell shake like an earthquake had hit the ground around the castle.

"Do you think," Amanda began to ask. "Do you think that noise is..."

"Yes, child," answered Gee. "I do believe that my dear old friend Hemlock has come to our aid."

Then, Amanda heard the rattling of one of the guard's keys approaching.

"Too late on getting out of here," Amanda said disappointed, "I hear a guard coming now."

Amanda waited for the guard to approach her cell. The darkness of the dungeon once again prevented her from seeing anyone who wasn't directly in front of her face. The sound of the guard's keys grew louder and closer. She waited, clinching tightly to the bars on the cell door.

Funny thing, Amanda thought, *I don't smell that nasty Boarilla smell like I did before.*

The keys could be heard right in front of her. Amanda looked and saw no one. Then the keys were heard right next to her, inside of the dungeon cell, and she shivered in fright as to how that could be. She glanced to her side to see how the Boarilla could possibly have gotten into the cell with her and Gee.

"Why, you little stinker!" exclaimed Amanda. "Your obsession for collecting keys really does pay off."

What Amanda saw next to her was not a Boarilla, but a much friendlier beast. It was Lawrence. And in his mouth was a set of keys to the dungeon cells that he somehow managed to steal from the hip of one of the Boarillas.

"So you were able to squeeze out of here?" smiled Amanda. "I'm so proud of you, Lawrence. This is our way out. And you are the one who found it. Now let me have them." Amanda reached for the keys and took them from Lawrence's mouth. "Mister Lassy, we have a way out of here. Lawrence managed to find his way back and he brought keys with him. Dungeon keys. Did you hear me?"

"Yes child, I heard," answered Gee with much weakness in his voice. "I heard everything you said. Leaving this cell will be the easy part. Getting away from this castle will not be quite so easy. And I have little strength. You should leave this dungeon. Go on without me. I will only hold you up child."

"Go without you?" Amanda asked bewildered. "There's no way I'm leaving here without you. You cared for me for years, watching all of my dreams. You protected me. You kept me safe. I owe you so much. I will be leaving this dungeon, but I'm not leaving it without you."

"I understand," said Gee, "but be warned, I am not my usual self. Gamirathen has caused great harm to me already. It will take all that I have to keep up with you. There is also one other thing."

"What?" asked Amanda. "What is the one thing?"

"If I go with you and since you have the keys," replied Gee, "I ask that you open the other dungeon cells and release what is left of these children's dreams that are held in them."

"Oh my gosh!" exclaimed Amanda. "I had almost forgotten about them. I feel so selfish. What am I thinking? I'm only concerned about saving myself and forgot about all the other children."

"Don't be upset that you forgot, child," Gee encouraged. "It's easy to forget many things when one is faced with such obstacles and challenges. That's why we make such a wonderful team. We help each other."

"Yes we do," agreed Amanda. "We make a splendorific team. Now let's get going before any of those guards return."

Amanda made numerous attempts placing various keys from the key ring into the dungeon cell lock and turning until she found the right one. But one key did work and the lock clicked open. Amanda then helped Gee to his feet and picked up Lawrence, tucking him inside her navy blue jacket, where the Dream Diary was still safely secure.

"Ok, here we go," Amanda said as she took a deep breath. Then, she opened the dungeon cell door and exited with Gee following right behind her.

Amanda had to walk slowly, unable to see far ahead, due to the low light from the Toucandles along the dungeon walls. She hoped she would not to run into a Boarilla along her way. Amanda approached the first cell with a captured dream of a child inside.

"Don't worry," Amanda said to the child's dream, "we're not here to hurt you. We're here to help you. You can be free now. Free to return to your child and let them find you."

Amanda sampled the keys, as she did on her cell door, until she found the correct key for the cell. The cell door unlocked and Amanda opened it. The captured dream was now free to leave.

"There," Amanda said proudly. "You are free to find your child."

But the dream didn't move.

"What's wrong, Mister Lassy?" asked Amanda. "Why isn't it leaving? Why is it just sitting there?"

"I'm afraid it has been cursed too, child," answered Gee. "This is again Gamirathen's doing and only he can break the spell, much like he did with the Veil of Darkness. I'm afraid there are not many options to save them without the spell being broken - unless..."

"Unless what?" Amanda asked quickly. "What? Can we somehow break the spell?"

"Not we, child," answered Gee. "But, you can. Even if I were at my full strength, I cannot battle Gamirathen anymore. I am much too old. But remember, that is what you are here for. And by destroying Gamirathen, or by weakening him. Then, any spell he has previously cast, will no longer hold its power."

Amanda gulped. "So I'm guessing that means we can't just sneak out of here?"

"No, child," Gee answered. "There is something you must do before we leave this castle."

Amanda said no more and continued through the dungeon, unlocking every dungeon cell she could find with a child's dream locked inside. As before, not one of the children's dreams left their dungeon cell, being frozen to stay under the spell cast by Gamirathen.

Amanda's thoughts were focused on freeing the children's dreams, as well as facing Gamirathen. After all dungeon cells were opened, she and Gee made their way back to the steps that had led them down into the Dungeon of Darkened Slumber.

Amanda peered into the throne room and saw that it too was empty. There were no Shadow Knightmares to be seen anywhere and Gamirathen was no longer sitting at his throne. Amanda and Gee slowly made their way to the foyer of the throne room, with Gee in an extremely weakened state.   Sounds of fighting were heard coming from the castle grounds.

BOOOOOMMMMMM!!!!!!

Amanda looked at Gee upon hearing the cannon sound blast from outside.   They both knew that Master Hemlock and his crew had made their way to Gamirathen's castle, and were fighting a battle, that was sure to have odds stacked against them.   It was now their turn to join the battle.

Amanda blinked her eyes and looked faint for a moment and then swallowed in an effort to regain her composure.   Amanda then opened the door to the castle grounds.

The castle grounds were full of Shadow Knightmares posting themselves into defensive positions, in efforts to avoid any cannon gum balls being launched in their directions.   There were also dozens lined along the outer walls of the castle.   Some of these had catapults that were launching large balls of a boiling black tar-like substance at Master Hemlock's ship. The corner towers of the castle, where the roofing was alive, were firing flames of black tar from their mouths at the *SS Sweet Dreams*. Master Hemlock's voice could be heard yelling out orders as he tried hard to avoid any attack that the Shadow Knightmares or the castle's roof beasts might throw at him.

The Boarillas were also among the crowd within the castle grounds, although the dungeon guards and their newly formed union known as DarkO, was not quite as organized as the Shadow Knightmare's army was. Most of the Boarillas were moving quickly in a frantic pace and yelping a hideous growl of fright. This activity caused them to sweat profusely, which in turn, caused their stench to be even more unbearable. They had resorted to hurling rocks and throwing sticks into the air, trying to help fend off Master Hemlock's attack, but having no success. Instead, their rocks and sticks hit nothing more than the castle walls, a Shadow Knightmare, or each other.

Amanda stepped out into the castle grounds, staying close to the edge of the circular building she and Gee just exited, hoping not to be seen. After only a few steps, a chuckle could be heard from behind her.

"Where could you be off to angel?" smiled Gamirathen. "Was there a problem with my hospitality?"

Amanda turned around to see the nightmarish grin on a very confident looking figure of evil sitting on a ledge just slightly above them, enjoying the view of battle from his perspective.

"What do you think? Does your pirate friend have a chance?" asked Gamirathen. "I mean he has about 100 or so in his crew, and I have well over a thousand in my army. Not to mention the roof beasts of mine. Don't you just adore the architecture here?"

"Master Hemlock is a fighter," responded Amanda. "You'll see. He isn't going to give into your army or to you."

"Oh no?" retorted Gamirathen. "I truly beg to differ. See right there."

Gamirathen pointed up to Master Hemlock's ship as it was hit by a shot of the burning tar-like liquid. Several of the pirates ran over to the burning portion of the ship that had been hit in an effort to make a quick repair.

"A few direct hits from my boys like that one and I'd say that ship of his will no longer be flying," gleamed Gamirathen.

Amanda knew that Gamirathen was right. Master Hemlock just didn't have the numbers in his crew to fight the Shadow Knightmare army. But what could she do? How could she help Master Hemlock? Amanda stared at the ship and thought hard. Then, Amanda saw something. Something was approaching from the air in the distance. She couldn't quite tell what it was, but it looked like a swarm filling the sky.

"What's this?" Gamirathen asked with concern in his voice.

"Oh yes!" screamed Amanda. "Thank you! Thank you! You didn't abandon me. You were just going to get help."

"Yee Haw!" yelled Monroe as he came flying into the battle area riding XR-27. "The calvary is here." However, Monroe and XR were not alone. Amanda could see Sebastian riding on another dragon. In fact, there were hundreds of dragons, perhaps Monroe's entire farm, most flying solo.

Now, Master Hemlock had the much needed backup. The Shadow Knightmares looked almost scared as they froze in their attack. Amanda turned around to face Gamirathen.

"It looks like things have taken a turn for the good guys," boasted Amanda.

But Gamirathen was not there.

Amanda looked around to see him nowhere. "Mister Lassy, where did he go?" she asked.

"I do not know, child," answered Gee awestruck by the flock of dragons advancing their way onto the castle perimeter. "My sight was set on this incredible scene. It is something that these eyes have never seen before in all of my years."

Then she spotted him. Gamirathen was leaving the battle scene. He was heading up the spiral stairway that wrapped its way around the large circular tower. Amanda knew what she had to do. Follow Gamirathen.

Chapter 12
Putting a Nightmare to Rest

The battle scene on the castle grounds had now changed.
No longer was it so heavily one sided in favor of the
Shadow Knightmares. With the herd of dragons that had
just joined the battle, the sides had evened up nicely.

Several of the dragons immediately began blowing huge gusts of fire at the roofing beasts. Others began to pick up rocks, large sticks, and anything that might inflict damage, and dropped it on the Shadow Knightmares below. This was the help Master Hemlock needed. The crew now had plenty of time to make much needed repairs to the ship and to reload all of their cannons before they launched another set of strikes.

As for Amanda, she began to make her way up the circular stairwell which wrapped its way around the building in the center of the castle grounds, trying hard to keep an eye on Gamirathen, and trying not to leave Gee behind. She realized that the battle ground she approached at the top of the castle, may not be the best place for a ferret.

"Lawrence, I'm going to let you go now," said Amanda sadly. "If anything bad happens, run far away from here and don't look back. I want you to be safe."

Amanda set Lawrence down and continued climbing the stairs. Gee and Amanda had made their way near the very top and saw Gamirathen at the end of the stairwell, standing with one hand on his hip and leaning with the other on his cane, smiling the entire time. Gee and Amanda hurried to reach him, but as they climbed, the stairwell began to grow as more stairs appeared to have to be climbed, leaving them further from Gamirathen with each step. Their increased effort to climb the stairwell left Gee and Amanda exhausted.

"What's he doing?" asked Amanda. "We're never going to reach him."

"He's put a spell on the stairs," answered Gee. "I have to stop for I am growing too tired to continue. You must find a way to make it to the top."

Amanda looked at Gamirathen and continued to climb, even though her attempt left her further away from him no matter how hard she tried. Then, she thought and placed her hands on her jacket in the area where the Dream

Diary had been placed inside. Her eyes began to glow as she stared at the end of the staircase where Gamirathen stood.

Amanda fell into a trance as she remembered a dream she had that was similar to her current situation with this never-ending stairwell. In her dream, she was running down a dusty, gravel road, which stretched through the middle of a desolate, barren field. In the distance, she could see her mother and father standing in the center of the road, smiling and waving at her. Amanda ran toward them, but the faster she ran, the further from them she became. She tried harder. Her efforts were pointless. She could never reach her parents. As they began to slip from her sight, she screamed "No!" and leaped forward.

At this same moment, Amanda screamed "No!" toward Gamirathen and leaped forward toward the end of the stairs. Her body moved in one sweeping motion from where she was, to the top of the stairwell. And now, she was face to face with Gamirathen at the top platform, on the roof of the circular building where the dungeon and throne room were located.

"Bravo, bravo," cheered Gamirathen with a sarcastic golfer's clap. "You do have some tricks up your sleeve, now don't you?"

Amanda's eyes stopped glowing. She did not understand what had just happened. "I don't know how it ended," she wondered, as she stood nervously thinking of the dream she had flash into her mind of her parents at the end of the gravel road. "How did my dream end? And how did I make it to the top of this stairwell?" Looking up at Gamirathen, he winked at her. It was time to focus on the problem at hand. A problem named Gamirathen.

With Gamirathen's attention on Amanda, the spell on the never-ending stairwell stopped. Gee began again to climb his way to the top.

"So, where is it?" asked Gamirathen.

"Where's what?" Amanda asked back.

389

"Why, that Dream Diary, of course," replied Gamirathen. "You surely didn't climb all the way up here for anything else other than to hand it over to me, now did you angel?"

"I wouldn't dream of giving my diary to you, you beast," said Amanda. "I'm here to put an end to you."

"If I had a nickel for everyone who has told me that," snickered Gamirathen. "Even that glass friend of yours back there thought he could best me at one time. But that soon became a moot point. Isn't that right old friend?"

Gee had now made it to the top and was in the presence of both Gamirathen and Amanda. "You and I both know she is different," answered Gee. "You know who she is and what she is capable of doing to you."

"Oh, I do know who she is," agreed Gamirathen. "I know her very well. And I have an idea of how powerful of a Dream Caster she may be and what she might be capable of doing. I just need to see that diary, so I know for sure what her dreams really are - all of them."

"How is it he knows me, Mister Lassy?" asked Amanda. "How does he know me so well?"

"Yes, Gee," smiled Gamirathen, "how is it I know her?"

"Gamirathen, this has gone too far," Gee replied, avoiding Gamirathen's question. "Just look at the chaos you are causing."

"I tend to like what I see out there," Gamirathen responded. "It all gives my home such a festive mood."

"Festive?" asked Amanda. "How can you call this festive? They're destroying each other out there. This is not festive. This is wrong. You're wrong!"

"Wrong? Ok, maybe. But you do understand that this is all your fault angel?" clued Gamirathen.

"What could you possibly mean?" asked Amanda.

"You don't understand?" Gamirathen questioned. "Well, let me spell it out for you."

"Don't listen to him, Amanda," pleaded Gee. "He's trying to break your spirits."

"Oh am I?" asked Gamirathen. "Well then. It is I who used to also be a Dream Watcher much like your friend Gee there. I bet you did not know that now did you angel?"

"You were a Dream Watcher?" Amanda asked with much doubt. "Who could possibly allow such a hideous fiend such as yourself to watch their dreams?"

"Why, your father, of course?" responded Gamirathen. "I was your father's Dream Watcher. Where do you think you got your "gift" from? Dream casting is typically a genetic quality."

"My father?" Amanda asked. "You're lying. You don't know my father. I barely know my father. Mister Lassy, tell me he's lying. Tell me he never knew my father. Tell him my father is not a Dream Caster."

"Yes, Gee," grinned Gamirathen, "tell me I'm lying."

"I'm sorry, Amanda," Gee responded, "but he's not lying. Gamirathen was at one time your father's Dream

Watcher just as I am yours. And yes, your father is a Dream Caster. Just as you are."

"See, angel," Gamirathen said smiling, "I am a very honest person. I don't lie. I even have your father's Dream Diary tucked away nice and safe to be read at my leisure."

"Then why?" cried Amanda. "Why are you so wickedly evil? Why are you stealing dreams? Why can't you leave the children alone? Why can't you leave Maldderan alone? Why can't you leave us alone?"

"Me, evil?" asked Gamirathen. "Why, I'm only evil because you made me this way. You brought the evil out in me."

"What do you mean I did this?" Amanda asked. "How could I have anything to do with you and what you are?"

"Let me tell you," Gamirathen explained. "Your father had but one dream. I watched but one dream all of his life. He wanted nothing more to fall in love and marry a beautiful woman, have children, and build a warm and loving family together. But then came you. You had to come and ruin it didn't you? You show up and your mother dies. Your father couldn't handle it. He went crazy as his dream was shattered. I had nothing left to watch but nightmares and soon my sanity was questionable too. Yes, angel. Your mother is not here so that you may be. How's that for a dream? And it's all your fault. You're birth made me what I am. You made me."

"No, no, no," Amanda whispered under her breath crying. "This can't be true. Can it? Did I cause my mother to die? Is my father crazy because of me? Am I responsible for all of this? No, it can't be true. It just can't be. You are so wicked! So very wicked!"

Amanda's eyes glowed bright white, like two small stars, showing none of her pupil. There was no more time for talk. With her starlit eyes affixed on Gamirathen, Amanda again placed her hand over the area of the jacket where the Dream Diary was securely located, and dazed off into a dream about her birthday. In this dream, she had a cake with hundreds of candles placed on top, all lit and ready to be blown out. She was surrounded by many faceless people whom she did not know. Amanda made a wish and blew at the candles with the force of a tornado. She blew and blew and blew, but never could get all of the candles blown out.

At the same moment, as Amanda stood in front of Gamirathen, she held her hands out to her sides and blew out from her mouth. But the air coming from her mouth was not a normal breath of air. This was a huge gust, like the wind created in a typhoon, and it was directed at Gamirathen.

Gamirathen braced himself against the storm Amanda had created. "Oh, this is just terrible weather, isn't it?" he said laughing as he held on tightly to the edge of the castle wall where he had been blown. But it was no use. Amanda's gust was too strong. "Not fair," said Gamirathen as he fell off the side of the castle platform.

Amanda's eyes turned back to normal and she fell to the ground in exhaustion. "Mister Lassy, what just happened?" she asked.

"I do believe you used your dream casting power and blew Gamirathen right off of that ledge," answered Gee. "It was quite remarkable."

"I did start dreaming," said Amanda. "I was blowing candles out on a birthday cake. And I made a wish, but I don't remember what the wish was. I'm just glad I have the Dream Diary with me. With it, I was able to use the dream casting power."

"It's not the diary," said Gee. "You did it. You need to understand that."

But Amanda's efforts were not enough. A dark, hideous laugh was heard and Gamirathen floated up from the side of the castle where he had fallen. "You don't play fair angel. Not fair at all. Therefore, I think I won't play fair either." Gamirathen began to change from his somewhat human-like appearance into a large shadow beast. He was at least five times his original size and his body appeared as a dark shadow with no defined beginnings or endings. The blackness of his body boiled like smoldering tar. His hands were wickedly frightening. The tips of his fingers looked like black lightning bolts that could destroy anything they touched. His face was monstrous, as before, but more shadowy in nature. His teeth consisted of multiple rows of razor sharp fangs and his tongue had become slimy and serpent shaped in appearance. But his eyes - his eyes had not changed. They were still the two amber eyes that Gamirathen was famous for. The eyes alone made it obvious that this creature, although different in all other physical ways, was definitely Gamirathen.

A voice roared from the air, allowing all within the castle surroundings to hear. It was Gamirathen. He was able to speak without the use of his mouth. He was not happy. "Now, I will not play fair!" Gamirathen shouted as he lifted the form of his right hand and pointed it toward several of the dragons that were in pursuit of the castle. A blast of dark energy shot from his palm, hitting at least ten or more dragons, sending them falling to the ground below. He then lifted his left hand and did the same to another group of dragons, sending them plummeting to the ground. "How do you like how I play now?" he continued to roar.

Amanda didn't know what to do. Quickly, she pulled the Dream Diary from her jacket and began to open it.

"Oh, so it's been in your possession this whole time?" Gamirathen said as he struck Amanda's hands with a burst of the same dark energy that he had hit the dragons with. However, when the burst hit her hands, the diary appeared to absorb most of the impact. But that was enough to cause the diary to fly from Amanda's grasp and go flying away from the castle's area toward the Desert of Nod, well out of site of Amanda, Gee, or Gamirathen.

"No!" shouted Amanda. "Now what do I do?"

"Use your power child," answered Gee. "Don't worry about that book. I'll do what I can to protect the others."

Gee created a wall of light which covered Amanda, Gamirathen, and himself like a dome. His face showed his struggle as he gave everything he could with what little energy he had left in his body. The wall of light shielded the dragons and the pirates from any attack that Gamirathen planned to use, as long as Gee could hold it. And in his weakened stage, that might not be very long.

"Such amateur tricks my old friend," Gamirathen sneered as he hit Gee with a blast of dark energy. "It does not matter. I only want the child. You have become expendable to me."

"Gee! Please, leave him alone!" pleaded Amanda. "It is me you want. Not him."

"Well, well, well," taunted Gamirathen. "You two do have a special bond. Isn't that sweet. I have to say, I am sorry it came to this angel. You lost the diary, your dream watching friend has interfered one too many times, and now, I grow tired of you too."

Gamirathen hit Gee with another dark shot of energy causing Gee to scream out in pain.

"I can't let this happen!" screamed Amanda. "I can't let you suffer anymore, Mister Lassy. What do I do? Please tell me what I need to do."

"Don't you understand?" Gee asked. "The power was not in that book. That diary has no power. The dream casting power is inside you." Gee fell to his knees in pain. The power of the darkness was about to destroy him and he knew it. "Please child, trust in yourself. I plead of you. Use your dreams to save us all."

Amanda stared speechless at Gee. She was scared. Her body shook in fear as if shivering from severe cold temperatures. *This can't be happening!* she thought to herself. *None of this was supposed to happen. My dreams were supposed to come true, not be destroyed. How do I do this? How do I stop a nightmare?* Amanda felt lost and with her friends unable to help, she was all alone to fight. "How do I stop a nightmare?" she continued to ponder, as Gee groaned in agony.

Amanda closed her eyes.

"How do I stop a nightmare?" Amanda whispered.

Amanda opened her eyes and once again they began to glow like two shining stars.

A piercing light shot out of the curtain of darkness from the sky and through Gee's force shield, as if it were a door opening from outside. A stairway began to make its way to the platform where Amanda, Gee, and Gamirathen were in battle. A beautiful woman appeared at the top of the stairwell. She had a dark complexion with long brown hair, and wore a long white robe which illuminated like the opening around her. She looked down at Amanda and smiled.

"A woman?" Gamirathen sneered. "You send a woman to fight me? Of all possible choices you could have made, this is how you choose to defeat me? A woman? Pathetic."

"No," Amanda responded, "it's not pathetic. This is not just any woman. This is my mother."

"Oh, yes. I thought she looked familiar. And what do you think mommy is going to be able to do to little ole' me?" Gamirathen taunted. "You never even knew her when she was alive. You have no real memories of this woman."

"You just don't understand," Amanda explained. "I may not have any real memories of my mother, but I do have dreams. Many, many dreams. And I never forget any dream I have had of my mother. It's all that I have of her."

"So," said Gamirathen, "you dream of your mommy. Good for you angel. I'll destroy that dream too."

"You won't be able to," Amanda boasted. "I have been scared to fall asleep much of my life. Scared of my nightmares. And when I'm scared like that, I close my eyes and dream of my mother. I dream of her singing to me. I love for her to sing to me. The songs that she sings keeps nightmares from haunting me. It destroys them even before they have a chance to exist."

Amanda's mother began singing a beautiful lullaby that would soothe any child to sleep. Gamirathen tried to strike her with his shots of dark energy, but they passed right through her having no effect at all. However, her singing had a huge affect on Gamirathen. As she sang, portions of Gamirathen's body began to burn in glowing light and dissolve away. Gamirathen began to scream. The further his body dissolved, the lighter the area around them became. And the lighter the area around them became, the stronger Gee became.

Knowing it was safe, Gee removed his force shield and watched in amazement as Amanda used her dream power to destroy the evil beast. The dragons, pirates, Shadow Knightmares, and Boarillas had all stopped fighting. They were now gazing at the battle on top of the circular building. Gamirathen continued dissolving and screaming.

"There's no use to fight this Gamirathen," said Amanda. "You can't win. I'm not scared of you anymore."

"Curses," Gamirathen grumbled. He then screamed one last cry of despair and disappeared into the light.

"You are truly the chosen one child," said Gee as he approached Amanda from behind. "You did what you came here for. You have defeated Gamirathen and now all of Maldderan and the children of your world are safe."

Amanda did not respond. Her eyes were still like stars and were continuing to gaze upon her mother as she walked toward her. Amanda held out her hand and reached for her mother's hand. Her mother lifted her hand and just before Amanda was able to touch her, Amanda's mother faded away into the light.

Amanda's eyes turned back to normal and she began to cry.

"No mommy! No!" cried Amanda. "Don't leave me! Don't leave me again! Please, come back! I'm so sorry I was born and you had to die. Please, come back!"

Amanda fell to her knees in tears.

"She cannot come back child," explained Gee. "That was not really her. That was just your dream you saw. Nothing more."

"It was her!" screamed Amanda. "Don't you tell me that wasn't my mother. It was her and she was real!"

"I will not argue with you, child," Gee said. "Learning to use your power is not an easy task. Sometimes things are not always the way they appear."

A rumbling could be felt among the castle as the door to the foyer of the throne room shot open and hundreds of children's dreams came flying out from within like ghostly comets. But they weren't leaving. The dreams took aim at the Shadow Knightmares left on the castle grounds and shot through their bodies like a dagger through a heart, piercing the Knightmares and causing all that were struck to fizzle away like disappearing vapor.

The Boarillas that remained made their way to the front entrance and managed to open the gate. They ran frantically into the Desert of Nod, squealing the entire way.

Amanda calmed down as she watched the Shadow Knightmares reach their fate and the children's dreams soar off into the skies above.

"Come, child," Gee said. "It is over. We must go see about the others. Our friends."

Gee and Amanda headed back down the circular staircase. As they made their way down, Amanda could see Lawrence's tail sticking out from a cubbyhole within the rocks of the circular building, where the ferret had found shelter during the battle.

"Lawrence!" exclaimed Amanda. "You're ok! That's such a relief. I was so worried about you. I lost so much today. My diary - in a way, my mother - and I thought maybe you too."

"You lost nothing, child," Gee said. "Don't be so foolish. You have gained everything. That diary will be safe. It has a way of taking care of itself. You saw what it did to protect you."

Amanda and Gee made their way to the bottom of the stairwell that wrapped around the circular building to be greeted by Master Hemlock who once again approached Amanda and bowed at her feet.

"It is with great pleasure to have been able to fight alongside you today Madam," said Master Hemlock. "My crew hit them with everything we had."

"You are tops in my book Master Hemlock," said Amanda, "and please stop calling me Madam."

"Ok, well how about..." Master Hemlock said as he stood up.

"How about Amanda?" Amanda asked, finishing Master Hemlock's suggestion.

"Well, ok," answered Master Hemlock. "Amanda it is."

"Great!" smiled Amanda as she pulled Master Hemlock to her and hugged him tightly. "Amanda is definitely splendorific to me."

"Well, ya' dern pirates are pretty good at fightin'," said Monroe as he flew in on XR-27. Sebastian flew in behind him on another dragon. "I just wish y'all would stay out of my blessed gum ball crop."

"Oh," said Master Hemlock, "are those your gum balls? I honestly didn't know. I thought they were growing in the wild."

"Wild, my dorsal fin," replied Monroe. "It's ok though. 'Dem gum balls sure did go ta' good use. Feel free ta' use 'em anytime."

"I tell you what," said Master Hemlock, "I'll ask first from now on before I take any."

"Deal," agreed Monroe as he reached out his fin to shake Master Hemlock's hand.

"Monroe, you were wonderful," gleamed Amanda. "And so were you Sebastian. I cannot thank you two enough for coming and helping us. And all of your dragons. That was amazing."

"I must admit," said Sebastian, " I was wrong about you after our first meeting. You are the one who is amazing. I consider it a privilege to have known you."

"You two are so wonderful," said Amanda as she went up to hug both Monroe and Sebastian. "It has been my privilege to have known both of you." Then she turned to face XR-27.

"XR," Amanda said apologetically, "I have to say I'm sorry. I thought you abandoned me after we had been captured. I'm so sorry. I should have known better than to doubt you."

XR-27 put his head out and stroked the top of it against Amanda's cheek. His scales were still pretty rough, but it was a nice gesture.

"You're such a sweetie," said Amanda.

"Well, I hate to ruin a perfectly good moment," said Master Hemlock, "but my crew and I have to get going.

We have to get ready to leave. We must sail to Amanda's real world and do our "undercover" jobs soon. If we don't leave now, we'll all be late."

"I understand," said Amanda. "I'm sure I will see you at school. Just hold on to your keys or Lawrence might grab them."

"I'll be sure to remember that," laughed Master Hemlock leaning down to give Lawrence a pat on the head. "You have an interesting pet. Backpack and all." Master Hemlock shifted Lawrence's backpack from side to side, as if examining it. "Well, it's time I board."

Master Hemlock boarded the *SS Sweet Dreams* and shouted orders for the crew to prepare it for departure. As the ship lifted back off of the ground and began to sail, Master Hemlock gazed over the bow at Amanda and shouted, "Sweet dreams!" The ship made its way toward the skies above the Desert of Nod.

"I'll always have sweet dreams now!" shouted Amanda back at him. "Thanks to all of you, I will never have nightmares again." But then, it suddenly occurred to her. How was Amanda going to get back home? Gamirathen was defeated. She fulfilled her purpose. How was she to get home?

"Wait, Master Hemlock!" shouted Amanda. "You are returning to my world! How do I get there?" Amanda knew that if the Sandmen were able to come and go between Maldderan and her world, then there must be a way for her to do the same.

But Master Hemlock could no longer hear her. As she stared at the ship sailing away into the skies, she felt a huge feeling of disappointment. Would she ever return home?

That feeling quickly changed. A dark cloud began to form in front of the ship, as an evil chuckle filled the air.

Oh no! Amanda thought, *this can't be him – again!*

But it was. Gamirathen had harnessed together what little energy he had left and was creating a vortex of darkness in the path of Master Hemlock's ship. Amanda ran through the castle entrance toward the Desert of Nod, where the ship was traveling.

The vortex grew larger and looked like a black whirlpool in the sky. Master Hemlock had his crew fight desperately to turn the ship around and pull out of its grasp. It was no use. The SS *Sweet Dreams* hadn't enough power to avoid the pull into the vortex.

Amanda ran as fast as she could to try to catch the ship and save Master Hemlock and the rest of the Sandman pirates. "No! I won't let you take them! Come back!" Amanda ran faster and faster but the ship continued to be swallowed up in Gamirathen's shadow.

"Ha, ha, ha, angel!"

Amanda could hear Gamirathen's voice laughing at her from the skies above, but she ignored him and continued to run. The vortex began to close, swallowing the ship and the pirates as if they were its food.

It was her last chance. She ran faster than she ever had before. But then, Amanda tripped and fell, hitting her head on the ground. She closed her eyes and fell into a deep sleep. All because she tripped over an object lying on the ground outside Gamirathen's castle. The object was her Diary of Dreams.

414

Chapter 13
The End or the
Beginning?

"**A**manda. Amanda, wake up."

The words could be heard in Amanda's head, but coming out of her current sleep induced state, was no easy task.

"Amanda, you need to get up."

The voice finally registered inside Amanda's mind as she opened her eyes and sat up briskly. "Oh my gosh! Grandmother! It is you."

"Of course it's me," laughed Grandma Sneed. "Who did you think would be waking you up? The Sandman? It seems like I have to get you moving every morning." Grandma Sneed walked over to a pair of windows on the far side of Amanda's room and pulled the curtains back, allowing the sunshine to fill the room and causing Amanda to squint.

Suddenly remembering the events that took place before she went unconscious, Amanda wondered how she got back from Maldderan and into her bed. And what about Master Hemlock? What happened to Hemlock and all of the pirate Sandmen? Where did their ship, the *SS*

Sweet Dreams go? "Grandmother." Amanda decided to see if her grandmother knew anything about what might have happened to Master Hemlock. "Do you know if Master Hemlock is alright?"

"What kind of question is that?" Grandma Sneed asked staring back at Amanda.

Amanda realized that her concern for her friend placed her in an awkward position with her question. "Um, I guess you could say I had a strange dream with him in it and something bad happened to him. But the dream seemed so real that I wanted to make certain he was safe."

Grandma Sneed sat down on the edge of Amanda's bed. "Why wouldn't he be safe sweety? Your grandfather walked by his place earlier this morning. He mentioned something about the front door of his cottage being open."

If Grandpa Sneed had seen Master Hemlock's front door open, then he was probably home and had wandered outside to gather firewood or something. Therefore he must be safe. That would mean the entire adventure she had just experienced was nothing more than a crazy dream. But, what if it wasn't just a dream? Amanda needed to be certain. "So, was Master Hemlock ok, grandmother?"

"Well sweety, to be honest, I don't believe your grandfather ever saw him. At least he didn't mention it. He just said the front door of his place was wide open."

Amanda froze in fear. *Wait a minute,* she thought. *I left the front door open when I ran out back to make my wish. And if grandfather didn't see him, then maybe everything really did happen. Oh no!! If that's true, I need to find a way to help Master Hemlock. But how? And what about Gamirathen? I have to know more about him if I'm ever going to help Master Hemlock.*

"Could you tell me about my dad, grandmother?" Amanda asked. "What was he like?"

"Someone is certainly full of questions this morning," answered Grandma Sneed. "Your father, well, he was a good man. Growing up, he was a daydreamer, just like you. That's where you get it, I'm sure. He'd dream up all sorts of crazy things and talk about them all day long, as long as someone would listen to him. Come to think of it, he was a restless sleeper like you too. Probably because I always considered him a bit hyperactive. Well, after your mother died, things changed. Your father changed. Things became - what you would call - well, they became complicated. That's why he had to go away. That's why you have never seen him since you were born. It's just a bit complicated."

Amanda knew what her grandmother was really trying to say. Complicated meant crazy. She learned that from a so called nightmare of her own. A nightmare that would not go away.

"Come on sweety. Let's go eat. Breakfast is ready. You better come eat it while it's hot." Grandma Sneed stood up and headed on downstairs for breakfast.

"I'll be down in a minute grandmother." Amanda could hear her stomach growl in hunger. "Just let me get my clothes on and grab Lawrence. Then we'll be down."

Amanda looked around her bedroom for her furry friend. "Lawrence, where are you? Oh no. Please tell me you made it back from Maldderan with me."

Amanda heard a rustling noise coming from under her bed. She leaned over the side of the bed, with her head upside-down, to take a look. A furry, wet nose stuck out from underneath, directly in front of Amanda's face. "There you are you little furball." Lawrence licked Amanda's nose, showing his happiness to see her and the familiar scenery of the bedroom. "Come up here with me fella. We need to figure out what we're going to have to do next to help Master Hemlock."

Amanda lifted Lawrence onto her bed. "I'm glad to see you managed to make it back with your backpack." However, as she lifted the ferret, her eyes stayed affixed to Lawrence's backpack. "Oh no," Amanda said in shock. "Why is your backpack glowing?" Sure enough, a yellowish glow beamed out of the open corners of the flap of Lawrence's backpack. "This means..." Amanda set

Lawrence next to her and quickly opened up his satchel and reached inside. "Oh, now this is just splendorific!"

There was indeed a reason for Lawrence's bag to glow. "Then this proves it Lawrence." Amanda pulled out the object and held it up in front of her face, not taking her eyes off of it. "That was no dream. It was all real. And from the looks of things right now Lawrence, this isn't the end." Amanda had pulled out, and was staring at an object that was more than splendorific. Inside Lawrence's backpack, was another magical, gold coin, good for one wish at Master Hemlock's wishing well. "Lawrence, we're not done. This is just the beginning. We have another wish to make."